THE HOUSE THAT JACK BUILT

Jack Ryder #3

WILLOW ROSE

Cover design by Jan Sigetty Boeje

https://www.facebook.com/pages/Sigettys Cover Design

Special thanks to my editor Janell Parque

http://janellparque.blogspot.com/

Connect with Willow Rose:

http://willow-rose.net

http://www.facebook.com/willowredrose

https://twitter.com/madamwillowrose

This is the house that Jack built, y'all. Remember this house.

Aretha Franklin 1968

P R O L O G U E

THERE WAS A ROOM THAT

WAS FILLED WITH LOVE

1

MARCH 1986

"I'M SCARED a monster will come and take me, Mommy."

Carrie Kingston looked at her seven-year old son with a smile filled with love. It was the same every night when tucking Scott in for the night. He was afraid of the dark, of monsters in the closets or under the bed. The child had a vivid imagination. Sometimes that was a good thing, an excellent thing, his teacher in first grade told them, but just not when going to bed.

Scott suffered a lot from nightmares and almost every night he would wake up, walk down the hallway and climb into Carrie's bed. It was getting tiresome for Carrie and Scott's father, Jim, since they had to get up and get to work in the morning, and with Scott in the bed, they never slept that well. Carrie was okay with it for the most part. To be perfectly honest, she loved sleeping with her beloved son, but Jim couldn't stand it.

"It'll be fine," Carrie said and kissed her son's forehead, then stroked his red hair gently. How she adored those light blue eyes. Carrie had always wanted a son. She had always imagined having a baby boy. So, when she got pregnant the first time, she was certain it was a boy. It had to be. She was so sure she had bought only boy's clothing and boy's toys. What a disappointment it had been when Joanne came along. It had devastated Carrie, and for years they kept trying to have another child, but without success. Finally, when Joanne was six years old, Carrie had gotten her lifelong wish fulfilled. A little boy. A little adorable baby boy just like the one Carrie had seen in her dreams. And her love for him was so big she could hardly contain it. Carrie didn't mind admitting that Scott was the greatest love of her life. She loved him even more than she loved Joanne, even more than she loved her husband. Even more than she loved herself.

Scott stared at his mother, then at the door to the closet. "Are you sure? I thought I saw something just before."

Carrie chuckled. She tucked the blanket tightly around Scott to make him feel safer. Her mother had told her that's what she used to do when Carrie was afraid of monsters as a child.

"I'm very sure. Remember, monsters aren't real."

"They are to me," Scott said. "Very real. I see them every night, Mommy. They look at me through the window."

Carrie looked at the window. They had left it open because the AC was acting up again. It hadn't been able to cool the rooms down, especially not

Scott's bedroom, for a week now. Carrie knew they needed to get it fixed, but she also knew they couldn't afford to have it done right now. Not when they had to have the truck fixed as well, and that was more important, since without the truck Jim couldn't get to work. He needed it. Besides, it was still early spring, so the heat hadn't gotten ahold of them just yet. There was a cooler breeze at night to cool them down. But it wouldn't last long. Soon, they would have to have that AC fixed or it would be unbearable. Living in Florida, you couldn't get by without the AC. It wasn't like Ohio, where Carrie was from originally. This was very different.

"Can we close it, Mom?" Scott asked with fear in his pretty blue eyes.

Carrie shook her head. "I don't think that would be very smart. It will be unbearable in here. You need the air to cool you down."

"But the monsters, Mom. They can crawl through the window."

Carrie sighed again. It was hot in Scott's room and she felt how clammy her son's hands were.

"The screen will stop them," she tried.

"No, it won't, Mommy."

Carrie shook her head. She was getting tired of this. "Stop with the monsters, Scott. There's no such thing."

"But…"

"No buts. They don't exist. They're not real. It's all in your mind," she said, stroking her son's cheek.

"Now, go to sleep. You have a big day tomorrow, remember?"

Scott's face lit up. "The play," he said. He had been looking forward to doing the school play for weeks now. Scott loved the stage more than anyone else. He had landed the lead in the play because he was a natural on the stage and had received much praise from his teacher. It wasn't something that happened often.

"I can't wait," Scott said and closed his eyes. After a few seconds, he opened them again. "Could you close the door to the closet?"

Carrie got up from the edge of Scott's bed and walked to the closet door and closed it.

"There. Are you happy? No monsters can come in that way."

Scott nodded. A gust of wind came through the open window and grabbed the curtain. Scott gasped.

"It's just the wind," Carrie said. "Now, go to sleep."

Scott nodded and smiled. "Could you leave a light on, please?"

"If that makes you feel better," Carrie said, and turned on the small lamp in the corner of the room.

"It will. Thank you, Mommy."

Carrie smiled and kissed her son's forehead once again. "Now, sleep tight. There's nothing to be afraid of. This room is filled with nothing but love, and the Bible says love conquers all," she said and left the room.

2

MARCH 1986

IT WAS the light that caught his eye and drew him closer. It was shining from the window into the front yard and lit up the night. He had been watching it for several nights in a row. It was always the same. The window was left open and the light shone through the thin curtains.

It was like it was luring him in, telling him to come closer.

So, he did. With his heart pounding in his chest, he walked to the house and peeked in the window through the screen…just like he had done the night before and the night before that.

And just like the other nights, the boy was lying in his bed, sound asleep. He watched the boy for a little while and enjoyed how innocent he looked. It was breathtaking. The man had always been so amazed at how a little boy like that could seem so harmless, so blameless, when they were anything but that.

Just sleeping like he hasn't a care in the world. Doesn't have the faintest idea of the evil lurking right outside his window. But, guess what, little friend? Evil is everywhere. Even in the ones you trust the most.

The boy moaned in his sleep and kicked off his blue blanket. He was feeling hot. His skin was glistering.

There was a rustle from a bush and the man turned to look, but didn't see anything. There wasn't a car in the street. It was all so quiet. He loved the nights. In the nights you could roam free; in the nights, no one watched.

The nights are more alive and more richly colored than the day.

The man thought about the quote by Van Gogh, which had been written on the walls in a toilet booth. He had memorized it because that was exactly how he felt. Come to think of it, that was how he had always felt. Even as a child, he would often wake up at night and stay up for hours. He liked the quietness of the house when everyone else was asleep. As a child, he would go to his brother's room and look at him while he was asleep. He would just stand there and imagine hurting him. He would grab a pillow and pretend to put it over his head and just hold it down till he didn't move anymore. Smother him like Caligula did to Tiberius to succeed him as a Roman Emperor. Stories like that had always fascinated the man. He had devoured everything about the Roman Empire they had taught him in school as a child.

The boy mumbled in his sleep now, and the

man turned to look at him again. He turned to the side and groaned. His giraffe toy fell to the floor. The boy didn't notice.

The man looked at him and tilted his head to better see. He was smiling in his sleep now. Seeing him smile made the man lose it. He couldn't hold himself back any longer. He grabbed the screen and pulled it off the window, then he pulled the window up to make it completely open, and climbed inside the bedroom. He walked to the bed and leaned in over the little boy. Then he stroked him gently across the cheek.

"Having a nice dream, are we?" he whispered. "Enjoy. It'll be your last."

The sound of his voice close to his ear made the boy open his eyes. As he spotted the man, he opened his mouth in order to scream, but the man forced his hand over it and covered his nose as well. The small body tossed and turned underneath him. The boy's wild eyes stared at him in desperation. He held on to him till he passed out, then he let go. He waited a few seconds to make sure he was breathing before he lifted him up and carried him out the window and put the screen back on, before he carried the boy to his car.

He started the engine and took one last glance at the window where the light was still shining. He chuckled, thinking how ironic it was that the nightlight was supposed to keep the monsters away.

3

MARCH 1986

"Scott? It's time to get up!"

Carrie walked inside her son's room and found the bed empty. She walked to the bed, then to the closet, and checked if Scott was in there getting dressed. But it was also empty.

The bathroom. He's probably in the bathroom. Of course. He's nervous about today and has been up for a long time. Now his stomach is acting up like it always does when he is nervous.

Carrie chuckled then walked to the bathroom door and knocked. "Honey? Are you in there?"

There was no answer. "Scott? Are you okay?"

When there still was no answer, Carrie opened the door that she had always instructed her son to not lock. Her heart dropped as she realized the bathroom was empty. She looked in the shower, just to be sure, but knew in her heart that Scott would never take a shower voluntarily.

"Scott?"

Carrie's voice was starting to tremble. She didn't like this. Unease was spreading through her body like wildfire.

Where is my son?

Carrie walked through the hallway into Joanne's room.

"I'm up, Mom. You don't have to check on me," she snarled.

"I wasn't checking on you, Joanne," she said to her always-angry teenage daughter. "I'm looking for Scott. Have you seen him?"

"He's not in here," she said. "The midget probably hid somewhere. He's so childish. What a dork."

Carrie chuckled. Of course that was just it. Scott loved to play hide and go seek, especially when they were in a hurry.

"Now go, Mom. I have to get ready for school," Joanne said.

Carrie shook her head and scoffed. *Teenage-girls these days.* They were so vain and spent such a long time getting ready. When had that happened? It was just the times, she tried to explain to Jim, who didn't understand anything of his daughter's constant obsession with her own appearance. She was madly in love with Rob Lowe and wanted to look like Demi Moore and sing like that awful Madonna. When you had just turned thirteen like Joanne that was all there was.

"When I was her age, I worked from early in the morning," Jim would say. "At this time of day, I had fed the cows and the chickens and cleaned out the stables before I rode my bike three miles to get to school. And I didn't even have breakfast first."

Those were his stories, and they would grow more and more impressive each time he told them.

Jim was sitting in the kitchen with his coffee when Carrie came out to him. He grunted behind the newspaper.

"Have you seen Scott?" Carrie asked.

"No," Jim answered.

"I think he might be playing hide and go seek with me, and I don't have time for it this morning."

Jim looked at his watch. "Speaking of time," he said. "I gotta go. I'm late for the bus."

Carrie kissed Jim on the cheek, gave him his lunch, and watched as he rushed out the front door. She felt bad that he had to take the bus to work, but she needed the car to buy groceries and had to go to work all the way in Rockledge. She needed it more than him today.

We've got to get that truck fixed.

When he was gone, Carrie continued the search for her son.

"Scott, come on out now!" she yelled. "I give up. You win."

Still, she was met only by silence.

"I don't have time for this. Don't let me get angry with you."

When he still didn't show himself, Carrie started to pour cereal in his bowl, thinking maybe his hunger would lure him out. Joanne came out in

16

the kitchen, grabbed some cereal for herself, and started to eat.

"I don't think he's here," Carrie said anxiously. "He never hides for this long."

Joanne shrugged. "Maybe he already went to school?"

Carrie lit up. "The play. Of course, that's it. He must have been so excited he couldn't wait for the rest of us to wake up. He probably rode his bike to school or something."

"His bike is still in the driveway," Joanne said, glancing out the window.

"Well, maybe he walked," Carrie said and put on her shoes, grabbed her car keys, and stormed out the door.

PART ONE:

THIS WAS THE LAND THAT

HE WORKED BY HAND

4

MAY 2015

"Isn't it just perfect, kids?"

Shannon put her arm around my shoulder and looked at the kids. We had taken them to visit the lot where we were going to build our future house.

It had all gone through really fast. Once Shannon and I agreed that we wanted to buy the property, the deal went through within a few days. The lot had been vacant for many years, the real estate agent told us, and that was a shame when you thought about this wonderful oceanfront location.

I couldn't agree more. The lot was perfect for our purpose. There were still the remains of the old house that used to be on the property, but I was going to get that removed as soon as possible, and then start building our new house. The house that was going to belong to us, to our little family.

"What do you say, kids?" I asked and turned to look at the twins.

Abigail looked skeptical. "It doesn't look like much, Dad."

Always so honest. She was right. Right now

it didn't look like anything…just the overgrown ruins of an old house that had been torn to pieces by a hurricane in 2005 and never rebuilt. It had been in the hands of the bank for a long time.

Until now. Now it was ours. Well, technically, it was Shannon's, since she had paid for it, but we had put my name on the deed as well, so I would feel like it was just as much mine. She was also going to pay for all the construction of the new house. Meanwhile, I had told her I would make the drawings and design it along with an architect we had hired. I would also supervise the construction as soon as it started.

"You don't have to," Shannon had said. "I can just pay someone to do it."

"No, this is the way I want it," I had argued. "You contribute with money, I with my hours. If this is supposed to feel like my house too, then I need to do this. I need it to be my house too. I want to built the house of my dreams."

She told me she understood and we never discussed it again.

"It might not look like much right now," I said, addressed to Abigail. "But picture a house, a magnificent house with porches facing the beach, with a wooden stairwell that ends in the fine sand right when you step out of the house. Picture a living room with spectacular views, and picture a second floor with bedrooms overlooking the ocean as well."

Abigail closed her eyes. "It's hard to really

picture it, Dad."

"I can see it," Austin said.

"So, you really think it's a great idea for all of us to move in together?" Emily grunted.

"We're all going to be a family soon," I said and held a hand to Shannon's stomach.

"What?" Emily asked with a frown.

The twins looked at us as well. We hadn't told them the news yet, and now was as good a time as ever.

"That's right," I said. "Shannon is pregnant. You'll have a new little brother or sister soon."

All four kids stared at us. Angela's eyes widened. "You're having a baby, Mom?" Then she let out a shriek of joy. "I'm going to be a big sister? I always wanted to be a big sister."

"It's not that big a deal," Abigail said and looked victoriously at her younger brother by fifty-eight seconds.

"You might be a big brother instead if it's a boy," Austin said, sounding very clever.

I couldn't hide my laughter. Neither could Shannon. I looked into her eyes, feeling such a deep love for her. For just one moment, while we all looked out on the roaring Atlantic Ocean in front of us, holding each other's hands, we all forgot everything else in our lives. All the troubles, all the worries were gone for just this short moment. I, for one, couldn't wait for all of us to be a family.

5

CUBA 1959

SOME MOMENTS in your life you'll never forget. Hector Suarez had no idea today was one of those when he was sitting in his brother's restaurant in Havana with his girlfriend Veronica.

At the age of only fourteen, Hector didn't know much about politics or what was going on in his country. Born and raised on his parent's farm in Ternimo de Guanajay with nine brothers and one sister, Hector had always lived quietly and happily unaware of the impact a change in the political system could have on him and his family.

All he knew was that he liked Veronica, that he loved the Cuban sandwiches they were eating, and that he was wearing two different colored socks... one yellow and one black.

Hector took a sip of his beer and looked at the girl in front of him. Hector knew it was the woman he wanted to marry one day. He just knew it.

It was while taking the next bite of his sandwich that he heard the screaming. Loud voices in the street as someone ran inside the restaurant and started to yell:

"Castro is taking over! Castro is taking over!"

Not knowing what a life-changing event this was, Hector finished his food, grabbed Veronica by the hand, and escorted her home. He went to bed while his older brothers' loud voices were debating wildly in the living room with their father.

The next day at their Sunday dinner at the farm, where the family always gathered, the voices were still agitated. One of his brothers voiced his support of this new regime. Finally, their father ended the conversation with the single statement that Hector would end up remembering for the rest of his life.

"Government is no good."

That was it. His father had spoken and that ended all discussion and debate, much to his older brother's disappointment.

Just a few weeks later, Hector felt the wrath of this new government that they spoke so much of. His older brother Raul came to his room one night and woke him up. His face was sweating heavily and his eyes pierced with fear.

"Raul? What's going on?"

Raul sprang for the window and looked outside, then closed the curtains. He looked at Hector.

"I'm scared, Hector."

Hector sat up. Fear had not been a part of his life up until this day…only the fear of his father's wrath when he got himself into trouble. But this was different. This was a different kind of fear. It was deeper.

"What are you afraid of, Raul? What's going on?"

Raul sat on Hector's bed. "If I tell you this, will you promise to never ever tell father?"

It was a lot to ask. But with Hector, his loyalty to his brothers was always more important than his loyalty to his parents. It had always been like that for him.

"Of course. What's going on? Talk to me, Raul."

"I'm in trouble. I have done something. I need your help," Raul said.

"What did you do?"

"I helped two men get out of here. I helped them get into the Mexican Embassy," Raul said. "They got arrested. They'll tell them my name. I just know they will. They'll come for me. They'll arrest me too."

Hector didn't know much about politics or government, but he did know what his father thought of this new government and he did know when a brother was in trouble he needed to help him.

The next day, he dressed Raul up in some of his mother's clothing and smuggled him out of Havana in the back of his father's truck. As he left him with his friends in a small town where he could hide in an attic above a pharmacy, Hector shed a tear, wondering if he would ever see him again.

6

MAY 2015

"**So, are** you excited?"

Kristi looked at Shannon above her steaming cup of coffee. Shannon smiled and nodded. Yes, she was excited about buying this lot and finally settling down in Cocoa Beach. Since Joe was gone now, there wasn't any reason for her to go back to Nashville.

"I am," she said. "I'm very excited about everything. The house, the baby…it's all happening."

"Why do I detect a slight bit of worry in your voice?" Kristi asked.

A guy came out from inside the restaurant and placed their sandwiches in front of them. He looked shyly at Shannon. She was used to that. Cocoa Beach still hadn't gotten used to having her around. It was getting better, though, and lately she had been able to walk around freely in town, especially since the reporters left. She hoped they would stay away. She and Angela needed all the peace and quiet they could get.

"I am worried," she said and took a bite of the

sandwich. "How can I not be?"

Kristi sipped her coffee, then emptied it, and started her sandwich. It had become a regular thing for the sisters to meet at Juice N' Java for coffee and sandwiches on Monday mornings when Kristi was off from work. Shannon enjoyed it. She loved having her sister in her life again.

"I'm sure they'll find the gun," Kristi said. "It'll all blow over eventually. Just give it time."

Shannon felt tears pressing behind her eyes. She held them back. She couldn't stand this pressure that was put on her, especially not now that she was hormonal because of the pregnancy and everything. The police in Nashville threatened to charge her with murder of an old friend, Robert Hill. Her ex-husband Joe had left a letter when he died, stating she killed him by beating him to death with a microphone stand, when it was, in fact, him. She had only hit him the first time when he aimed that gun at them and told them he would kill Joe to be with Shannon because he was madly in love with her. Robert Hill had written songs for her first album, songs that had given her a breakthrough as an artist. Now the entire world believed she had stolen the songs, even though Robert Hill told her she could publish them without using his name. Now she risked going to jail over what Joe had done. If only they could find the gun he had held in his hand on that night. The police had told her that would make them believe her story. But they still hadn't, and it ate her up.

"What if they don't?" she asked. "What if they don't find the gun? It's the only evidence I have to let them know it was self-defense…that I didn't mean to kill Robert Hill. They already believe I stole his songs for my first album, when in reality he gave them to me. He didn't want his name on them."

"And, still, you put his name on them now. You did the right thing to change that, to make sure his legacy remains. It pleased his family a lot that you changed it. Nobody wants to see you in jail, Shannon. I mean, who would sing for us? The whole world loves you."

"Not everyone," Shannon said. She hated to feel this emotional, but it was hard not to. The doctor had told her to relax and be sure not to worry. It would affect the child, but it was so hard when facing a murder trial. What was going to become of the baby if she had to do time? She could get life for this. Would she even see her baby grow up? And what about Angela?

Shannon felt her blood pressure elevate quickly. Kristi saw it on her face and put a hand over hers.

"You have to relax. You can't get upset like this anymore," she said. "You have some of the best lawyers in the country working for you. It'll be fine."

"I just wish they would get it over with. I hate the waiting, you know?"

"But you have to go through it. It could take

months, maybe even a year before we know what will happen. You have to trust that everything will turn out fine, and then focus on the baby and your new life. Can't you immerse yourself in your music? That used to make you forget about everything else, like the time I graduated and you forgot to show up at my party because you were so caught up in your music, remember?"

Shannon laughed. She did remember. Vividly. Especially how Kristi had yelled at her afterwards. Back then, she hadn't understood why she was so upset. Now, she did. She understood that this was what she had always done to her sisters throughout their lives together. She had taken the spotlight and been too caught up in herself to celebrate their victories.

"I know. I have been writing a lot lately. The hormones have set off the emotional side of me, and the trial too, of course, and maybe the falling in love with Jack. I've said yes to doing a couple of concerts this month. I need to get out there and feel the love of my audience again."

"That sounds good. How does Jack feel about it?" Kristi asked.

"He knows how much my work means to me. He loves his job too and gets caught up in it. In that way, we're much alike. We both have a lot of passion for our work. Luckily, his parents are always there to take the kids if needed."

"Angela is always welcome at my house too, if you ever need it," Kristi said.

"I know," Shannon said.

"So, when do you start building the house?" Kristi asked, finishing the rest of her sandwich.

"As soon as the lot is cleared. There are remains from some old house that was taken down in a hurricane years ago. We need that removed. We should be ready to start in a few weeks. Jack is all excited. He wants this to be perfect."

"I'm sure it will be," Kristi said.

Shannon smiled. Her sister was right. Jack would make it just perfect. If only Shannon could be certain she would be around to enjoy it.

7

MAY 2015

WE WERE still trying to track down the last two Monahan sisters, the murderous sisters who called themselves the Angel Makers. They had murdered so many people thinking they were getting the world rid of child molesters and abusers. They had been four in total when they started out, one had died in the Bahamas, and another, Sarah Millman had been arrested, but released on bail. She was being kept under constant observation by us in the hope she would try to contact her two other sisters or they would contact her somehow.

But the trail was getting colder and colder. Meanwhile, Sarah Millman was awaiting her trial. I was trying to get her convicted of killing her husband first. Then her involvement in the other cases would come later. I had given all my evidence to the State's Attorney, Jacquelyn Jones, and hoped she would be able to make a case against her. Sarah Millman and her lawyer had already declared that she was mentally unstable and drugged at the time of the murder, and handed us an evaluation of her mental health. I knew this was going to be a hard nut to crack. But I hadn't lost hope yet. Neither had I lost hope that I would find the two other sisters, Angelina and Kelly Monahan. We had sent out a nationwide search, and so far the trail of Angelina ended in North Carolina, where she was seen two weeks ago at a restaurant. We were almost certain it was her.

I pushed the files aside on my desk and looked at the screen of my computer. I was fed up with this case and couldn't stop thinking about the house. It was all that was on my mind lately. My dream house. I opened an email from the architect and looked at the floor plan he had made so far. I liked it, but had a few changes I wanted to make, so I wrote him back.

When I had sent it, someone entered the room. It was Beth. It was her first day back at the Sheriff's office after the explosion that left her burned on a big part of her body. I smiled when I saw her. Everyone in the room stood up and started clapping. She limped heavily when she walked, but she held her head high.

"Ah, come on," she said as she moved to her desk and saw all the flowers. "I didn't die, you know. This looks like a damn funeral home."

I handed her a card that we had all signed. "From all of us."

Beth snorted and opened it. It was a gift card to a spa treatment. Beth burst into violent laughter. "A spa? Me? That's a good one."

"Well, we thought you could use a day off to

treat yourself a little," Ron said. "I am giving you any day off you want to go. Just let me know."

Beth looked at him like she didn't believe him. Then she shook her head. She scoffed, but I could tell she was moved.

"What are you all just standing here for?" she asked. "We got ourselves some female killers to catch, right Ryder? Where are we on that?"

I chuckled and sat down. Everyone returned to their desks. Ron had wanted to buy a cake and everything, but I had told him Beth didn't want any of that. She wanted everything to go back to the way it was. I had visited her every week at the hospital while she was there. That was what she had told me every time I came. I could at least give her that.

"So, how are the kids?" Beth asked.

"Good. They're all good, thanks."

"And the stomach is growing, I take it?"

I smiled at the thought. "Not much yet, but it will be. She is throwing up a lot, though. Not just in the mornings, but all day."

"Then, everything is as it should be," she said.

"It is. And everything is in place with the lot. It is ours and as soon as it is cleared, we start building."

"That sure sounds good, Ryder. Now, where are we on catching the Monahan sisters? Fill me in. I want to nail those murderous women."

I couldn't blame her. The explosion they had

caused had burned Beth's face, so the doctors had to transplant skin from her thigh to her face. Beth was never going to look the same again. I fully understood her anger. I think we all did.

8

MAY 2015

VERNON WAS brought into the courtroom wearing his orange suit and handcuffs. His belly-chains rattled as he walked, his heart in his throat like so many times before when he had appealed his case.

The judge looking at him from above her glasses knew him all too well.

"Mr. Johnson," she said, addressed to him, after they had sat down.

A tear left his right eye and rolled across his cheek. This was it. This was the moment of truth.

"Your name and the history of your case have been with me since I started this job. Now, twenty-eight years later, here we are again. New evidence has come to the light of day. A vital testimony has been recanted, and this clearly undermines the confidence the public might have had in the verdict that was previously rendered."

The words leaving judge Brydon's mouth resulted in a loud outburst from the spectators in the seats behind Vernon. He couldn't stop his tears from rolling and turned to look at his mother's face. She too was crying.

Then followed the words he had been waiting to hear for twenty-eight years.

"You're a free man, Mr. Johnson."

Vernon sobbed and looked at his lawyer from the Innocence-Project of Florida. This guy had fought his case since he was an intern. Now, he was a senior partner in the firm. He too shed a few tears and shook Vernon's hand.

"You did it, Vernon."

"No. You did it. Thank you. Thank you for believing in me."

A few hours later, Vernon had gathered his belongings and left the cell that had been his home for the biggest part of his life, since he was only eighteen years old. Now he was forty-six, and one of the few to leave death row alive.

What had gotten him this far? Hope. The undying hope that they would sort it out. He had believed they would. He simply refused to lose confidence that they would. When they had taken him in and asked him all those questions, he knew they had made a mistake and believed they would eventually find out. Even when they had been in the courtroom and the verdict had been stated, he believed it. On the bus ride to the prison, even when they gave him that suit, the one with the rear stripe on it that only inmates on death row wear, even then he had thought: *They'll figure out the truth. They're gonna straighten it all out. Someone will tell them they got it all wrong.* Like they did in the Perry Mason TV shows. Someone would soon yell:

Stop, he didn't do it!

Even when he walked the long catwalk to his cell with his hands cuffed, he believed there was still hope. It wasn't until they had closed the door and left him alone that it finally occurred to him.

This could be your last stop. This could be where it will all end. They might kill you here. Kill you for nothing.

But still, he had kept the hope. Even if it decreased as time went by. He had appealed his case many times and, finally, after eight years, they had changed it from death row to life in prison, since the body had never been found, but that hadn't been enough for Vernon. He wanted to be cleared of all charges. He wanted to be a free man. He knew he deserved to be. He knew he was innocent and he was determined to prove it.

Now it had happened. It had finally happened, he thought to himself as the glass doors opened and he walked outside in front of the TV cameras and photographers and people with microphones asking him *how he felt.*

"Unbelievable," he said, "It's simply unbelievable." Vernon grabbed his mother and hugged her so tight. Her small body was whimpering and hollering in his arms and he held her, feeling like never letting go again.

"I knew they would realize your innocence sooner or later," she said through the tears.

Microphones were pushed in her face as they started to walk out. Vernon's arm was solidly planted on her fragile shoulders, tears gushing across his cheeks.

"Do you feel anger?" a reporter asked.

Vernon shook his head. "Right now, I just want to go home."

All the reporters burst into a laughter, but his mother didn't. She looked into the camera and pointed her finger at it.

"I do have one thing I want to say," she said. "Vernon had twenty-eight years taken from him. An entire lifetime. Meanwhile, the real killer is out there somewhere. He got to live his life, while my Vernon was held in here for something that other person did." She paused for effect. "So, if you're watching this, better get ready. Your time is up. It's time to pay your dues."

9

MAY 2015

On my way home, I stopped by at Oceansurf Surf shop across the street from my parents' motel.

"How's my baby coming along?" I asked as I entered.

The owner smiled. "It's coming along great," he said. "I'm done shaping it and have made an appointment for the glassing. All I need is to do the paint job."

"Ah, I can't wait to take her into the waves. And you'll do the rainbow colors as I asked?"

The owner shrugged. "It's your board."

"Great," I said and smiled. I wanted my new board to be colorful. "So, when do you think it'll be done?"

"Two weeks time."

"Perfect," I said on my way out the door. "If it turns out to be a good board, it might not be the last I buy from you."

The owner smiled. I was glad to be able to help him out a little. I knew his shop was struggling. He had been asking me for months to let him shape a board for me. He surfed with the rest of us at my parents' break often. I thought it was a good idea to support one of the locals.

The entire family met up at my parents' motel for dinner, as usual, sitting out on the deck overlooking the beach. Abigail and Austin told us everything about their day at school, while my parents complained that times were slow at the motel. They were always slow at this time of year, I told them.

Shannon seemed pensive while everyone else was caught up in the talk, and I looked at her for a little while without her noticing it. I liked to look at her. It made me so happy inside. I loved that she had put on a little weight and her cheeks were fuller now. It gave her a cute look. We hadn't told the press the news yet, but it wouldn't be long before they noticed, and then they were going to be all over it. I was enjoying this moment before hell broke lose again. I just hoped they weren't going to occupy our building like they did last time. It would all be better once we had our own house and property that they weren't allowed onto. A big fence surrounding the property would keep their noses out.

I could tell Shannon was worried, and I knew why. I called my colleagues in Nashville almost every day, asking them for news on her case, but so far, no luck. All they needed was to find that damn gun and then it would be all over. But, so far, they had dug out the entire backyard where the body was found and they hadn't found anything yet.

It was driving me crazy.

Shannon was innocent. She wasn't even the one who killed the guy; Joe was. But he was gone, and we had to provide them with something to make them believe what she said. The gun, preferably with Robert Hill's fingerprints all over it, would do just that. It would show them Shannon was telling the truth.

"So, Angela, how was your day today?" I asked, to try and involve her a little in the conversation. My kids always spoke so loudly and dominated the entire conversation so that no one ever heard what Angela had to say. I wanted her to feel at home. This was, after all, her new family.

"Good," she said and blushed a little.

"We saw her at recess," Abigail said.

"Yeah, we played the shark-game," Austin said.

"Did you, now? Well, that sounds like fun," I said, as my eyes met Shannon's. She forced a smile through her worry.

"Did anything exciting happen at your job today, Dad?" Austin asked. He always hoped I had caught some bad guys or maybe been in a car chase. For some reason, he thought that was all I did.

"Not really. Beth came back," I said.

"That's good," my mom said. "She is a fighter, that girl. I tell you. Just like her mom was."

My mother was born and raised in Cocoa Beach and knew about everybody around there.

"She sure is," I said and ate more of my fish taco. A set of waves was rolling in on the beach now, and I couldn't wait to go out after dinner for a little sunset surfing. If I was lucky, I could get a good hour in. The kids were planning on playing volleyball on the beach with my parents. Shannon said she wanted to work on her new song.

They were all good plans for a nice Monday night, but as it often is with plans, they tend to change. And so they did this evening when my phone rang in my pocket. I was inclined to not pick it up, but when I saw whom it was, I knew there was no way I could ignore it. It was Sheriff Ron.

"Ryder. Whatever you're up to, stop it. You're needed down in Sebastian. Pick up Beth on your way."

10

MAY 2015

THE SUN had almost set when we arrived at Sebastian Inlet, thirty-four miles south of Cocoa Beach. Beth seemed tired and I wondered if she had come back to work too early after the procedure. I also wondered if she was all right or if she was afraid. Last time she was called out, she had almost lost her life. I knew she had to be feeling something, but I also knew she would never admit to it. That was just the way she was.

"So, what do we have?" I asked, when we got out and Ron greeted us at the scene. We had been called out to a construction site where they were demolishing an old condominium building to build a new and bigger one.

"Construction workers stumbled over it around four this afternoon. They weren't sure what it was, so they called for their supervisor. He called us right away."

The scene was already packed with police, medical examiners, and technicians combing through the area in their blue suits. Ron led Beth and me to an area where something had been spread on a white sheet. I knew right away what it was. I said hello to Yamilla Díez from the ME's office.

"The workers found this small pile of bones," she said. "Our guys found the skull."

I kneeled next to it and looked at it thoroughly. "Looks old," I said.

"It is," Yamilla said. "There is nothing left except the bone. No clothing, no hair, no nails, nothing.

"Well, the building was built in nineteen ninety-three," Ron said.

"It could have been buried here before that," I said.

Ron nodded and looked around. One of the technicians brought in more bones and put them on the sheet. Yamilla went over to them immediately and began trying to put together the skeleton. It was starting to look like a person.

"It doesn't look like it was an adult," I said, when looking at the femur.

Yamilla shook her head. "No."

"A child?" Ron said.

I shook my head. "No. It's too long to be a child. I'm guessing a teenager." I looked at Yamilla, who nodded again.

"That's more likely. But a young one. Not fully grown, so no older than fourteen, I'm guessing. We'll know more once I get him to the lab."

"It's a he?" Ron asked.

44

"Yes," Yamilla said. "This is, of course, only based on my assumptions. Later examination will determine if I am correct. But a common way in which you might differentiate between male and female is quite simply bone size. This, of course, is not always accurate, but for the most part male bones are larger in size than female bones and are that way because of the addition muscle that may built up on the male body through adolescence and into adulthood. The pelvic area is another good way of differentiating between the sexes. A female will have a larger sub-pubic angle than that of a man, and this is obviously indicative of child bearing requirements in the female that are not required in the male of the species. This difference is noticeable across all species in nature, where birth is from the womb. The male's sub-pubic area is less than ninety degrees whilst the female's is more. The area around the pelvic inlet—in the middle of the pelvic bone—is larger in females than in men, again with relevance to child bearing."

I stared at the human remains that were starting to shape into a real person in front of me. A person who once had a life, a mom and a dad, a school, and friends. It was all just about to begin when it had somehow ended so abruptly. As I looked at the bones on the sheet, something struck me as off.

"What's wrong with the back?" I asked.

Yamilla looked at me. "I've been wondering about that too," she said. "I keep thinking I might have put it together wrong or that some parts are missing."

"What is it?" Beth asked.

"The spine," I said. "It's curved. Like he suffered from spinal stenosis, something you usually see in older people."

11

MAY 2015

IT FELT strange being on the outside. It was nothing like Vernon had expected it to be. It was funny, he thought to himself while sitting on the couch in his mother's small condo in Rockledge; it was funny how many times he had imagined how life would be on the other side, what things would look like, what life would be like, and now that he was out, he had to realize it was nothing like anything he had pictured.

The day after he was released, they had driven back to their old neighborhood, back to where they used to live, and everything was so changed. It used to be old worn-out houses, and some of them you could barely call shacks. Now, it was all brand-new cookie-cutter houses with two car-garages and pools. Even the house Vernon used to live in with his mother had been torn down and another had been built there in its place. Children were playing in the street and all the front yards looked well maintained.

It was nothing like the neighborhood he had grown up in. Nothing.

They had cruised down to the beach at Vernon's request, and they had walked with bare feet in the sand like he had dreamt of so many times while in prison. He had felt the water on his feet and shins and closed his eyes and breathed in the fresh ocean air. The beach looked a lot like it used to, except for the many condominiums that had been built since Vernon was last there. The old motel was still there, though, except it was called Albert's now.

"So, what are you going to do today?" his mother asked on her way out. She worked at the Publix, packing grocery bags.

Vernon smoked his cigarette and shrugged. In front of him was a big flat-screen TV that he had bought for his mother the day before. TV he knew from the inside. It was familiar to him. It felt like home.

"I think I'm just going to sit here for a little while," he said.

His mother nodded and sighed, then walked to the front door and left. He knew she didn't want him to just sit there and stare at the TV all day, but right now, it was all he knew how to do. He liked to look out the window at the blue sky, but walking around out there was a little intimidating. It was like it was too overwhelming for him. Like the fact that that his space was no longer limited frightened him somehow. It made him feel unsafe and insecure. Inside in the living room in front of the TV with a cigarette in his hand, he felt safe. He felt at home. Out there in the world, there was too much noise, too much turmoil. When he went for a coffee at Starbucks one of the first days out, he had seen nothing but people staring at their phones or computers. Nobody talked anymore. It was like anything you needed to say to someone could be contained in a text message. Vernon didn't like it. He liked looking into people's eyes. He didn't like the coffee either. It was nothing like the coffee he was used to. He had bought himself a burger he really liked, though. That was something he had missed on the inside. A really good burger.

They had paid him a million dollars in replacement for wrongly incarcerating him. That meant Vernon didn't have to work for the rest of his life. Neither did his mom, but she wouldn't hear of it.

"Any honest man or woman should work if they can," she said.

Vernon had a feeling she enjoyed her job too much to let it go. That was the only explanation he could think of for her rejecting his proposal to support her for the rest of her life. He could easily do that with this kind of money. The condo she lived in was cheap, and they didn't have many expenses. But living a life without having anywhere to go every morning after working your entire life wasn't his mother's idea of a great life.

"And do what all day, do you propose? Stay here with you and watch TV? No, thank you."

She liked that she was needed. She liked having a purpose, something to do. He respected that.

Now, Vernon had bought the TV he had always wanted, he had eaten the burger, and had put his feet in the ocean. Now, what was he supposed to do with himself? He had no idea.

Except there was one thing he had dreamt about doing for every day of the twenty-eight years in prison. There was one person he had dreamt of seeing again.

12

CUBA 1969

TEN YEARS after his brother ran away, Hector Suarez still hadn't seen Raul again. The family mourned the loss of one of their sons, and especially Hector's mom took it hard. Two years passed without a word from him until one day when they heard the rumor that he had been moved to another village after having been hidden in the attic while the police searched for him and his face was on matchboxes all over the country.

A year later, Hector heard his brother had been moved to yet another village, and later smuggled out of the country and managed to make it into the U.S. Where he was today was uncertain, but Hector had a feeling he was somewhere safe. And soon after he heard about his brother making it to the U.S., Hector started dreaming about following in his footsteps. He too wanted to get away and provide a better life for his family.

Veronica and he married when they turned eighteen, and soon after she was pregnant with their daughter, Isabella. Isabella was the love of Hector's life, especially after Veronica died. She became sick only a year after the birth of their daughter and never recovered. Now, Hector was alone with his daughter and dreaming of a better life for her. The government had taken his father's farm and their family was poor now. Two more of Hector's older brothers soon did what Raul had done and escaped to the U.S., where they believed a better future awaited them. They all dreamt of the land with streets of gold.

Hector was determined to follow them. Only, he had a daughter, and he was scared of what would happen to her there. He had no idea what life would be like for a little girl, and mostly he was afraid of the trip there. Would it be safe to bring her along? He wasn't sure.

In 1965, Hector decided he was ready to make his own journey to the United States. He forged a birth certificate, since he was only twenty-two years old, and men between the age of fifteen and twenty-five weren't allowed to leave the country. To earn his visa, he was forced by the government to work in the sugar cane fields. There he was, working along with lawyers and doctors, all of them trying to earn their visa to go to the Promised Land. While working the fields, Hector's hatred towards the government and the dreams of a better future increased rapidly. When he lay in his tent at night in the camps where they slept, he would remind himself over and over again that it would come one day, soon. The dream wasn't far away. While working in the fields, Hector only saw his daughter once a month.

As the years passed, he started to wonder if it was worth it...if he would ever get the visa. There was a lot of tension in the country, and the stories of people who tried to get away, but were incarcerated or killed instead were many. Yet, he didn't feel there was any future for him in Cuba anymore, and especially not for his daughter. They weren't told how long they had to work the sugar cane fields in order to gain the visa, and Hector was beginning to wonder if they would ever get it.

Until one morning, after four years in the fields, when his foreman came up to him. Hector was sweating heavily in the heat and his hands were bloody from the hard labor. The foreman looked at him with a disgusted look, then said the words Hector would never forget for the rest of his life.

"Suarez. You're done here. You can leave Cuba."

Hector decided to leave Isabella with her grandmother until Hector had found his brothers and gotten a job to be able to provide for her. She was too young to endure this travel and their future in the U.S. too uncertain. He would have to send for her.

The very next day, Hector was put on an airplane by three of Castro's soldiers. Right when they let him go, one of them stopped him and said:

"If you ever come back to Cuba, we will shoot you."

13

MAY 2015

"I have an ID."

Yamilla sounded excited on the other end of the line. I shared her enthusiasm. A week had passed, and we still had no idea who this little boy who was found on the construction site in Sebastian was. It had been driving me nuts. I had been going through old cases of missing teenagers in the beginning of the eighties for days, but had come up with no results.

"Finally. Who was he?"

"It was the teeth that gave him away. Dental records show me this is the body of Scott Kingston, who, according to the file, disappeared from his home in Cocoa Beach in 1986."

"1986?" I repeated and noted the name. "That's a lot earlier than we expected."

"And he was a lot younger when he disappeared," Yamilla said. "Only seven, according to our records. His dental records were only a match on the two front teeth. The rest had fallen out and new ones grown in."

"So, you're telling me he wasn't killed in 1986?" I asked.

"No, definitely not. This boy we found was older. I'm guessing thirteen or fourteen years old. He had developed all of his permanent teeth."

"So, he lived several years after he disappeared, then," I said, and wrote everything down.

"That's safe to say, yes," Yamilla said.

"Thank you."

I hung up and went into Ron's office. He was on the phone, but finished his call when he saw me.

"What's up, Ryder?" he asked.

"We got an ID on the boy."

"Finally," he exclaimed.

"His name was Scott Kingston, disappeared from his home in…"

"Scott Kingston?" Ron said very loudly. "*The* Scott Kingston?"

"I take it you know more than I do," I said, and sat in the chair.

Ron drew in air between his teeth. "It's one of the greatest mysteries in our district. The little boy was taken from his house in the early morning hours while he was asleep and simply vanished. Later, a guy was convicted of having kidnapped and killed him, but the body was never found."

"How was he convicted if there wasn't a body?"

"I believe there was a witness or something. Someone saw him, but you might want to look into that. Come to think of it…" Ron went through his pile of papers on his desk and pulled out a newspaper.

"Here." He showed me an article in *Florida Today*. He pointed at the picture of a guy in the arms of his mother under the headline "A Free Man: Vernon Johnson to leave prison 28 years after a lie helped put him behind bars."

I remembered reading about this guy.

"Vernon Johnson here was just released about a week ago, after spending twenty-eight years behind bars for killing Scott Kingston in 1986," Ron said. "He was convicted in 1987."

"But, wrongly? It says here the witness recently admitted to having lied about seeing Vernon Johnson with the boy. The witness was a paperboy and doing his early morning rounds at five o'clock, when he saw Vernon Johnson carrying the boy to his car in front of the Kingston's house. The witness, a boy who was only sixteen at the time he gave his testimony, is now terminally ill, and told a priest recently that he had never been sure that it was Vernon he saw back then, even though he told the police he was certain. The priest then convinced him to tell the police the truth. He told them he had felt coerced by the police to testify that he was certain it was Vernon Johnson he saw, when he had his doubts." I looked at Ron and put the paper down. "So, they based the entire case on a sixteen-year-old's testimony? They took twenty-eight years of a man's life just like that? That's crazy."

"I know. Times were different back then. But, once the boy came forward and told them he wasn't certain and never had been, that was when the Florida Innocence Project took up Johnson's case again and went through the evidence. It was all only based on that one eyewitness testimony. The judge had no other choice than to let the guy go."

I looked up at Ron. "And now we have the body? The body of this boy that apparently was still alive for several years before someone buried him at the construction site of the new condominiums."

"Looks like we just blew the case wide open," Ron said. "And it's all yours."

14

MAY 2015

NOAH LOVED his new room. It was painted light blue the way he preferred it. Noah was a real boy. His favorite toys had always been trucks and cars and his favorite place to go for his birthday was the airport to watch the planes take off and land.

His mother and father gleamed with pride as they looked at him standing in his new room with pictures of trucks on the walls.

"Do you like it?" his mother asked.

"I looove it!" Noah said, turned, and hugged his mother's legs. "Thank you, thank you, thank you."

Then he threw himself in the beanbag in the middle of the room and just laughed. The bed was the best part, he thought. It was shaped like Lightning McQueen from the movie *Cars* and had a steering wheel and everything.

"We're glad you like it, son," Noah's dad said. "Your mother and I spent many hours painting it, and especially your mother spent a lot of time decorating it. We want you to feel at home in our new house."

"We know it's been hard on you with the move and everything," his mother said, and looked at her husband who nodded. "I mean, with the change of school and everything. Hopefully, this will help make it easier."

Noah grabbed one of his monster trucks. When his parents left, he found another truck and let them smash into each other with a loud noise.

Noah played with his trucks, and soon he was lost in time and space, and forgot everything about the fact that he missed his old friends at his old school on Merritt Island. It was the first time Noah didn't feel sad being in the new house in Cocoa Beach. Since they had moved there two weeks ago, he had hated every moment spent in it and every moment he spent in the new school, where the teachers seemed to correct everything he did.

Noah set up train track and began rolling trains across it. He grabbed a sword and pretended he was a zombie-fighter and started fighting his toy elephant and tiger.

"Ha! Take that, Evil Ely Elephant," he said, stabbing it with the sword.

"And you too, Tiny Tiger!" he yelled and stabbed the tiger in the stomach as well, causing it to fall backwards.

"Ha!"

"Don't you know that zombie-tigers can only be killed with a light saber?" A strange voice asked.

Noah gasped, then turned to face the open sliding door. Behind the screen, a set of brown eyes were staring at him. The man smiled. Noah remembered having seen him before and wondered if he was one of the neighbors.

"You do have a light saber, don't you?" the man asked.

Noah bit his lip, then shook his head.

The man lifted up a black sword, just like the one Robert from his class had. The one he had brought to school once and everyone had admired. The one Robert had never let Noah touch. Noah gasped again.

"May I join you?" the man asked.

Noah looked back at the closed door leading to the hallway and the rest of the house where his parents were. Would they mind? The man did seem awfully nice and he had brought his own sword. Maybe he would even let Noah use the sword?

He turned and looked at the man, then nodded. "Sure."

15

MAY 2015

"HE REALLY loves his new room, huh?"

Steven Kinley looked at his wife, Lauren. "We haven't heard a sound from him in hours. He must be having a great time."

"I'm so happy," Lauren said. "It was all worth it. Did you see his face? It was priceless."

Lauren looked through the hallway at the closed door at the end of it. It was a relief for the both of them to finally see their son with a smile on his face.

The move from Merritt Island to Cocoa Beach had been hard on all of them, but mostly on Noah. He had no siblings, so his friends were his everything, and back at their house on Merritt Island they had lived at a cul-de-sac where both neighbors had kids that he played so well with. Where they lived now, their neighbors were elderly people, who didn't care much about children. The house was much nicer and it was better for Steven to be closer to his job at City Hall in Cocoa Beach. Plus, it was a better school, they believed. It was better for Noah in the long run, but that was hard to see when you were only eight years old and had to leave all of your best friends.

"So, should I start making dinner?" Lauren said and looked at the paperwork in front of her. As the director of Minutemen Preschool, she always had a ton of work to do.

"That would be wonderful," Steven said. "I, for one, am starving."

Lauren put the chicken in the oven, then chopped up some vegetables, and roasted them in the pan. She kept wondering about Noah and how much this move had affected him. She deeply hoped it wasn't a mistake. Noah had seemed a little depressed lately and didn't like his school at all. The teacher had more than once had to call Lauren to let her know Noah wasn't behaving well in class. It wasn't like him to act like this. They did have a lot of tests, Lauren thought, and it made Noah constantly anxious. There had been more than one time he had to stay home from school because of a stomachache. It worried Lauren, while Steven kept telling her it would pass, that Noah simply needed time to adjust to his new reality. He hadn't made any friends in his class yet, and Lauren had started to wonder if he ever would. What if nobody liked him? What if the teacher was mean to him? Was that why he was constantly having nightmares?

Lauren shook the thought and set the table. No, everything was going to settle soon, and then they would be very happy here in their canal-front house. There were so many fun things for them to do here. They could go kayaking or paddle boarding, or he could fish with his father. They even had a pool now, and Lauren knew how much Noah had wanted that while they lived at Merritt Island. He had been begging for one for years. Now that they finally had one, he hardly used it. Well, at least not yet. Maybe he would, later on, when he was more settled in.

It'll come. It'll come. Just give it time.

"Dinner is ready," Lauren said, addressed to Steven, who had his nose buried in his iPad. Probably playing Candy Crush, she thought to herself and walked towards Noah's room.

She knocked on the door. "Noah? Dinner's ready. Come and eat."

There was no answer, and Lauren figured Noah was simply too deeply buried in his playing to answer. She was certain he had heard her and returned to the kitchen to get the chicken out and start cutting it. When Noah still hadn't come out, she looked to Steven, a bad feeling starting to nag at her from the inside. She decided to ignore it. It was silly.

"I'm kind of busy here, could you?" she said.

"I will," he said, slightly annoyed, then walked to the door and knocked. "Noah. Your mom said it was time to eat." He grabbed the handle and walked inside. "Noah?" he called. "Noah!?"

Whether it was the fearful pitch to his voice or simply an awful premonition inside of Lauren that made her drop the plate with the chicken on the tiles, she never knew. But she did know why she started to scream as she entered her son's room to find it empty, then ran into the yard, screaming his name in anguish and terror.

Because that was the only thing she could do. That was the only thing anyone could do when their worst nightmare suddenly was realized.

16

MAY 2015

WHEN SOMEONE loses a child and never knows what happened to him, something happens to them, something indescribable. You can see it in their face, in their glassy eyes. It's like they're in this constant haze, like they're not really living and not really dead. I had seen it before, and now I was staring right at it again.

"Carrie Kingston?" I asked, looking at the woman in the doorway. My first impression was the she didn't look at all like herself, like the woman I had seen in the old newspaper clips from 1986, or in the recent articles written about her when the man who was imprisoned for the kidnapping of her son had been freed a few weeks ago.

"I feel awful about the whole thing," she was quoted saying. "All this time, I thought they caught the guy, and now it turns out that he didn't do it."

Mrs. Carrie Kingston was thinner now, a lot thinner. Her eyes were dark with hollowed sockets. Her skin colorless. Gray wasn't a word that fully covered it.

"Yes?" she asked hardly looking at me.

"Detective Jack Ryder, Brevard County Sheriff's Office. This is my partner Beth. May we come in, please?"

"Naturally," she said and let us in. She moved as if she was in slow motion.

We sat down in the kitchen. The house in Palm Bay was neat and clean, but smelled stuffy and confirmed my suspicion that Carrie Kingston didn't go out much. According to our research, the Kingstons had moved away from Cocoa Beach two years after their son disappeared. They were both retired now, while their oldest daughter lived up north.

"Where is your husband?" I asked when I sat down.

She looked at the clock on the wall. "He's out golfing. He should be here any minute now."

I looked at Beth. "We'll wait for him, then."

"Can I offer you some coffee while you wait?" Carrie asked.

We accepted and she poured each of us a cup. It was late in the afternoon, and I needed a shot of caffeine to keep me awake for the drive back. Luckily, we didn't have to wait long before Mr. Kingston entered the door through the garage. He stared at us, startled, then put down his sports bag.

"What's going on here? Carrie?"

"These nice detectives are here to talk to us, Jim. We've been waiting for you."

Jim looked skeptical. "What about? Is it about that bastard Johnson? 'Cause if you ask me, he should never have been let out."

"It is not about Johnson," I said. "Please, just sit down, Mr. Kingston, and we will get to it."

Reluctantly, Jim Kingston pulled out a chair and sat down.

"You have to excuse my husband," Carrie said. "But we have been through a lot, especially lately with Vernon getting out and everything. The hard part is not knowing. We have no idea what happened to Scott. At least, up until now, we thought we knew who took our son from us; we believed he had received his punishment, but now it turns out, we didn't. It's very frustrating to never get closure."

"I have closure," Jim snorted angrily. "I know that bastard did it, and somehow he fought the system and got out. He was supposed to have been killed. But he managed to work the system. He is clever, you know. Now he is a free man? After all he has put us through? There is not a day where we don't think about our son."

"I understand your anger," I said and looked at both of them. "But that is not why we are here. We are not here to discuss Mr. Johnson."

Carrie Kingston looked into my eyes and gasped. She cupped her mouth. "Oh, my God." Her eyes welled up. "You found him, didn't you?"

I nodded with a sigh. "Yes."

A change went over Jim Kingston's face. He

was no longer fuming with anger and despair. Tears were welling up in his eyes as well. It was hard for me to hold mine back.

"Where? How?" Carrie asked, her voice shaking.

"At a construction site," I said. "In Sebastian Inlet. The building has been there since 1993. We believe he was put in the ground before then."

Carrie Kingston didn't move. She simply stared at me, holding a hand to cover her mouth, while years of sorrow and frustration left her body. Her torso was trembling.

Jim Kingston sank in his chair. After years of having his shoulders in this tense position under his ears, he finally let them go with a deep sigh. Tears streamed across his cheeks. "And you're sure, right? You're sure it's him this time…? I mean, so many times we've thought…"

I nodded. "Yes. A few years after Scott disappeared, a body was found in Cocoa Beach that we believed might have been Scott. DNA profiling was the new thing back then, and you were asked to provide us with hair from Scott's brush. We found out it wasn't a match, but we kept his information, and to make a long story short, the ME ran a DNA test again this time. We had the result this morning, and it was a match."

"I can't believe it," Carrie said. "After so many years of not knowing. Of constantly staring at every little boy you see in the street or at the beach or in Wal-Mart. Even later, I kept looking for him everywhere. In crowds. He would have been thirty-seven this year, and just the other day, I stopped myself from staring at this man in his mid-thirties, just because I wondered if it could be him, or what he might look…in case…well, in case he wasn't dead. You keep hoping. That's what hurts the most. I guess I had accepted the fact that he was gone, but there is a part of you that wonders. What if he isn't dead? What if he is out there somewhere…alive? But, I guess…I guess we know for sure now."

"There is something else," I said. "We do believe he was alive for a couple of years after he disappeared. The body we found matching your son's DNA was older. Maybe up to seven years older."

I could have sworn I heard Carrie Kingston's heart stop. Her eyes widened, and she kept staring at me. Then, she burst into tears, and Jim couldn't hold his back anymore either.

"You mean to tell us he was still alive? You mean to tell us we could have found him if we had just looked harder?" he said, his voice trembling with a mixture of furor and unbearable terror.

"There was nothing you could have done differently, Mr. Kingston," Beth said. "Everyone did all they could."

Carrie Kingston was no longer listening to the conversation. She kept shaking her head in disbelief.

"No…No," she said over and over again, her voice breaking. "I knew he was alive. I knew it all this time. I kept looking for him, but you told us it was over. You people told us to let it go. To move on. That the guy who had hurt our son was in prison. That the case was closed and we should leave it alone. I kept telling everyone it wasn't over, that my boy was somewhere, alive, but they wouldn't listen. It was unlikely that he was alive still, they said. Vernon Johnson had killed him and there was a witness. But, there's no body, I kept saying. But still they wouldn't listen. And all this time…all this time, I could have been looking for him. You could have been looking for him. We could have found him. I know we could have." She clenched her fist in desperation. "Seven years, you say? I can't believe it!"

Jim looked at Carrie. I could tell the many years of wondering had taken its toll on their marriage. There was no affection to trace between the two of them. They were simply two people living together in mourning.

"So…so what happens now? Will Vernon Johnson go back to jail?" he asked.

"We don't know," I said. "We're reopening the case."

"How?" Carrie asked.

"Excuse me?" I asked.

"How? How did he die?"

I cleared my throat. "Well, since the body has been in the ground for a very long time, it's hard to determine the cause of death just yet."

Beth and I exchanged looks and both got up

from our chairs. It was time for us to go. We had done what we came for. As painful as it was, we had to leave them to their sorrow.

"Again, I am so sorry, Mr. and Mrs. Kingston, for your loss," I said and shook their hands. "We'll be in touch."

17

MAY 2015

WE DROVE back in silence. I had an awful taste in my mouth. I couldn't get Carrie Kingston's voice out of my head.

All this time…all this time, I could have been looking for him. You could have been looking for him. We could have found him. I know we could have.

The realization was devastating. To think that the little boy had been somewhere in the area for up to seven years. For seven years, he had been so close they could almost have run into him. But, where had he been? Had he run away and hid somewhere? Or had someone taken him? According to the report, the screen to the window had been taken off. It was put back on so loosely it had fallen off as soon as someone touched it when the police were called. So, there had to have been someone. But who? And where had he kept him all those years? And why?

"A case like that makes you think, huh?" Beth finally said, when we hit the bridges and drove towards the barrier islands where we both lived. It had gotten dark and the lights from the boats on the Intracoastal looked like fireflies in the water.

"Sure does," I said. "Especially when you have kids of your own. How are you holding up, by the way?"

"If you mean am I drinking again, then no."

"Good. I don't mean to pry, but I know that going through hard times can set you back," I said, and thought about Shannon and her falling off the wagon recently. Luckily, the pregnancy had changed all that. I knew that as soon as it was about more than just her own life, she would never do it.

I stopped at the red light.

"But I won't lie to you, Ryder," Beth said. "I have been tempted more than once while being at home all alone waiting to get better. It feels good to be back. Drove me nuts to have to just sit there and rest all the time. Ugh."

I chuckled. It wasn't often Beth ever shared something about herself with me. I liked it. Usually, she kept people at a distance. Usually, that meant people had a lot they weren't too proud of to share. But we all had that. We had all done things we weren't happy about. That was life, right?

I completely understood what she was saying. I liked to stay busy too. Staying at home with nothing to do but rest would drive me nuts. I had thought about it since Shannon suggested I stopped working. She had enough money to provide for the both of us, she said. But that wasn't my thing. What would I do?

Build a house, yes, but once that was done, then what? No. I needed this job and the force just as much as it needed me. It was my second home. But the truth was, at moments like these, when driving back from having given news like this to already suffering people, kicking them when they were already down, in moments like that I did consider leaving the force. Maybe I should just do what my dad had done, retire before I hit fifty and follow my dream. But what was my dream?

I had no clue.

I drove Beth back to her house and dropped her off. "Take it easy, partner," I said and meant every word. Beth needed to rest.

I drove back up A1A and stopped at my parents' motel to pick up the twins. Emily had texted me that she was at home. Angela and Shannon were visiting her sister Kristi for dinner.

The light was still lit on the deck overlooking the beach. I walked up there, thinking my parents were probably sitting outside talking the day through over a beer like they usually did before bedtime. As I came closer, I spotted my mother, but she wasn't sitting with my dad. She was with another man. Someone I didn't know personally, but had only seen in the newspaper. I stopped before they saw me and decided to walk inside the bar instead, where I found my dad behind the counter. He was closing up the bar while looking out at the two of them on the deck outside.

"What's going on, Dad?" I asked.

He drew in a deep breath and looked at me. "An old friend of your mom's showed up today."

I stared at him, startled. "Old friend? Vernon Johnson is my mother's old friend?"

"Not just friend," my dad said and looked into my eyes with a tender yet slightly fearful look. "I never told you this, but your mother once fell in love with someone else. You were six years old when it happened. She was very young when she had you and still was when she met him. That was why we left Cocoa Beach and moved to Ft. Lauderdale back then. Your mother decided to stay with me for your sake, but she loved him. They were deeply in love when he was arrested for having killed that kid. Your mother never got over him."

18

MAY 2015

Noah Kinley opened his eyes. At least he thought he had, but it was still as dark as if his eyes were still closed. He blinked a few times. No, they were open. He felt rested, but had a strange unease in his body. He didn't feel like waking up yet. He wanted to sleep more. Maybe it was still night?

He felt hungry. He felt so thirsty, his throat dry as sand. Noah coughed. His body felt almost numb. He blinked his eyes again and again, but the darkness wouldn't go away. Usually, he could see at least something from the light coming from the window, but there was nothing.

Had he gone blind? There was a kid on Noah's old street who was blind. She walked with a stick and had eyes that had rolled back in her head. She was weird and looked scary, Noah thought.

Oh, my God. Am I like her now? Have my eyes rolled back in my head too? Am I going to walk using a stick to find my way too? Oh, God, please, please don't let me be blind.

Noah sobbed and touched his eyes. As he did,

his hand slid across something. Noah reached up with both of his hands and felt it. It was like a roof or something, but very close to his face. He tried to lift his head, but it hit the roof with a thud and he put his head back down again. Then he felt around him to the sides and realized it was everywhere. It was surrounding him everywhere. He could hardly move.

What was this?

"Mom? Mooom? MOOOOOM??!" Noah finally screamed while slamming the palms of his hands on the roof. And now he couldn't stop screaming.

He banged on the sides and on the bottom and on the roof. He was scared to death. What had happened? Where was his new blue room? Where was his soft bed with the steering wheel? Where were his pillow and Ely the Evil Elephant?

Where are my mom and dad?

Noah screamed again and cried for hours, then he felt tired and weak and floated out of consciousness for a little while before he woke up again, only to realize nothing had changed. He could still open his eyes, but it felt no different than when he kept them closed. The darkness was still everywhere, enclosing him completely.

"Mooom? Where are you? I'm scared."

Noah was crying again. He felt so confused. Then he remembered something. He remembered having fought zombies in his room. He remembered the nice man who came to play with him with the sword. It was all very foggy. He had played with the nice man; they had been fighting with their swords, then he drank a soda that the man had given him. Noah's had tasted strange and afterwards he had felt sleepy. So incredibly sleepy all of a sudden. He had told the man he needed to take a nap before they could continue the game. He had smiled and tucked him in the bed. He had even caressed his hair till he fell asleep, just like Mommy used to do. He had been so nice to Noah.

But where was the man now? And where was Noah? Was this darkness ever going to end?

Noah banged his fists at the roof again. "MOOOOMMY! HELP! MOMMY. MOMMY! HEEELP!"

He cried and screamed desperately till he wore himself out, then had to stop. Noah felt so weak. So hungry and thirsty. And he had to pee. He had to pee really bad.

19

MAY 2015

SHANNON LEANED over and kissed Jack on the lips. He had been awake most of the night, worrying about the case he was working on. She knew him well enough by now to know what the groaning and constant tossing were all about. He had told her he had visited the parents of the boy whose body they had found just the night before, and after hearing the details, Shannon completely understood why it bothered him so much.

"Let me make you some breakfast," she said and looked deep into his eyes.

His eyes went from worried to relaxed. "Just some coffee would be great," he said and kissed her nose.

Shannon got up and walked into the kitchen. All the kids were still sleeping. In a few minutes, they would be all over the place, looking for shoes and backpacks and fighting. Shannon had learned to enjoy those small moments in the morning before hell broke loose.

From the kitchen, Shannon could hear Jack

pull the curtain like he always did first thing in the morning. To check out the waves. It had been very windy lately and a storm system was in the Atlantic, they said on the radio. It was still very far away from Florida. They didn't know yet if it would turn into a hurricane and maybe make landfall. It worried Shannon, but not Jack. He told her it was very rare they made landfall and they hadn't had one since 2005.

"It might get windy for a few days, but after that it'll pass. Don't worry."

Shannon tried hard not to. She had enough to worry about as it was. She was trying to get used to the chaos of being a big family and trying to get past the constant all-day sickness from the pregnancy, while battling the anxiety of possibly going to jail. It was a lot to take at once.

Jack crept up behind her and put his arm around her. He kissed her neck. Shannon closed her eyes.

"So, no surfing today either?" she asked.

"No. Not with that wind. It's nasty out there. Big waves in the back, but it's not worth the effort to try and paddle out. It's all blowing out. But with a little luck, we might get some awesome conditions on the backside of this system. Once it passes us out in the Atlantic, the wind will shift to off-shore and that's when the surf is perfect."

Shannon nodded and handed Jack the coffee. She had heard him talk about off-shore winds being perfect for surfing before. She felt like such a novice when it came to the ocean. She didn't understand why today wasn't a perfect day for surfing when the wind was blowing forcefully onshore and creating all these waves, but according to Jack, wind was a bad thing when it came to wave-surfing. She still didn't fully get it. But she did enjoy surfing with him and had come to the point where she could catch a wave on her own. But now with the pregnancy and all, she wasn't going to be surfing for a long time. She couldn't risk it. She didn't dare to, even though both Jack and the doctor said it was perfectly safe.

There was a noise coming from behind them and they turned to look at Angela, who had come into the kitchen. Shannon smiled and kissed her.

"Good morning, sleepyhead. You want some breakfast?"

She sat down at the table with a sleepy nod. Soon after, Abigail and Austin stormed inside and fought about sitting next to Angela.

"Hey, I wanted to sit there," Abigail whined, when Austin grabbed the chair.

"Sit on the other side of Angela," Jack said and poured cereal into bowls.

"No," Abigail said and crossed her arms in front of her chest. "Austin took my chair."

Jack sighed and looked at her. Then he told Austin to move away. Shannon felt a sting in her heart. She wanted to speak up and tell him Austin hadn't done anything wrong and that it was unfair, but bit her tongue. It wasn't her battle.

Austin refused to move.

"But, Daaad. I was here first."

"No, I wanted to sit there," Abigail claimed victoriously.

Abigail could be quite the handful, and Shannon couldn't help thinking that Jack maybe let her get away with too much. She never said anything, since she didn't want to hurt him. Neither of them ever commented on the other's education of their children. It seemed to work for now. But she wondered how it was going to work out once they started living in the same house. Right now, they lived in separate condos and Shannon and Angela could go downstairs and be on their own every now and then, even though they did hang out at Jack's place most of the time. But what was it going to be like when they were together like this every day? Shannon and Angela were used to it just being them. Shannon wasn't used to all these children and all their conflicts. Would she be able to never say anything? Would it be expected of her to help raise his children as well? Or was she supposed to just stay out of that, even though it affected her life as well. Standing in the kitchen and watching Jack try to solve this little problem, Shannon suddenly wondered how on earth they were going to do this and with a baby on top of it?

Shannon was staring helplessly at the many half-eaten bowls of cereal and screaming children when Jack's phone suddenly rang and he picked it up. He left the room, and Shannon had no idea how to manage the two arguing children.

"You're mean," Austin said to Abigail.

"No, I am not!"

"Yes, you are!"

"Am not!"

"You are. You're a meanie."

"Daaad. Austin called me a meanie!"

Shannon stared at the two of them for what felt like ages with no idea what to do or how to handle them. Finally, Jack returned with the phone in his hand. Shannon drew in a breath of relief. He was back, now he could take care of the two, while she focused on her baby girl, who just like her mother had no idea what to say or do. They simply weren't used to these kinds of conflicts. Shannon smiled when she saw Jack, but then her smile froze. He looked at her seriously.

"It was Ron. I've gotta hurry to the office. Something has come up. Could you please make sure the kids get to the bus on time? Thanks!"

Before she could open her mouth and argue, he had run into the bedroom, put on his uniform, and left, blowing a quick kiss to all of them.

Austin and Abigail had stopped fighting and were eating now, but just for a few minutes before Abigail poked her elbow into Austin's side and Austin wailed, "Abigail hit me!"

"No, I didn't. You were just sitting too close to me. If you had picked the chair over there, then maybe this wouldn't have happened."

"I was here first! Shannon?"

Shannon stared at the three children. She had never had more than one child at a time. This was certainly different. She forced a smile and avoided getting in the middle of their discussion.

"Finish up your food and get ready for the bus. It leaves in ten minutes."

"Yeah, hurry up, doofus," Abigail said to Austin.

"Abigail called me doofus."

"Because you are a doofus, doofus."

Only ten more minutes, Shannon. Only ten.

20

MAY 2015

RON PLACED a picture on the whiteboard next to Scott Kingston.

"Noah Kinley," he said and placed his finger at his nose. "Disappeared from his home yesterday. According to his parents, he was playing in his room in their new house, but when they went inside to tell him it was dinnertime, he was gone. The sliding door to the yard was left open to get some of the fresh breeze that we've had lately. The parents had turned off the AC and left the doors open instead. The screen door was shut, but open when the parents came into the room. They looked for him everywhere. We had a team search the canal and the entire neighborhood for most of the night. Not a trace of Noah. It doesn't look good."

"You think he was kidnapped?" Beth asked.

"We don't know yet," Ron said. "He could have just run away. But when children are involved, I don't take chances. I'm putting all my men in to look for him."

We all nodded. No arguing that it was

important. I stared at the little boy next to Scott Kingston on the whiteboard. The similarities were obvious. Little boy, almost the same age, disappeared from his room where the window or sliding door was left open. No one in the room wanted to say it out loud, but we were all thinking it.

Vernon Johnson had just been released and now it happened again?

It could be a coincidence. It might not be. We didn't know just yet. When Ron ended the meeting and told us to go to work, I went back to my desk with the pictures of the two little boys flickering for my inner eye. Carrie Kingston's voice was roaming my mind.

All this time…all this time, I could have been looking for him. You could have been looking for him. We could have found him. I know we could.

I couldn't bear it. So many years this boy was still alive after he was kidnapped. We weren't going to make the same mistake again. That was for sure. I was determined not to let that happen.

I looked through the newspaper, where Shannon's upcoming concert in Orlando in two weeks was announced. She had said yes to doing a couple of concerts in the coming months. I hoped it wasn't too much for her. I wanted her to rest. She was, after all, carrying our child. She had been throwing up a lot lately and I wondered if she was up for it. Could it affect the baby? All the loud music, screaming fans, and Shannon straining herself? I wasn't happy about her doing it, but I also knew it was her passion and her entire life, so I hesitated to say anything when she told me about her plans. Now I wished I had. Now that it was too late.

I flipped a couple of pages in the newspaper, then stopped at an article that made my heart pound. I grabbed the paper, then ran into Ron's office without knocking. He looked at me, perplexed.

"What's going on, Ryder?"

I threw the article on the desk. He looked at it.

"Two people were found killed yesterday in Daytona Beach," I said. "These two."

Ron gave the picture an extra glance. "So? It's out of our area."

"Their story. Look at their story. It's a couple. According to the article, they were being charged after their little girl was found locked in basement in *deplorable* conditions. Deplorable conditions. Look at what it says: *a school nurse reported that a nine-year-old student may have been the victim of abuse after the girl was sent to the nurse's office because she smelled strongly of urine. The girl told the nurse that her private parts hurt, so the nurse conducted an examination and found her vaginal area to be red and irritated. The little girl also told the nurse that she wasn't allowed to go to the bathroom in the house and was forced to go to the bathroom outside because her family didn't want to contract the infections she had. When Sheriff's deputies responded, the victim's father and his girlfriend acknowledged they locked her in their unfinished basement with little food and water during the day as punishment for a recent school suspension. The basement door was secured with a lock and chain. He and his live-in girlfriend and her biological son live upstairs, while the little girl lives in the unfinished basement. He said they kept her downstairs because of her lack of bladder control, saying he "cannot afford to keep cleaning up after her."*

I put the paper down and looked at Ron. He looked at me like I had completely lost it. "Where are you going with this?"

"They're dead. They were shot outside of their house yesterday. Both twice in the heart."

Ron's eyes widened. Finally, he understood. "The Monahan sisters?"

"You bet."

21

FLORIDA 1969

WHEN HECTOR spotted his brother in the crowd at the train station in Orlando, he started to cry. Raul yelled his name and started to run closer.

"Hector! Hector!"

Seconds later, they were in each other's arms. The trip from Cuba and been long and hard, and finding Raul had taken months. But through other Cubans in Miami, he had heard that Raul had settled on a small island up in Central Florida called Merritt Island. As soon as Raul had polished enough shoes to make enough money for the train ticket, he had written to Raul at the restaurant that he had heard he worked in, and once he was on the train, he could do nothing but hope that Raul would be there. And so he was. Tears were streaming across his cheeks.

"Dear brother. Look at you. You are too skinny!" Raul said and clapped him on the back. He put his arm around his shoulder and pulled him close.

Raul took Hector to the restaurant where he

worked. It was a small Cuban place, and the smells and music inside of it made Hector sick with longing for his daughter, Isabella, whom he had left.

At the restaurant, he was also reunited with two of his other brothers who had escaped Cuba the year before. The reunion was tearful, yet joyous.

"We have a job for you here," Raul said. "The owner is Cuban too and he told us you could work with us. You can live with me as long as you want to. After all, I owe you my life, dear brother."

Raul smiled and wiped a tear from his eyes. Then he laughed and patted Hector on the shoulder once again. Hector's other two other brothers, Alonzo and Juan, joined in and they all hugged again. Hector's heart was heavy in his chest. He was so happy to finally be there, to finally be in the U.S., but now that he had reached his destination, he was confronted with the fact that he had left everything back in Cuba. Four of the brothers were together, but the rest of the family wasn't. He feared for their lives.

Hector soon started working in the kitchen of the restaurant, and as the days passed, he got used to life in the U.S. without his daughter and parents, even though he missed them every day, every minute. He started to make a decent living and soon was able to get his own place. A condo on Merritt Island soon became a house on Merritt Island, and his job in the kitchen at the restaurant soon led to a job as a butcher in Cocoa Beach, and two years later, he had saved enough money to be able to open his own Cuban restaurant in Cocoa Beach.

Little Havana was the love of Hector's life, after his daughter Isabella, naturally. He wrote her letters every day and hoped they would reach her, but knowing how things worked in his homeland, he also knew it was very unlikely. The political tensions were getting worse, even though Hector didn't understand what it was all about. He knew things were getting worse back home; he heard many stories of people being imprisoned for speaking up for themselves, for defending the right of speech, or if they tried to leave, and he started to wonder how he was going to get his daughter out. He wanted to get his parents to come as well, and the rest of his brothers, but for now he focused only on Isabella. She was the one who deserved a better future. She was the one he was responsible for. She was the one he was being eaten up from the inside with longing for.

Sometimes, he would drive down to the beach after closing up the restaurant or before they opened, and he would simply stare out into the Atlantic Ocean, thinking she was out there somewhere. South of where he was. Breathing in the same air that he did. Maybe swimming in the same ocean. Every day, he wondered if it would be possible to simply take a boat and go get her. But he knew he would be shot if he was caught. They had made themselves very clear. He could never set foot in Cuba again.

22

MAY 2015

I IMMEDIATELY called up my colleagues at Volusia
County Sheriff's Office, who covered Daytona
Beach. They gave me the details of the case and I
told them my concerns.

"I believe it might be connected to a case we're
working on down here," I told the detective on
the case, and then gave him the details about the
sisters.

I hung up and then called Sarah Millman's
lawyer and asked him to bring her back in. Two
hours later, she was sitting in the interrogation
room as Ron and I entered. He wanted to hear
what she had to say.

"My client is not saying anything," the lawyer
said before I even opened my mouth. "What are
the charges?"

"She's not under arrest," I said. "At least not
yet."

"So, why are we here?" the lawyer asked. "My
client is still only a suspect, as far as I have been
informed."

I threw a picture of the couple from Daytona Beach in front of them. "These two were killed outside their home yesterday. It has the scent of the Monahan sisters all over it. They were being charged with child abuse, and they were each shot twice in the heart."

Sarah Millman shook her head. "I don't know anything about this. I was at home yesterday. The guard at the gate can tell you. I haven't been to Daytona for years."

"Have you spoken to your sisters lately?" I asked. "Maybe they're in Daytona?"

"I hardly think so," she said. "It's a very noisy town."

"I wasn't asking if they were there for the speedway," I said.

"I know what you're asking," she said. "But you also know I haven't heard from them. After all, you're tapping my phone, aren't you? You have a tail on me twenty-four-seven. Isn't that what you call it? Don't think I haven't noticed that I'm being followed everywhere."

"Well, it's hardly a secret that we're trying to catch your sisters, so I don't expect you to be surprised," I said.

"I'm not."

"We have a proposition for you," Ron said. "I talked to the State Attorney and they're willing to lower the charges against you if you help us find your sisters."

The lawyer leaned forward. His facial expression told me he believed in her guilt as well. He knew she had a bad case. "What are we talking about?" he asked.

"Assisting murder instead of homicide," Ron said.

It hurt inside of me to know that she might get away with killing her husband, and only being charged with assisting to it, but it was worth it if it meant we would get the two others.

Sarah Millman leaned back and crossed her arms in front of her chest. Her lawyer looked at her. She shook her head.

"It's a good deal," her lawyer said.

Sarah Millman was thinking about it. I could tell this might be a way to get to her. She was afraid of going to jail. She doubted if it was worth it…if it was worth covering for her sisters.

"What about Christopher?" I asked. "If you go in for murder, he'll have to grow up without a mother or a father. You say you fight for the children…against injustice and abuse. But what about your own son? Is he the one who will be lost in all this? 'Cause you're going to jail. I spoke to Jacquelyn Jones this morning, and they're getting ready to press charges. She even believes she has enough evidence to charge you with being an accomplice in the attack on my partner. And that's bad. You know how they get when an officer is involved. They always go for the worst punishment. Even if it was your sister Natalie who set up the bomb, you knew about it. That's what they'll argue. They might even say you planned it along with your other sisters. And then there's the matter of Stanley Bradley, who identified you as one of the women holding him captive and trying to kill him. It doesn't look very good, sweetheart. It's only a matter of days before we'll be taking you in again. And this time, it's for good. It's up to you how badly you want this to end for Christopher."

"Would they agree to us pleading that my client was under the influence of substances while planning or committing the crime?" the lawyer asked.

Ron nodded. "Yes. If she talks."

"I'm not saying anything," she said. "I don't know where they are."

I sighed and got up from my chair. "That's too bad, Sarah. We were just trying to help you out here. Now, we'll just have to settle for whatever we found in your house when our people went through it while you were here talking to us."

"You searched my house again?"

The lawyer was about to speak, but I showed him a copy of the warrant. "Yes, we did," I said.

"This is beginning to look like harassment," the lawyer said.

"You won't find anything this either," Sarah Millman said.

I got up from the chair and walked to the door. I grabbed the handle, then turned and looked at her. "I guess you have nothing to fear, then."

23

MAY 2015

NOAH KNEW he was in the worst nightmare in his life. As a matter of fact, it was worse than any nightmare he'd ever had. And Noah used to have many. Especially since they moved to the new house. He never liked the house much. There was something about it that made him scared, especially in the dark.

"It was just a nightmare," his mother would whisper when she came to his room after being awakened by Noah's screaming. "Go back to sleep. It was just a bad dream."

But Noah kept having the same dream over and over again; it haunted him even when he was awake.

Where are you, Mommy?

He had no idea if it was night or day. Wherever he was, there was no light. Only walls surrounding him on all sides. Wooden walls that he knocked and knocked on, but had no answer. He had no idea how long he had been lying like this, but he did know he was very, very thirsty.

He had wet his pants and the smell made him sick. The hunger and the thirst ate him up from the inside.

I'm so thirsty, Mommy. I'm so hungry. Where are you? Help me, Mommy!

Did his mom know he was gone by now? She had to know. He had been gone for a very long time. Noah closed his eyes. It didn't matter if he had them closed or open. The darkness surrounded him anyway. Every now and then, he broke into a panic thinking he was never going to get out of this thing. Then he would scream and knock and call for his mommy, but nothing happened. No one came.

Have they forgotten about me?

Sometimes, Noah felt like back when he had been lost at J.C. Penney's at the mall. He had been only five years old, but remembered it vividly. He had been holding his mother's hand, then spotted something, a sweet alligator toy, and let go of his mother's hand for one unforgiving second. When he returned and spotted his mother again, he grabbed her hand and looked up, only to realize it wasn't his mother anymore. It was some other woman wearing the same white pants.

"Hello there," the woman said and knelt next to him.

"You're not my mommy."

"No, I'm not."

Noah had let go of the woman's hand, then run away, getting lost between rows of women's clothing. He had looked and looked but not been able to find his mother anywhere. He had ended up asking a security guard to help him. The guard had found her. Finally, he was back with his mother again and promised to never ever wander off again. It was an easy promise to make, since Noah never ever wanted to feel that feeling again.

But now, it had happened again. He was lost, he was in trouble, and he couldn't get himself out of it. He had no idea how to. There was no nice security guard he could ask; he was all alone, alone in this…this thing.

Noah sobbed and felt sorry for himself, when suddenly, he was interrupted by a sound coming from outside.

Someone was there.

There was a fumbling on the other side, sounds, and then someone saying something, calling his name.

"Noah…Noah…"

Strong light from above blinded him. He held a hand to his face to cover his eyes. But he wanted to see who it was. Was it his mom and dad? Was it the police?

Noah smiled with relief and felt his heart race in his chest. Finally, someone was here. Finally, he was getting out.

A silhouette blocked out the light. Noah couldn't see their face.

"Mommy?" he cried. "Is that you, Mommy?"

A hand reached down and he grabbed it and sat up. Then he was helped up, but it was hard for him to stand, and he kept falling. An arm grabbed him and finally he saw the face of his savior. Only, when he looked into his eyes, he realized with terror that he wasn't here to rescue him. He was the one who had put him there.

24

MAY 2015

"I HAVE something!"

Richard yelled through the room. I looked up from my computer. Outside, the windows the dark gray clouds hung heavily. The storm was still forecasted to stay off the Florida Coast. It was still far away, but it was bringing bad weather to our area already. So far, it wasn't even a tropical storm yet, but it was building. I was keeping a close eye on the radars. The wind gusts made people's clothes and hats fly in the streets. Still, they all wore flip-flops and shorts, since it was very hot.

I walked to Richard and stood behind him, looking over his shoulder. Twenty-four hours had passed since we had searched Sarah Millman's house, and so far, we hadn't come any closer to finding her sisters.

Until now.

"What did you find?"

"I've been through all of the stuff on her computer, and I mean everything. Search history, all her emails, anything she looked at for the last forty-eight hours before we took her computer in. Just now, I was going through her iPad, and I finally came upon something. You are familiar with Snapchat, right?"

I shrugged. "I've never used it myself, but I've heard about it, yes. Emily uses it with her friends."

"Well, basically, it's an app where you send a photo or a video or a text message to someone and users set a time limit for how long recipients can view their Snaps. The time limit ranges from one to ten seconds."

"And afterwards, it's deleted; I know that much," I said.

"Yes, that's how it works. When the ten seconds are up, the pictures are hidden from the recipient's device and deleted from Snapchat's servers."

"Why am I sensing there is a but in here?"

"'Cause there is," Richard said with a smile. "Most people think it's perfectly safe to send their boyfriend a Snapchat of themselves naked because no one else will ever see it and it will be deleted immediately afterwards. But, that is not entirely the case. Snapchat's own documentation states that the company's servers retain a log of the last 200 "snaps" that were sent and received, but no actual content is stored. The documentation further explains that if the file is not viewed by the recipient, it remains on Snapchat's servers for 30 days. Furthermore, a forensics firm in Utah discovered a way to find the so-called deleted pics, and created a way to download them from the 'hidden' location a few years back. Apparently, there's a folder on the device, where all the photos are stored. The team then developed a process of extracting the image data. It takes about six hours, on average, to get the information. Look what I found. This was received in Sarah Millman's Snapchat two days ago."

I stared at his screen. Then a smile spread across my face. In front of me stared Sarah's two sisters back at me. The picture was a selfie taken in front of the house in Daytona where the couple was shot later that same day. The sisters were smiling. The caption read: SHOWTIME!

"You've got to be kidding me," I exclaimed.

"I know. They all make mistakes at some point, right?" Richard said. "I have only seen a little bit, but this is definitely what they have been using to communicate with one another. I'm talking dates, names, everything. It tells us everything they've been up to. I even found a text telling Sarah that they have Stanley Bradley, then a photo, followed by the sisters with his lifeless body in the crashed car before they pulled him out. This is good stuff." Richard opened another picture. "This was taken three days ago."

I looked at the photo and smiled even wider. The picture showed them in front of a resort in Daytona Beach. The caption read:

THE ANGEL MAKERS JUST CHECKING IN

25

MAY 2015

WE DROVE to Daytona just before sunset. Volusia County Sheriff, Ned Farinella, met us outside the Hotel Tropical Winds. Ron was with me, since Beth was too emotionally involved in this case, and I was afraid of her reaction when facing these women that were responsible for her severe disfigurement.

The sun was setting beautifully into a thick layer of clouds over the mainland, coloring the dark clouds over the Atlantic with its last breath before it disappeared. I stared at the darkness on the horizon, wondering if the storm would make landfall or just come close enough to give us the swell I was longing for. Waves had been picking up all day because of the strong winds. The low-pressure had turned into a regular storm-system now, but it seemed to have stalled. It was still very visible, even this far north of Cocoa Beach. It was a big storm. It now had a sixty percent chance of turning into a hurricane, according to the meteorologists. I just hoped it would stay off the coast. It had been many years since we last had a storm make landfall. Last time it happened, the roof was blown off my parents' motel. This winter had been rough on them financially. They couldn't afford for it to happen again.

"I got all my people here," Ned Farinella said, as we shook hands.

I looked at the many cars parked in the parking lot of the hotel. I just hoped the Monahan sisters hadn't looked out the window of the hotel.

"I spoke to the owner," Ned Farinella said, as we walked up to the front. "They say the sisters are in room 333. They checked in as Amy and Michelle Childs. Told the receptionist they were sisters travelling together. The receptionist recognized them from the picture we sent them. According to the receptionist, they're in their room right now. They came back this afternoon and she hasn't seen them leave."

I felt the handle of my gun while my heart rate went up. We entered the lobby of the hotel and Ned talked shortly with the receptionist before we found the elevator and got in.

"Still there?" I asked.

Ned nodded. "As far as she knows, they're still in the room, yes."

"Good."

I felt the heavy gun between my hands and tried hard to calm my nerves. I hated this stuff; so much could go wrong, and more often than not, someone ended up getting killed. But, at the same time, I was eager to get these women. I wanted them to pay for what they had done to Beth, but

I didn't want anyone to die. I wanted them to face justice.

We walked up to the door of the hotel room and I knocked, holding my gun in front of me. "Angelina Monahan? Kelly White?" I yelled, not knowing if the last sister went by her married name or her maiden name since her divorce.

There was no answer, nothing but a loud noise that told me that something was going on behind that door.

"They're trying to escape," Ron yelled.

I kicked the door in, and within seconds, we were both inside the hotel room. My eyes moved slowly across the room, scanning it for any sign of movement. Suddenly, there was something near the balcony. The curtain was blowing. The sliding glass door was open; someone ran through it. It was a woman.

"Stop! Police!" I yelled, then stormed after her. I caught up with her on the balcony, just before she was about to climb the rail and climb down. Her sister was already hanging underneath the balcony and now managed to land on the balcony below, from where she could jump to a grass area next to the building. I threw my arm around the woman's waist and grabbed her. The woman screamed and yelled and tried to fight me off, but I fell backwards with her on top of me.

"The other one is getting away!" Ron yelled.

I spotted her running across the grass, just as the woman on top of me managed to push her elbow into my face so hard I saw nothing but stars for a few seconds, just long enough for her to get out of my grip. She jumped for the rail again and I held up my gun.

"Stop, or I'll shoot," I said.

She froze in the middle of her movement, then turned and looked at me. I recognized her as Angelina Monahan.

"You won't get far. Neither will your sister," I continued. "There are police everywhere down there. It's over, Angelina."

Angelina looked into my eyes, then a smile spread on her face. She shook her head slowly with a scoff.

"It'll never be over, Detective. Don't you realize that by now?"

She turned around with the intention of jumping. Beneath us was pavement. She risked getting killed if she jumped directly down from the third floor without landing on the balcony below first, like her sister had. Either she'd kill herself or she would end up getting away. Neither worked for me. My breathing was getting harder by the second. I felt steadier than ever. Then I pulled the trigger.

Angelina Monahan screamed as the bullet hit her shoulder. It was intentional. I didn't want to kill her, only hinder her escape. Stunned, she turned and looked at me while placing a hand to her shoulder, just as she lost her grip on the railing and fell backwards.

"No!" I yelled and got up to grab her, but my

hand just missed hers as she fell into the air. Seconds later, she hit the pavement below, headfirst.

26

MAY 2015

I DIDN'T get back to Cocoa Beach until way past midnight. Angelina Monahan was dead. Her sister Kelly was still on the loose. I was so angry with myself and had a feeling everyone else was going to be too. Especially Emily. She had a spring concert at the school, and for the first time she had told me to come. I had been so excited, since she never wanted me to come to these things, and I had never heard her sing.

My mom was waiting for me on the deck of the hotel. They had closed the bar long ago, but she was still sitting outside with a book and a glass of water. Just like she had when I was young and went out at night. I couldn't help but smile.

"Hey, Ma," I said and sat next to her on the wooden bench.

She put the book down with a sigh. "You missed it," she said.

I closed my eyes. "I know. I feel so bad."

"You should have seen her face when she received your text, telling her you weren't coming, right before she was supposed to go on. I could have killed you right then for doing this to her. She had looked forward to this, you know. It took a lot of courage for her to ask us to come. Especially you. She wanted to impress you."

I inhaled deeply, feeling the guilt eating me up. No one could make me feel like an awful dad like my mother.

"I know," I said. "You don't have to tell me I screwed up."

"I get that your work is important. Believe me, I was married to someone a lot like you once. Until he finally retired and started to live his life with me and not constantly making excuses for not being there. You have to decide how long you think this will work for you and your family. Not all cops have three children to take care of alone, you know."

I looked at my mother and nodded. She was right. I had a huge responsibility on my shoulders. On top of it, I now had a chance to change things radically. Being with Shannon and moving in with her gave me a new opportunity I had never had before. Shannon had told me she wouldn't mind if I didn't work. She could support all of us. It was a huge advantage for me. But I had no idea if that was what I wanted. I loved my job. But I didn't love what it did to my family. I didn't love missing out on nights like this one, where my teenage daughter tried to impress me.

"No one would blame you for choosing your family," my mother said. "The kids, on the other hand, will blame you for the rest of their lives if you miss out on their childhood. One of my dear friends works at a hospice in Orlando and she tells me the thing people there regret the most is not that they didn't work more; what they regret is not spending enough time with their loved ones. Think about it. You have a real chance of starting over and creating a whole new family. Not everyone gets a second chance like that."

I nodded and leaned back against the wall. I kept trying to avoid having to make a decision. I knew if I quit my job at the force, I could never come back to the same position again. Reaching homicide had taken many years for me. If things didn't work out for some reason between me and Shannon and I had to go back to work, I would never get back into homicide easily again. It was a big chance to take. What if I missed it too much?

We sat in silence for a few minutes while I let my mother's words linger on my mind. She had a way of always being right. It was annoying.

"Are the kids here or at the condo?" I asked as I got up.

"Emily and Shannon took them home after the concert. I think they all decided to sleep at your place."

"I better get back there, then, and get some sleep," I said and leaned over and kissed my mother.

I started walking back to the car when my mother turned her head and said, "She was amazing, by the way."

I smiled and nodded. "I had a feeling she would be."

27

MAY 2015

BEING OUTSIDE the walls certainly wasn't all it was cracked up to be, Vernon soon realized. He had no idea what to do with himself. At least while on the inside, they had told him what to do, every day. He had no choice but to do what they told him to. Now, all of a sudden, he had all these choices. He was a free man and could do anything he wanted to.

Nothing frightened him more.

What did people do with themselves all day? Worked? Vernon never had a job in his life. Being only a teenager when he went in, he never had an education either. He had tried taking some college courses while on the inside, but never managed to finish them. He had nothing to offer a workplace. Besides, they had given him enough money so he didn't have to work. But, what else was there to do?

He went to the local Wal-Mart a couple of times a week, and to him that was more than enough. Being around people scared him, to be frank. He had no idea what they expected of him or if they knew who he was and feared him. He didn't feel like they even belonged to the same race or era. It was like he was still living in the eighties, where everything was much slower and people actually looked at each other and not into their small screens constantly. It was like the world had stopped communicating.

Vernon liked to take a walk every day. He would go to the park and walk or take the bus to the beach and take a long stroll with his feet in the water. Somehow, the ocean made him calm. It was the one thing that hadn't changed one bit since he went in. He loved the calmness of the ocean. And there was one thing more he loved about the beach, especially Cocoa Beach. He loved the fact that Sherri lived down there. His one and only. The one he had been dreaming of every night while waiting on the inside, waiting for them to finally figure out that they had made a mistake.

Vernon knew she was married now, but he just couldn't stay away from her. Now he was standing outside her motel and waiting for her. He had taken the bus there and been there twenty minutes earlier than they had agreed, just to make sure he wouldn't be late. He felt nervous. He was so excited to see her again. Today, she had promised to take him to see Kennedy Space Center. He had dreamt of seeing it for so many years, and she had told him she would take him. For old time's sake, she had said. She felt like she owed him that much.

Vernon didn't know how she felt about him, but to him, she was the only bright thing about being outside again. She was the only one he knew and the only one, except for his mother, who still cared for him after so many years. She had always known he was innocent, she had told him. And it was her great sadness that she had been unable to prove it to the police. She had ended up marrying an officer, and now her son was a detective too.

Vernon smiled as his eyes met hers. She was still beautiful, even after so many years, he thought.

"Are you ready?" she asked.

Vernon took his cap between his hands. "You look beautiful," he said.

Sherri blushed. "Vernon," she said with a slight reproach in her voice. "I'm a married woman."

Vernon smiled and bowed his head. "I know, Miss Sherri. I know."

"Now, get in," Sherri said and opened the door to her car.

Vernon nodded and got in. Sherri started the car. Vernon was impressed by how quiet the engine was. A lot had happened to cars. This one even had a back-up camera that made an awful lot of noise when Sherri backed out of the parking lot.

Just as she was about to drive into the street, a police car from the Sheriff's Department drove up and stopped her. A deputy got out and walked up to the car. Sherri rolled the window down.

"What's going on, Officer?" she asked.

He lifted his cap. "I'm sorry Mrs. Ryder, but I need to talk to Mr. Johnson."

PART TWO:

IT WAS THE DREAM OF AN UPRIGHT MAN

28

CUBA APRIL 1ST 1980

ISABELLA SUAREZ was wearing her Sunday best. She knew everything had been carefully planned by her grandfather and her uncle Amador, the only one still left in Cuba. The rest of them had all fled to the U.S., going through Costa Rica or even Spain. But it was getting harder to get out, her grandfather had told her. And they had to try now to get the rest of the family out before everything closed up completely. Being only sixteen years old, Isabella didn't understand much of what was going on, other than what she heard her uncle and grandparents discuss with low voices at the dinner table. But she did know one thing. She desperately wanted to go to her father, who had left her eleven years ago. She had received one letter from him during the many years and knew he was with his brothers in the U.S. She had put his address in the pocket of her dress on this night when her grandfather grabbed her hand and took her suitcase. He put it in the back of their old truck. Isabella grabbed her grandmother's hand and they exchanged one anxious glance before getting in the car.

They drove to downtown Havana, then left the car and got on a bus. The bus driver was a friend of Amador's, and Isabella remembered having seen him at the house several times in the past weeks while they were carefully planning this.

After driving around downtown for a few minutes, the bus driver stopped the bus several blocks from Embassy Row in downtown Havana.

Isabella held on to her grandmother's hand and looked into her eyes. She could tell she was worried. The woman had been the closest Isabella had to having a mother. Isabella knew when she felt anxious. She knew her every movement and recognized any unusual behavior, just like any child did with their mother.

"It'll be fine," Isabella whispered, and held her grandmother's hand tightly in hers. The old woman tried to smile.

"The bus is broken down. Everyone needs to leave the bus immediately," the bus driver said, addressed to the rest of the people on the bus.

It wasn't an unusual event. The old buses driving downtown broke down constantly. So, no one thought of it as being strange or even complained about it. The other passengers left the bus, and as soon as they were gone, the driver closed the doors and looked at Isabella, her grandparents, and Amador.

"You ready?"

Isabella swallowed hard and bit her lip. Her

grandparents and Amador all nodded. Isabella hesitated. She wasn't sure what it was she was agreeing to. But she was sure she wanted out of here.

Then she nodded too. The driver smiled. She detected a slight nervousness in his smile. He was trying to hide it.

"Okay," he said, his voice trembling. "Let's do this."

The driver started the bus up. He reached the Peruvian Embassy, then looked in his rearview mirror and looked at Isabella and her grandmother. "Get down now," he said. "Everyone."

They all threw themselves on the floor of the bus. Isabella's body was trembling in fear while her grandmother's arm landed on her back and she felt her creep close to her. She petted her across the hair and whispered in her ear.

"Sh. It'll all be alright."

The bus continued towards the fence of the Peruvian Embassy, and seconds later, the sound of shots being fired at the bus burned themselves into Isabella's memory as she closed her eyes and screamed, drowning out the sound of the bus crashing through the fence.

29

MAY 2015

SHANNON BENT over the toilet once again and gagged. Nothing came out. It was the seventh time this morning she had thrown up. There was nothing left. She slid to the floor and caught her breath. The nausea was killing her. She didn't remember it being this way with Angela.

There was a knock on her door. "Ten minutes to showtime," a voice said.

Shannon got up and splashed water on her face. It had been a busy couple of days. Jack had been very occupied with his case and been away in Daytona, leaving her to deal with the kids, and this morning she had flown out to Austin, Texas to do a concert. The stadium was completely sold out. Around thirty thousand people were expecting her to go on stage in ten minutes.

Was it nerves? Could it be that she was simply so nervous it made the nausea worse? Or was this just a different pregnancy than with Angela? She had been throwing up for weeks now. Her doctor told her it would get better...usually, after around three months into the pregnancy, he had said.

Well she was more than three months in now, and it didn't seem to have any intentions of calming down.

She also felt so tired every day. Like she was completely drained of energy. She wasn't used to feeling this feeble. Shannon had always been a person with great energy.

She looked at herself in the mirror. She was so pale. She found some make-up and tried to cover up the redness around her eyes and nose. No one knew about the pregnancy yet, and she wasn't ready to tell. Not until it showed. Then she would have to. But she wasn't looking forward to it. The press was already all over the fact that she had bought the property in Cocoa Beach. The covers of the magazines this week told everyone how she was *building her love nest with her hunk-lover, Jack.* Others were really mean and wrote that she had barely buried her ex-husband Joe before she moved on. Some still called her the *murderess country-star,* even though she hadn't even been charged with anything yet, let alone convicted.

Shannon finished putting on her make-up, then smiled her stage-smile, grabbed her hat, and put it on. From afar, no one could see how bad she felt on the inside.

There was another knock on the door and Shannon knew it was time to go out. She went to grab her guitar, but as she leaned down to get it from the box, she felt a pain in her stomach. Like a pinch, but just worse. Shannon leaned against the wall to not fall. She gasped in fear.

It didn't feel right.

She felt her stomach as the pain disappeared. Shannon breathed hard. She felt anxious and looked at her phone. Should she call Jack and let him know?

No, he is busy today. Besides, he'll only worry and tell you not to go on. This is what you love. You need this to not go insane.

It had been a lot lately…taking care of all the children, and Shannon wasn't sure she was made for taking care of children. She loved them, yes, but she needed more in her life.

Shannon opened the door and stepped out. In the distance, she could hear the crowd calling her name. She closed her eyes and smiled. She started walking towards the stage area, deciding to forget everything about the pain in her stomach, children, houses, murder charges, and being a mother and simply do what she did best, what she knew she could do.

Sing.

30

MAY 2015

I FINISHED my report on the Daytona shooting and handed it to Ron. There was still no news about the last sister, who seemed to have vanished. Meanwhile, Richard was pulling all kinds of evidence material out of Sarah Millman's Snapchat account, and it was starting to look really good. It was obvious they had thought they were safe using this media to share their pictures, but now it served as excellent evidence. I couldn't have been happier.

After a long day of work, I decided to leave early and go to the lot to see if they had made any progress. They had started to clean it out the same morning and were still at it when I arrived. The bulldozers were cleaning out the yard and tearing down the remains of the old house that had been there since the storm knocked it down in 2005.

I spoke to the workers, who told me it all went according to plan, but that they might need a day or two more than anticipated. I figured they would.

"The old house will be gone in a couple of days, and then you can start to build your own," the foreman said.

I was looking very much forward to that. The architect and I had agreed on the floor plan, and I had asked him to make a bigger deck outside towards the beach, but other than that I was very satisfied. I couldn't wait to see my dream house materialize itself. I couldn't wait for my family to live there. Just me and Shannon and all of our kids. I could imagine all the fun we were going to have. So much joy and happiness.

I had started to dream about the baby and what it was going to be like, holding it in my arms. I couldn't believe I was going to be a father once again. I had thought I was done with that part.

But, with life, you never knew.

I left the lot and drove back the two blocks to my parents' place, where the twins and Angela were putting up a kite on the beach. My dad was helping them and I watched as they got it in the air. I walked up to my dad and stood next to him while watching the kite soar.

"So, where is Mom?" I asked.

My dad didn't look at me. "She's at Kennedy Space Center," he said.

"At the Space Center? What on earth is she doing there?"

"Showing that Vernon character around. Apparently, he's never seen it and really wanted to. After twenty-eight years in jail for something he didn't do, I guess your mother feels like she owes it to him or something."

"Doesn't that upset you?" I asked.

125

He shrugged. I knew him well enough to know it did bother him.

"After so many years of marriage, you just gotta trust one another, right?" he said, not sounding very convincing.

"Dad. It bothers you. I can tell. Why don't you just say something to her? Tell her you don't want her to see him anymore."

My dad looked at me, then laughed. "I can tell you don't have much experience with the institution of marriage. If I say that, I'll only make things worse. I don't tell your mother what to do and what not to do."

"But, at least, you should be able to tell her it bothers you," I said.

The kite fell to the ground and Abigail ran to fetch it. They all helped each other to get it back up again. A woman walked past with her dog on the beach. It wasn't on a leash. It annoyed me, since dogs weren't allowed on the beach. But many dog owners did it anyway, and now people had started calling the Sheriff's office to complain about it, and Ron had to send some of his deputies to the beach to give them fines. It happened every day now, and took a lot of our resources that we would be happy to use otherwise to maybe, say…solve murders. I understood why people wanted to walk their dogs on the beach. It was a great place to walk, and at this end of the beach, there weren't that many people. But the least they could do was to keep them on leashes so they wouldn't bother people.

I decided not to care, since I was off duty, and turned to spot Emily. She was sitting in the shade on the deck staring at her phone. I left my dad and the kids and walked up to her and sat down. She didn't look at me.

"So, I hear you were pretty amazing last night?" I said.

She didn't look up from her phone, or answer.

"Listen, I understand you're mad at me for not coming. I can't blame you for being mad. But you must believe I really wanted to be there more than anything in this world. Shannon told me all about it. She said you sang so beautifully. I feel so awful for missing it. It's been eating me up all day. You must know I feel bad. I'll be at your next concert. I promise I will."

Emily sniffled and continued to look at her phone. I grabbed it out of her hands and forced her to look at me. I loved her beautiful brown eyes, and looking into them always made me go soft. Teenager or not, she was still my little girl, the same little girl I had taken in and taken care of since she was six years old and her mother died. I loved her like crazy. It was insane.

"Give me that back," she said.

I held it in the air, so she couldn't reach it. "Not till you tell me you forgive me," I said with a grin.

Emily crossed her arms in front of her chest with a sigh. She rolled her eyes. "Okay," she said. "I forgive you."

"You gotta mean it," I said. "Say it like you

mean it."

Emily rolled her eyes at me again, but a smile was slowly spreading. "I forgive you, okay? Now just give it back to me. I need my phone."

"Alright," I said and handed it back to her. "I know how you teenagers can't live without your precious phones."

As she reached for the phone, I noticed her collarbone seemed more visible than usual in the opening of her shirt. I looked into her face, feeling suddenly struck by worry.

"Emily? Are you losing weight?"

She stared at me with an angry look. Then she shook her head and pulled up her shirt to fully cover her chest. She was wearing an awful lot of clothing for a day like this with temperatures in the eighties. Come to think of it, it had been a very long time since I last saw her in shorts or even a swimsuit.

"What's going on here, Emily?" I asked.

"Nothing," she said.

That was when I noticed her face had changed as well. Her cheeks had sunken in and her eyes were protruding.

"Are you alright? Are you having trouble in school?"

She looked into my eyes intensely. "Dad, I'm fine." She paused and looked away, then back at me with a smile. "I really am. I'm just tired, is all. School is hard lately. Lots of work." She sighed and rolled her eyes again. "Would you stop with that look? I'm fine. I really am, Dad."

I nodded. "Okay. Just checking."

Emily paused, then looked at me again. "So, Shannon said I was good?"

Seeing her smile made me relax. Maybe I was just overreacting. "Yeah. She said you are a really good singer. She's very hard to impress, so there must be something to it."

31

MAY 2015

My mom still hadn't come home when it was dinnertime, so I went in the kitchen and threw together a lasagna that my dad and I ate with the kids. I kept an eye on Emily and noticed that she hardly touched her food.

"You don't like your lasagna?" My dad asked her.

"You know I don't eat meat," she said and put down her fork.

"I'll have it," Abigail said, and grabbed Emily's portion as well.

"I'll just make something else for myself," Emily said, and walked into the kitchen. She didn't return. The kids finished their plates and asked if they could run down to the beach and play ball before sunset. I told them they could, and soon it was just me and my dad left.

"I'm worried about her," I said.

"Who, your mother?" he asked.

I smiled. "Why don't you just call her and ask her when she will be back?" I asked. "No, I meant

Emily. She seems to be losing weight."

"Ah, Emily. It's just a phase, son. Teenagers are scrawny. They grow so fast, their bodies can't keep up. You were so skinny you looked like you could snap in two." He looked at my stomach. "Guess you've outgrown that like the rest of us."

"I'm not fat!" I protested.

My dad laughed and tapped my stomach. "No you're not, son, but you're getting older like the rest of us. It happens around forty. The hair recedes, the stomach pops out. It's nothing to be ashamed of. Just shows me you're alive and well."

I couldn't help feeling a little offended. I was still only thirty-five. I had always been skinny, and, yes, I had a little stomach now, but I believed I looked great. I was in great shape and surfed almost every day. Well, almost. Lately, my job had been taking up all of my time.

"Be careful," I said with a smile. "Don't forget you're talking to Shannon King's surfer hunk."

My dad laughed and shook his head. "That's right. I forgot. That's what they call you now."

"Well, something like that," I said and sipped my beer.

We sat in silence for a little while and enjoyed the nice breeze from the ocean. The storm was still out there somewhere and created strong winds on shore and choppy waves, but we couldn't complain. It was overcast, but the temperature was very pleasant.

"Any news on the storm, yet?" My dad asked.

I grabbed my phone and looked at my storm-tracker-app. "They have given it a name," I said. "Anna. First tropical storm of the season."

"Anna, huh? Well let's hope Anna stays off shore," my dad said.

A car drove up to the motel. It was my mother. She was alone. I looked at my dad as she approached us on the deck. He avoided looking at her.

"There you both are," she said.

My dad sipped his beer with a grunt.

"You made dinner, Jack?" she asked and looked at the lasagna in the middle of the table and the many empty plates.

"Yeah, lasagna," I said.

"I'm sorry I missed it. I had to drive Vernon back to his condo. I met his mother and she talked my ear off." My mother laughed. "They invited me to eat with them. I couldn't say no. Didn't you get my message?"

My dad shook his head. He never had his phone with him. He never saw any reason to.

"Well, be grumpy if you like. I had a great time," she chirped, then walked inside.

I grabbed a couple of empty plates and followed her. She stood behind the counter and poured herself a glass of water. I placed the plates on the counter, then looked at her.

"Mom. What are you doing?"

"What's that?" she asked.

"What are you doing with this guy? Staying away all day and not showing up for dinner? Dad is very upset. I can't say I blame him."

"Ah, he'll get over it. He's just grumpy because I wasn't there to cook for him. Well, if he's that hungry, he can cook for himself."

I stared at my mother, completely baffled. I had never seen her like this. She had always taken care of all of us. If she ever died, my dad would die right along with her of starvation. There was no way he could ever cook anything.

"But, I need you to do me a favor, son," my mom said and clasped my hand. "I need you to talk to those colleagues of yours. Tell them to back off. They are harassing Vernon. This morning, they stopped us as we were driving out. They asked him all kinds of questions and delayed us. They keep showing up at his mother's condo asking him all kinds of questions or bringing him in for interrogation. They have searched his home several times. And, Vernon, sweet as he is, never even asks them for a warrant. He just lets them walk all over him. They never give him a reason or anything. It's harassment, Jack. The poor guy was in prison for twenty-eight years for something he didn't do. He is so afraid of the police that he'll do anything they tell him to. It's not fair, Jack. You've got to talk to them."

"I can't do that, Mom. We're investigating the possible kidnapping of an eight year old boy. We're pretty desperate. You have to admit, it is kind of odd that just as he is released, another child disappears."

My mother grabbed my arm hard. She forced me to look into her eyes. "He didn't do it, Jack. Just like the first time, he is innocent."

"Why do you keep protecting him?" I asked.

"Because he is innocent. Because he is my friend. Because I let it happen once and I am not going to let it happen to him again. It has been haunting me for twenty-eight years, Jack. I knew he was innocent back then too, but there was no way I could prove it. Now, I feel like it's happening all over again. I can tell he's scared."

"But what if he isn't innocent, Mom? What if he did do it?" I asked.

"What happened to innocent till proven guilty? You and the rest of this small town have him stigmatized. You all believe he's guilty, even though you have no proof to back it up. Tell me this, Jack. You just found the body of the poor boy he allegedly kidnapped and killed back then. I read in the paper he was older than the seven years he was back when he was kidnapped. At least a couple years older when he was killed, right?"

"Right."

"So, who killed and buried him? Can you tell me who did that? 'Cause it wasn't Vernon. He was already in jail."

She was making a strong point. I'd been wondering that myself. Only I didn't want to tell her she was right. I wanted Vernon Johnson to be guilty. I don't know why. I just did. But I couldn't keep ignoring the facts.

"I'll talk to Ron about it," I said, just as the phone in my pocket started to ring.

32

MAY 2015

Shannon had collapsed. It was her manager Bruce that called to tell me. With my heart in my throat, I asked my parents to look after the kids while I got on the last plane to Austin. I arrived right before midnight and was let in through the back door of the hospital to avoid the press. I was met by her doctor outside her room.

"She needs all the rest she can get," Dr. Stanton said. He was her private physician from Nashville that she insisted on keeping, even though he was very far away from Cocoa Beach. He was the best, she insisted, and she never wanted anyone else. He had been called right after it happened.

"What happened?" I asked. "Is she alright? Is the baby alright?"

"Let's sit down," Dr. Stanton said and pointed at the chairs behind us. "She is sleeping now. Which is good. The baby is fine. Shannon will be too. But she can't keep doing what she's doing. She needs more rest. She was severely dehydrated when they brought her in. She had been throwing up all morning, and then with the travelling across the country and going on stage with all the heat from the lights, well she collapsed on the stage."

I breathed a sigh of relief. "Thank God she's alright," I said. "So, it was just dehydration?"

Dr. Stanton paused. It wasn't a nice pause. "Well, there is more. She experienced some pain, she told me when she woke up. Abdominal pain. Now, it might be nothing, but I think it's her body's way of telling her to slow down. I'm not taking any chances with this baby, and I have to order her to stop working for the rest of her pregnancy. She needs rest, she needs to eat better, and make sure she gets enough liquids. She has a history of not being very good at taking care of herself, so it is up to you and me to make sure she does. Now, the press is down the lobby waiting. We need to get them out of her way. She needs her rest and to not have this pressure and stress on her shoulders. How do you suppose we do that?"

Bruce, her manager, was sitting next to me and I looked to him for help. I had no idea how to handle the press.

"I know she wanted to wait to tell them till it showed," I said.

"It would be best if she told them herself," Bruce said. "To show them she's not really ill. If she could do so tomorrow, then we might avoid the ugly headlines. There'll still be a few out there, stating that she's terminally ill or that she has bent under the pressure of being charged with murder. I think it would be best if we avoided too many headlines, for her health."

"I agree," I said. "She gets really upset when they write bad things about her."

"Alright," Dr. Stanton said. "I'll allow her to do one press conference, as soon as she feels up to it, then no more press, no more concerts or anything that is stressful. I want her to take long walks on the beach and play songs on her guitar, spend time with her family, that's it."

I was allowed into her room and spent the rest of the night sleeping in a chair next to her. In the morning, I woke to the sound of her voice.

"Jack?"

I grabbed her hand in mine and got up from the chair. "How are you feeling? Are you hot? Cold? Do you need anything?"

"I'm fine," she said with a smile.

"You scared me, Shannon," I said.

"I know," she said. "I scared myself. I'll be good from now on. I promise."

"No more concerts," I said.

She sighed and the smile disappeared. I knew it was hard on her. She loved to perform.

"No more concerts," she repeated. "No more stress. I promise."

33

CUBA APRIL 1980

ONE OF the Cuban guards in front of the Peruvian Embassy was killed when the bus crashed through the fence. He was shot in the crossfire as the guards tried to stop the bus. Isabella remembered seeing him being removed from the ground and carried away at the same time as she was being helped out of the bus by Peruvian soldiers and brought inside the Embassy. They were met by a Peruvian diplomat. Isabella was still shaking and fought hard not to cry when he spoke to them.

Given the desperate measures the five of them had taken to ask for political asylum, they were granted it by the Peruvian diplomat in charge of the embassy. He promised he would take care of them and make sure Castro's soldiers couldn't reach them.

They could hardly believe they had actually succeeded. Their plan had worked.

The next day, the Cuban government asked the Peruvian government to return them, stating they would need to be prosecuted for the death of the guard. The Peruvian government refused.

"We're protected. The diplomat kept his word to us," Isabella's grandfather said and hugged her when they were told the news.

"Castro won't give up that easily," her grandmother said.

And she was right. Four days later, Castro declared he was going to remove his guards from the Peruvian Embassy. Isabella woke up the next morning to the sound of people screaming and yelling. When she looked outside the windows of the embassy, she saw crowds of people running in the streets towards the embassy's gate. They had temporarily patched the area where the bus had driven through the fence, but hundreds of people now stormed it and broke it down.

"What's going on?" her grandfather asked, coming up next to her.

"This is exactly what we feared," her uncle said. "This is exactly what Castro wanted."

"So, what do we do now, Papa?" Isabella asked anxiously. She spotted women and children among the people outside. It was everyone for himself. They were being pushed and trampled.

"We help them," he said.

That day, seven hundred and fifty Cubans gathered at the embassy in Havana and asked for diplomatic asylum. People were coming in so fast they climbed the walls, since the gate was too full. Isabella, her uncle, and grandparents helped people over the fence one by one as they rushed inside. Outside the fence, news spread by word of mouth and by the second day there were more than ten thousand people crammed into the tiny embassy grounds. People occupied every open space on the grounds, some were even climbing trees and other structures and refusing to abandon the premises. New Cuban guards arrived and now blocked the entrance so no one could get in or out. The embassy grounds were jammed with people. Everything had turned to chaos. Isabella tried to help everyone, and along with her grandmother, she passed out water to the people. At some point, they spotted three trucks pull up outside and dump rocks into the street. They saw everything through the destroyed fence. Isabella looked at her grandmother. Then she felt her uncle pick her up as more people gathered on the outside of the fence and started throwing the rocks at them.

"Traitor! Traitor!" they yelled while the rocks flew everywhere. From atop her uncle's shoulders, Isabella watched the chaos unfold while gasping for breath. She saw a woman with the most beautiful blond hair. Their desperate eyes met, just as her hair went from blond to red.

Isabella screamed as she saw the woman fall to the ground. She was carried away and put on the ground where a wall would protect her. Most of them would sleep there lying close on the floor. She lay all night staring at the stars above, trembling and cursing her own vulnerability. In the street outside, trucks with speakers rolled past and yelled at them, keeping them awake.

"Traitors, Traitors!"

The sound of machine guns being fired in the air caused her grandfather to throw himself at his exhausted family. While lying on the hard ground all night, Isabella heard him murmur a prayer, asking that none of the bullets would rain down on them from this beautiful treacherous sky.

34

MAY 2015

NOAH WAS taken out of the box once a day. He was given food, and was allowed to go to the bathroom if he hadn't already done so in the box. He was even allowed to walk around a little and move his legs and arms. Every day, he looked forward to the lid being lifted, the light entering, and being let out. Even though it was that creepy man with those piercing eyes that took him out. It was the highlight of his day.

His legs were hurting so badly from lying still in one position all day and night, and he felt how he was getting weaker and weaker as the days passed. There was one small window in the room where he was being kept, and every day when he was let out, he looked to it, to take in as much sunlight as possible from the small window under the ceiling.

It wasn't long that he was allowed outside the box, only enough time for him to eat and drink a little, then go to the bathroom and walk two rounds around the wooden box that he had learned to dread so terribly.

Then, he was put back in and the lid closed

again. Those were the terrifying moments, when Noah would cry and plead and beg for the man to not put him back in there, but he showed no mercy. Noah even tried to fight him, but it was no use. He lifted his hand, and with one slap across Noah's face, he let him know just how much stronger he was than Noah.

He didn't give him much food…a few slices of bread and a glass of water every day. It was far from enough for him, and Noah was constantly starving. He felt dizzy even when lying down, and soon he started to sleep a lot. He dreamt about his mother and father and being back at the old house with his old friends and neighbors. He dreamt himself back to where he had last been happy, where he had last felt safe. It didn't take long before he decided he would rather stay in his dreams than be awake in the nightmare he was living.

His guardian never spoke much. He only commanded him to eat, drink, or go to the bathroom. He tried to speak to him to maybe convince him to not put him back in the box, but he wouldn't even look into Noah's eyes. It was like he didn't want to talk to him.

"Please, Sir?" he asked one day when walking around the cold room. As usual, the man was sitting in a chair by the door, watching him as he walked in circles around the box. "Please, tell me your name?"

"Walk. No talk," he said and turned his head away.

"Please, can't I sleep outside on the floor instead of in the box?" he asked.

He didn't answer. He stared at him with his piercing dark eyes.

"I can sleep right over there? I won't bother you. I won't cry or scream. I won't try to escape."

He slapped Noah across his face and Noah fell to the ground. "Walk."

Now, Noah was crying. Tears rolled across his cheeks and he refused to get up. He simply couldn't do this anymore. He refused to.

The man stomped his feet in the ground. "Walk."

"No! I don't want to," Noah said defiantly. "I want to go home. I want to see my mommy!"

The man rose to his feet with an angry movement. He grabbed Noah by the arms, lifted him up, while he was screaming and kicking, then put him inside the box again and closed the lid.

"Please don't. Please don't leave me here!" he screamed.

But he did. And he didn't return until three days later.

35

MAY 2015

I TOOK Shannon home to Cocoa Beach the next day and put her on my couch with orders to not move. I made her lunch, then kissed her forehead and looked into her eyes.

"Now, promise me you'll take it easy while I'm gone, okay?"

She smiled wearily. She still hadn't regained her strength after the collapse. Dr. Stanton had gone back to Nashville, but promised to come down later in the week to check on her. I, for one, was worried madly about her and the baby.

"What am I supposed to do all day?" she said with a sigh. "Just sit here and watch TV?"

I went to my bookshelf and pulled out five books that I placed on the coffee table.

"Here. Once you've watched all the movies, then read these books. The kids will go to my mother's when they are dropped off till I pick them up this afternoon. We'll have dinner here at the condo, so you can stay put for now. I have to go to work for just a little while, but call at anytime, alright?"

Shannon nodded. She didn't seem too pleased at the prospect of spending the next days on the couch, but I hoped she knew how important it was that she did. For the baby and for her own sake. We couldn't risk any more collapses.

"Will you be alright?" I asked and kissed her again.

"I was just dehydrated, Jack. Will you stop acting like I'm dying? I'll be fine. Go, do your job."

I left, feeling like I'd abandoned her. I wasn't going far, though. I was meeting Beth at the Kinley's house on 4th Street North.

The mother, Lauren, opened the door and let us inside. "Steven," she said, addressed to the husband. He was sitting in a chair in the living room, staring out the window. He didn't react when we came in.

"He's been like this ever since it happened," she said. "I can't get him to do anything. He won't even eat. They keep calling him from the office. They say he is going to lose his job if he doesn't come in, but how can he? None of us can do anything. We keep wondering. Where is he?"

"I understand," I said.

"Please, tell me you have news," she said as we sat down.

"I'm sorry, Ma'am. I don't," I said. "We're here because we need you to tell us more about Noah. It will help the investigation if we know him better."

The disappointment was visible on her face. "Well, I guess no news is better than bad news," she mumbled.

"Have they arrested that Johnson fellow yet?" Steven Kinley suddenly said from his chair. I looked at him. He still stared out the window.

"No, we haven't, Sir," I said.

"But, it must be him," Lauren Kinley said with a slight whimper. "It all fits. He was just released, and then our son disappears, just like that other boy all those years ago. I called the station and told them to look at him, you do have…You have checked him out, right?"

"We have searched his home several times, Ma'am, and we've had him in for questioning more than once. If he has your son, we will find out," Beth said. "Don't you worry."

I could tell she believed Vernon Johnson was guilty as well. It made something turn inside of me. After my talk with my mother, I had realized I had been busy trying to make him guilty as well. But the fact was, he couldn't have kept or buried Scott Kingston, since he was in jail at that time. It would only be possible if he hadn't worked alone. There was nothing placing him at the scene of the crime when Scott Kingston was kidnapped. Only one boy's testimony, which had now been withdrawn, because he wasn't sure it was actually Vernon he saw.

It was my idea to try and have another talk with Noah's parents…to maybe try for another angle on the case. I seemed to be the only one doubting Vernon Johnson's guilt.

"As long as we haven't found your son, there is still hope he is alive," I said. "That's why we need you to tell us everything about him. Even the smallest of details that you think might not be of interest might help us."

36

MAY 2015

Do you have children, Detective?"

Lauren Kinley looked at me intensely. Her husband Steven had come closer and was sitting with us while we spoke about Noah. It seemed like talking about him made Steven Kinley warm up to us, made him feel better, and got him out of this state of apathy he seemed to be caught in. When speaking of his son, he lit up, and so did his wife. They appeared to be very loving parents and to still have deep affection for one another, even with all they were going through. I couldn't help comparing them to Scott Kingston's parents. Would the Kinleys end up like them in twenty-eight years? I couldn't bear the thought. We had to find this boy. This wasn't going to end like it had back then. I kept wondering if there was anything about the parents or the family that made the kidnapper choose them. Was there anything linking the two cases, other than the fact that the boys were both taken from their own rooms?

"Yes, I do. I have three and one on the way," I said. It felt good to finally be able to tell everyone that Shannon and I were having a baby. Shannon had held a press conference earlier this morning, just before we left the hospital, and now the news was everywhere. I felt very proud.

"Jack is the guy dating the country singer, Shannon King. She's pregnant," Lauren said, addressed to her husband. He didn't look like he cared. "I'm sorry," she said, addressed to me. "I watch a lot of TV. Keeps me from thinking all the time. Steven prefers to sit still and worry. I can't stand the silence in the house these days. I need to have some noise around me."

I could vividly imagine how hard it must be to have to wait for news about your son, not knowing if the next call on the phone would be the police asking you to come down to ID your own child. The very thought made me shiver.

"The teachers at his school tell us Noah had a little trouble," I said, looking at my notepad. I haven't gotten much out of my talk with them so far. Noah seemed to be a very ordinary boy, who had a tendency to get himself in trouble at school, played baseball on Wednesdays, and had guitar lessons on Thursdays. Nothing really struck me as out of the ordinary. Some of my colleagues had already spoken to his best friend's parents, back on Merritt Island, but found nothing suspicious in any of their statements.

"Yes, he did. He was having a hard time adjusting to the new school," Lauren said. "But he is the sweetest of boys. Just missing his old friends, that's all."

I looked at the picture of Noah that the parents had given us and tried to compare it to that of Scott Kingston that we had at the office. The two boys didn't seem very alike. Scott was redheaded, while Noah was blond. Scott was slightly overweight, while Noah was small and skinny. If this was the same guy, then what triggered him about his victims? How did he meet them? Why these two boys of all the boys around here? And why wait twenty-eight years between them?

"Did anything happen in his life up till his disappearance that we might need to know? Did you see anyone suspicious in the street watching your house? A car that was maybe parked close by? Anything?"

Lauren looked at Steven, who looked like he could break down any moment now. The thought that they might have been able to hinder the kidnapping if they had been more alert had to be eating them alive. I knew I would be wondering constantly. Was there anything I could have done differently?

"Not that we can think of, detective," Lauren said.

"Noah did have nightmares a lot," Steven said.

"Well, we had just moved," Lauren said. "The move seemed to affect him a lot. He kept dreaming the same thing over and over again."

I leaned over and looked at both of them. "What did he dream?"

"Just the usual stuff. He believed a man was looking at him through the sliding doors. But it was just a nightmare. I kept telling him it was."

37

MAY 2015

I COULDN'T stop thinking about the Kinleys when I got home and all the next day. I didn't like that we had no trace of their son whatsoever. As the days passed, the probability of him turning up alive became smaller and smaller.

I was going through my notes and everything on the whiteboard when Ron suddenly stormed in. He looked at me and I knew something was up.

"They found something," I said, while images of the Kinley's horrified faces flickered for my eyes.

Please don't. Please don't let it be Noah, God.

Ron nodded. "A body showed up at another construction site. At the A1A just past Sixteenth Street, where they're building those new condominiums. Let's go!"

We drove there with our hearts in our throats and met with Head of the Cocoa Beach Police Department, the woman we called Weasel, in front of the site. She greeted us as we stepped out of the car. "It was Yamilla who believed this would be of interest to you," she said.

Weasel escorted us to Yamilla. She asked us to come closer and look at what they had found. I was relieved to see it wasn't a recently buried body. It was just bones. It couldn't be Noah.

"It hasn't been in the ground as long as Scott," Yamilla said. "But I'm guessing maybe ten years, give or take some."

I stared at the bones and especially the femur. I swallowed hard. It wasn't very long. "A child?" I asked.

Yamilla nodded. "Looks like it. I don't know much yet. I'll let you know when I know more," she said.

We let her work and drove back to the office. I stared at the whiteboard for a long time, wondering how I was supposed to crack this case open. If it turned out this was another one by the same guy that had killed Scott Kingston, then there was no way this could be Vernon. Everyone had to see that. Were we chasing a killer that had been abducting and killing small children since the eighties? Who the heck was he, and how had he managed to get away with it for this long? How many others were out there? How many more bodies were we going to find?

The thought made me sick to my stomach.

I decided to call it a day and drove back to my parents' motel, grabbed my board, and jumped into the water. Nothing could clear my mind like an hour of surfing. Waves were good. The storm in the Atlantic had moved closer the last twenty-four hours and had given us some very sizable waves. My dad was watching the storm anxiously, while I enjoyed the waves it produced. The forecasters didn't agree on what it was going to do next. Most models kept it off the coast, but a few of them had it hit right on. It was still moving closer very slowly and was threatening The Bahamas now. It was expected to make landfall there tonight. The area it covered over the Atlantic was so big we'd had rain and clouds for days now. It was so rare for Florida to have this kind of weather. I hoped Anna would continue up the coast, so it would continue to produce waves for four or five days still, and then give us off-shore winds as it continued north. That was how we surfers felt about storms. We loved them as long as they stayed in the ocean.

My friend Tom came out to surf with me and we caught waves together for about an hour and a half. It was nice to talk about something else for a change. Noah Kinley was all that had been on my mind all day. Especially his parents. I found it hard to bear that they still hadn't gotten their son back. I couldn't accept the fact that I hadn't been able to help them yet, to bring back the boy. I was so relieved that it wasn't Noah's body we had found on the construction site, but it still ate me up that I had no answers for them. My colleagues were looking for Noah everywhere and had had the dogs out searching the area for the third time, but still with no results. No trace of the boy.

When we were done surfing, Tom and I grabbed a beer on my parents' deck, while the twins threw themselves at him. My kids loved Tom and had known him since they were born.

"So, when are you getting your new board?" he asked.

"I checked on it a week ago," I said. "It's coming along, but still needs the paint job."

"And they're shaping it at OceanSurf? How come? You usually always use the same shaper."

I nodded. OceanSurf was the surf shop across the street from my parent's motel. It was owned by a guy that I had surfed with often. He had talked about shaping a board for me for a very long time.

"I know. I made a nice deal with the owner. He's a surfer himself. I buy so much stuff over there all the time, and a few weeks ago when I was in there, he saw me looking at one of the boards he had shaped. It was very nicely done. He told me he could make me one exactly the way I wanted it for less than four hundred. I had to try."

"That is very cheap," Tom said.

"He makes beautiful boards. Have you seen them over there? He used to be a carpenter or something; he's very crafty with his hands. I'm pretty excited to see how it's going to be."

"Will you stay for dinner, Tom?" Abigail asked and looked at him with pleading eyes.

"Yes, Tom, stay," I said.

38

APRIL 1980

"CUBA IS open."

Hector stared at his brother Raul. He had knocked on the door to Hector's house early in the morning.

"It's true," he said. "We can go get them. We can get our family. They just announced it on the radio. Castro opened the port of Mariel. Anyone can leave if they have someone to pick them up."

Hector couldn't believe it. It had been eleven years since he had left Cuba and left his daughter, Isabella. Every day since, he had dreamt of holding her in his arms again. Could this really be? Was this really happening?

"Pick them up? But how do we do that?" Hector asked.

"We get a boat," Raul said, grinning. "We go down south and get a boat. Then we pick them up."

Hector and Raul jumped in the car and headed to Miami. When they arrived, there were Cubans everywhere—just like them—trying to find a boat.

"It's impossible," Raul said, discouraged by

seeing the hundreds of people crowding the harbor. "There aren't enough boats."

"Let's go to Key West," Hector said.

The drive from Miami took six hours. They were driving in long lines all afternoon, every car packed with Cuban exiles with the same mission as Hector and Raul. Hector felt so frustrated and cursed loudly. Raul felt the irritation as well. It was hot in the car, and at the pace they were driving, they weren't going to make it till dark. At the same time, Hector started doubting if they would be even able to find a boat. If everyone in these cars was going to try and get a boat, there wouldn't be any left once they got down there.

"You gotta keep the hope up, brother," Raul said, and pressed the horn on the car for the fifteenth time. The traffic had almost stalled and they were sweating in the car. Hector leaned out the window. They had water on both sides of the car. He could see nothing but cars as far as the eye could reach.

"Think about Isabella. Think about seeing her again."

Hector nodded. Raul was right. Seeing her again would be worth all of this. He was just so worried that he wasn't going to succeed.

The car in front of them moved and soon they were back into a little more speed. At least they were moving ahead.

"Everything good comes to he who waits," Raul said. "Trust me. By this time tomorrow, you'll be holding your daughter in your arms. I promise you."

Hector looked at Raul. He felt like throwing up. He was so nervous. Not only because he feared he wouldn't be right, but also because he feared that he was. How was Isabella going to react when seeing her father after this many years? Would she even be able to recognize him? Would she be angry with him for leaving her? Would he be able to become the father he always wanted to be?

It was dark when they reached Key West. Just like in Miami, Cuban exiles were everywhere. They searched for a boat until it was almost midnight before they finally found one. Hector wrote the owner of the boat a check for ten thousand dollars. Just after midnight, they jumped in the boat and took off without having the slightest idea where to find their family members that they hadn't seen in eleven years. They didn't know if it was true—or just a rumor—that Cubans were now allowed to leave the island, or if the two of them would even be able to return to Florida again.

All they had was their undying hope.

39

MAY 2015

SHANNON WAS already so bored she had no idea what to do with herself. Dr. Stanton had told her she had to rest as much as possible, and that was all she had done all day. He had been by and checked up on her and told her she was doing much better. But she still had to stay still, probably for the rest of the pregnancy. Everything inside of her had screamed. *Six more months like this!*

It had only been two days.

The good part was, she had written two songs the last two days and played her guitar like crazy. It seemed to be the only thing that would take her mind off of worrying. She seemed to be worrying about everything, but especially the murder case. She couldn't believe they hadn't found that gun yet and started to fear they never would. She was also very concerned about the entire building-a-house-together-and-moving-in-project. She loved Jack's family like crazy, but it was a lot. It was a big change for her and for Angela. And it was going to be an even bigger change once the baby arrived.

Now, she was getting out of Jack's condo for

the first time in two days. She was going to have dinner with the rest of the family at the motel. The doctor had told her it was all right to go out and walk a little every day from now on. That was at least something.

Shannon enjoyed letting the warm breeze hit her face when she stepped out into the sand. She walked barefooted with her shoes in her hand to the motel. She breathed in the fresh air and stared at the dark horizon where Anna was roaming. The ocean looked like an angry monster baring its teeth at her. The sky above the water was so dark it looked like it was the end of the world out there, or maybe a scene from *Lord of The Rings*. Maybe she had just been watching too much TV lately.

Jack greeted her on the deck with a kiss and a hand on her stomach. "Is everything well?" he asked.

"Everything is fine," she said.

"And does Dr. Stanton agree to that?"

"Yes, Dr. Stanton agrees. He told me I can start taking walks every day now."

Jack smiled. His hair was still wet from being in the ocean. It fell to his face and made him look like a drowned puppy.

"Dinner is served," Jack's mother said and rang the ship bell like she always did to call the children.

Seconds later, they were everywhere. Angela hardly noticed her mother. She was way too busy with the twins. It was amazing to Shannon how fast Angela had adapted to her new family. They acted like they had known each other all their lives. Shannon felt emotional and pressed back her tears. They were coming so easily lately. Probably just the hormones.

Jack grabbed a beer from the bar inside and returned. He brought Shannon a soda. She sat down next to him with a soft sigh. This was all good. Everything was good right at this moment. It amazed her how she didn't even crave a drink anymore. Not since she discovered the pregnancy. Just the thought of alcohol made her feel sick.

Jack's friend Tom was eating with them and Shannon enjoyed having an adult conversation for once. Tom and his wife Eliza had recently decided to separate, and he really needed to talk. Shannon was happy to lend him an ear.

"So, you guys are building a house, huh?" he said, once he had finished pouring his heart out.

Shannon looked at Jack, who nodded. "Yes," he said. "I just approved the floor plan today."

"You did?" Shannon asked, surprised.

Jack nodded while sipping his beer.

"You didn't even let me in on it?" Shannon asked.

"We didn't make any major changes since the first draft," he said. "I figured you had enough on your plate."

"I had nothing to do all day," Shannon said. "I could easily have looked at them."

Jack looked perplexed. Shannon fought her

anger. She didn't like to be kept out of things. She felt like she was being treated like a child.

"I'm sorry," Jack said. "I thought I was helping you out."

Shannon inhaled, then drank from her soda. She decided to let it go. Meanwhile, Jack showed Tom the floor plan on his iPad.

"It is going to be truly amazing," Tom said. "I am so glad someone finally bought that old lot and didn't care about that old story."

"What story is that?" Shannon asked.

"Yeah, what story?" Jack said.

Tom looked at their faces.

"You don't know?"

"No," Jack said.

"I thought you knew," Tom said. He looked at Jack. "I mean…with the case and everything."

"What case? What story?" Shannon asked. She felt an unease spreading fast in her body.

"Jack's case," Tom said. "The kidnapping."

Jack frowned. "The Noah Kinley case? What are you talking about?"

"No. The other one. Scott Kingston. It used to be their house on that land. The house that used to be on the lot was where Scott Kingston was kidnapped from. They abandoned the house when they realized he wasn't coming back. They couldn't live there anymore. But they couldn't sell it either. Everyone knew the story. No one dared to buy the house where a kid was stolen in the middle of the

164

night. So, the bank took over and later a hurricane destroyed the house. I thought you knew."

"Well, we didn't," Jack said.

"You didn't see the address on the old case files?" Tom asked.

Jack shook his head. "I guess I didn't notice." He looked at his mother, who was sitting next to Tom. "Did you know about this?" he asked. "You did, didn't you? Of course you did. You know everything around here."

His mother shrugged. "I didn't think it was important," she said.

"Not important? How can it not be important?" Jack asked.

Shannon could tell he was getting himself all worked up now. She herself didn't know how to react. She had heard about the kidnapping from Jack, but to actually live where it happened? She wasn't so sure she wanted that. Not that she usually was superstitious, but still. It just didn't feel right.

"It was so long ago, Jack," Sherri said. "I thought it was such a shame that lot was still empty. It's a great location. Where else in this world do you have water this close on both sides? You said so yourself. You love it here, son. What does it matter that something bad happened there almost thirty years ago?"

Shannon didn't say anything, but to her it mattered. It mattered a great deal.

40

MAY 2015

SHANNON WAS visibly upset and I tried hard to convince her it didn't mean anything, that it wasn't important for us if a boy had been kidnapped from the property almost thirty years ago. She didn't seem to agree.

"I can't live in a place where kids are not safe," she said, when we got back to the condo. "What if he returns? He hasn't been caught yet and might just have stolen another kid here in Cocoa Beach."

"Exactly," I said. "Don't you see? It doesn't matter what house or property we're in."

"Not an argument that helps a whole lot," she said.

"It has nothing to do with the place or property," I said. I didn't understand why she was freaking out about this so badly. I mean, I was upset that no one had told us, but I had let it go right away. It wasn't that big of a deal. But to Shannon, it was, apparently.

"I just don't like it, Jack. I really don't."

"So, now you don't want to build a house, after

all, is that what you're saying?" I asked.

She sighed and threw herself on the couch. I told the kids to get ready for bed. Emily had already gone to her room and closed the door. I hadn't talked to her all day and had planned to do so when we got home. Maybe even watch *The Tonight Show* with her before bedtime.

"I don't know what I'm saying," Shannon said.

I sat down next to her. "You're tired. Maybe we should continue this talk tomorrow when we've had a good night's sleep."

Shannon looked at me angrily.

Uh-oh. What did I do now?

"Please don't talk to me like that, Jack. Please don't patronize me. It's bad enough you make me feel like a child by not including me in decisions. Don't start talking to me like I'm a child too."

I sighed and closed my eyes. I felt so tired. Pleasing everybody was a lot of work. Shannon was very emotional right now, and there was no way she was capable of making any important decisions. I had never seen her overreact like this and blamed it on the pregnancy.

We sat in silence for a little while. I had no idea what to say to her to not upset her further and decided to not speak at all. After about ten minutes, I got up.

"Where are you going?" she asked.

"I'm going to Emily's room to watch *The Tonight Show*."

"So, that's it? You're leaving in the middle of an argument?" Shannon asked.

I sighed again. "I don't know what to say to you. I want this house. I have dreamt of building this house all of my life. I want us to be a family. I don't want a stupid thing like this to destroy everything."

"Well, I don't think it is stupid," Shannon said.

"Let's talk about it later," I said.

I walked into Emily's room. She smiled when she saw me. She had already turned on her TV and I guessed she thought I wasn't going to come. This was our tradition and I wanted to honor it for as long as she would let me. After all, I didn't have many years left with her before she would leave the nest. It was all about enjoying every moment.

Naturally, Jimmy Fallon only made it past his monologue before I fell asleep.

41

MAY 2015

SHANNON AND I didn't discuss the matter further the next morning. The mornings were way too busy with getting the kids fed, dressed, and to the school bus on time. Shannon was nauseated and spent most of the morning in the bathroom throwing up, while I took care of the kids.

As soon as they were off on the bus, I jumped in my car and drove to the office. I wanted to get there as early as possible, since Yamilla had called me yesterday and asked me to come to the ME's office today. I had to finish some paperwork, answer a few emails, and then I was off.

Yamilla greeted me in the lobby and told me to come with her downstairs. I hated going there, the smell alone made me sick to my stomach. I simply didn't understand how Yamilla did it, how she could work in a place like this.

"I have news on Scott Kingston," she said and approached a table where she had put the bones together so it almost looked like a skeleton. A few bones were still missing and hadn't been found... probably taken by animals over the years.

"Great," I said.

"After thorough examination, I have finally found a cause of death. I believe he starved to death."

I stared at Yamilla. "Starved to death?"

"I see serious signs of malnutrition in the bones. They're not developed properly. Around the age of seven, something went wrong. His body stopped developing and his growth slowed down drastically…signs of severe malnutrition or starvation. It also shows in the skeleton's spinal curvature. The bones have rickets and his teeth were affected. There is no trauma to the bones or skull indicating the death could have had another cause."

"How old was he when he died?"

"I believe he was fourteen."

It fit with the fact that the building he was found under was constructed in ninety-three. It had been a construction site at that point. An easy way to dispose of a body.

"So, we know for sure now that the kidnapper kept him alive for seven years?" I asked. It still surprised me. How the heck was this even possible without anyone noticing? Someone must have seen the boy. Neighbors? The kidnapper's family? Where had he been for seven years?

"I think he did. I think he fed him just about enough to keep him alive. For some reason, he didn't want to kill him right away. I believe he kept him in a small place. A place he couldn't stand upright. If you look at the spine, it is so curved, I believe he must have been kept in very small room or something like it. He was crouched for a long time while his body tried to grow."

I drew in a deep breath. Starvation? Kept for seven years in a small room? Who was this creep?

Yamilla cleared her throat and approached another table with a microscope.

"We also found this in the dirt," she said. "Close to the body."

I looked in the microscope and saw tiny splinters.

"Wood?"

"Yes, searchers found pieces of birch bark in the ground next to him. This type of birch bark isn't commonly seen around here. It's very sustainable and takes a long time to decompose. I think the splinters might have been in his body, maybe in his fingers and under his nails."

"From scratching," I said, my heart in my throat.

"Yes. Maybe on a wooden door," she said.

I wrote it down while Yamilla continued to another skeleton. I recognized it as the remains we found on the construction site a couple of days ago.

"We just got a positive ID on this one. Say hello to Jordan Turner," she said. "Jordan was thirteen when he died. Also from starvation. We found the exact same signs in his bones as in Scott Kingston. This one was also kept in a small room and suffered from a severe vitamin D deficiency from the lack of sunlight. He is from Rockledge. He was reported missing in September, 1999."

42

MAY 2015

NOAH HAD no more tears. He couldn't cry anymore. His legs were hurting from being in the box, his mouth so dry he couldn't swallow. He was so thirsty it made him delirious. Being in constant darkness made him sleep constantly. Now, the lid to the box was opened and he was being pulled out. His body felt so weak he couldn't get up on his own. The light from the window hurt his eyes.

The man placed Noah on the ground. Noah blinked his eyes. A slap across his face woke him up. Noah cried; his cheek was burning. He looked at the man in front of him. His nostrils were flaring; his eyes burning with fire. Noah gasped. He had seen this look in the man's eyes before. The last time he had looked at him like this he had beaten him with a stick. Noah still had stripes on his back.

"Thirsty," Noah whimpered. "I'm so thirsty."

The man laughed loudly. "Thirsty, huh? I bet you're hungry too."

Noah nodded feebly. "Yes."

Violently Noah felt the man grab him by the

hair, and soon he was pulled forcefully backwards. Screaming, he was dragged into another room, where he was placed in a shower and stripped of his clothes.

Noah smiled when he saw the showerhead above him, thinking finally he was getting a bath, finally he would get water. He opened his mouth, thinking, hoping, and dreaming of the soft water streaming at him from the showerhead. He closed his eyes and laughed in anticipation of finally getting all the water he could drink, of finally getting rid of this awful smell he was in constantly from his own body rotting inside the box. When he opened his eyes, the man was standing in front of him holding a bucket in his hand. Noah looked surprised at the bucket and managed to think in the split of a second that maybe the showerhead was broken and the man would just give him a bath using water from a bucket, when a second later he was hit in the face with something ice cold. So cold it hurt when it touched his naked skin.

Noah screamed and cried, while the man laughed, lifted another bucket up and threw it at Noah. The ice cold water felt like needles to the skin when it landed all over Noah, who bent to the ground in terror, crying and screaming his heart out.

Water dripped from his nose. His body trembled. He tried to get some in his mouth and cupped his hands to gather a handful and drink it, but he was so cold his hands couldn't be still long enough for him to hold on to the water.

174

"Please, stop," Noah cried. "Please, stop this. I want to go home. I want to go home to my mom."

He fell to his knees and pleaded while another bucket of ice cold water hit him on the head. He screamed and cried while the man laughed and laughed at him. Seconds later, yet another bucket landed on top of his head. Noah shivered and screamed.

"Help me," he cried. "Please, help me."

"No one can help you, pretty boy. No one can help your rich little ass now. Your mom and dad are gone; they left you to rot in here," the man hissed, then grabbed Noah's ankle and started to pull him across the floor.

Noah felt his body be lifted from the ground and soon he was put back in the small wooden box and the lid closed. Noah cried and screamed for help, fighting the lid so it wouldn't close, but it was no use. The man left without a word, leaving Noah alone again with nothing but the cold as companion.

43

MAY 2015

"**Jordan Turner**," Ron said and hung up an old picture of the boy from the case file, taken in 1998, the year before he disappeared.

"A black kid that disappeared on his way home from school on September tenth 1999. The case was investigated as a runaway, since Jordan had gotten himself in trouble at school and was facing his parents' punishment when he got home. It was believed he simply never wanted to come home. He was nine at the time he disappeared. Friends talked about a car with a man inside of it that had been parked at the school. The driver had asked Jordan for directions outside of the school. Jordan spoke to him shortly, and then walked home alone as usual. Jordan was reported missing the next day to Rockledge Police, but as I said, they believed he had run away and the case was never closed."

"But they didn't do anything to solve it either, I'm guessing," I said, thinking a black kid from a bad neighborhood running away didn't get much attention.

Ron shrugged. "Those are the facts."

"What do we know about the driver of that car?" I asked.

Ron looked at the case file. "Not much. The man was black, the car was an old beat up Ford, uh…that's about it."

"That's not much," I said, leaning back in my chair. "They didn't make a drawing or anything?"

Ron shook his head. "Like I said, they treated it like a runaway. So many kids run away from home every year…"

I knew what he was saying, even though I didn't like it. I wrote the details on my notepad, while Ron closed the meeting. I went back to my desk. I checked the radar. I had been doing that all day. Anna was getting closer and closer to the coast, and the forecasters were getting anxious. It had done a solid amount of damage to The Bahamas when it went through there. If it decided to make landfall, we would have to evacuate the entire coastline. We were all holding our breath.

Meanwhile, I had this knot in my stomach from last night. Shannon and I still hadn't talked things out, and I was worried what was going on between us. Was it just the pregnancy? The fear of the future? I could understand if she was worried and nervous about it. So was I. But wasn't it always like that when you were expecting, when big changes came in your life?

I feared she was going to say she didn't want to live on the lot. That would be the worst.

I opened the floor plan from the architect and

looked at it. It was truly my dream house. I had even added a sundeck as a surprise to Shannon, since I knew she would love to have one. From up there, you would be able to look over both the ocean and Intracoastal. It didn't get anymore beautiful than that.

I sighed and closed the document, then looked at my phone. She hadn't called yet. Beth approached my desk. She threw me the keys to one of the cars.

"You ready?"

I sighed and looked at her. "Don't think I ever will be."

We got in and drove to the address in Rockledge where Jordan Turner used to live. It was in one of the worst parts of town, the same place we had more than often been called out to drug related shootings. The house was from the fifties, and hadn't been maintained for many years. It was located right next to a road where cars drove past at forty-five miles an hour. Not exactly a safe environment for a kid to grow up, I thought to myself. On the porch sat an old woman on a chair. I approached her.

"Excuse me, Ma'am. We're looking for Mrs. or Mr. Turner. Do they still live here?"

The woman nodded. "That's my daughter," she said. "She's inside."

44

MAY 2015

"THEY'RE CHARGING you with murder. I just got the news."

Shannon stared out the window of the condo, but didn't really see. Instead, images of her in an orange jumper with her hands in cuffs flickered for her inner eye.

"Excuse me?" she asked her lawyer on the phone. "They can't do that!"

He sighed. It wasn't a good sign. "I'm afraid they can," he said. "They have Joe's letter stating you killed Robert Hill with the microphone stand. I don't know what else they have yet, but they seem pretty sure about this, about your guilt."

"But I'm not," Shannon said. "I'm not guilty."

She felt dizzy and sat on one of Jack's chairs. Outside, the storm was moving closer and it was pouring down rain. She saw lightning on the horizon. "I'm not guilty, John. You know I'm innocent. How can they do this to me? I told them everything."

"They think you're lying, Shannon. They

believe they have enough material to convict you. That's how these things work," John said.

Shannon had stopped breathing. She felt how the blood was leaving her head. Her stomach turned into a huge knot.

They're going to convict me, aren't they? They're going to put me in jail and I am going to have my baby in jail. Oh, my God, they'll take my baby away from me. I won't get to see my baby grow up, will I?

"Now, Shannon, it's important to take it easy. Nothing is decided yet. There will be a trial, and that's when we'll do everything we can to prove your innocence. I still believe there is hope, and you should too, Shannon. But we need to be smart about this. I need you to try and stay calm and keep your head cool, alright?"

Shannon gasped for air. She was panicking. "I…I…I'm so scared, John. I'm terrified."

"Of course you are," he said. "Now, take it easy and breathe, and when I hang up you call Jack and ask him to come home and help you stay calm. We can't have you collapsing again, Shannon. We have to think of the baby. I might be able to push things back. I'll be pleading that they wait till the baby is born before we go to trial. I'm going to try for that first. That should give us at least six months, if not more, since I will argue that you need time with the baby and physically won't be ready for trial till several weeks after the birth. Plus, you can't breastfeed in court. I think we're looking at trial around Christmas, if all goes well. That gives us a lot of time to figure out our defense strategy."

"Will they arrest me?"

"I have spoken to the State's Attorney and convinced them you are no flight risk. You've already paid a quite huge bail amount, so I think we're good for now. Just don't go out of the country the next couple of months. I need you to stay put."

"That's not going to be a problem," Shannon said.

"Okay. Now, take it easy, then call Jack and I'll be in touch as soon as I know more details. No panicking, you hear me?"

Shannon took in a deep breath. "Alright."

"Talk to you soon."

As soon as Shannon hung up, she felt the tears well up in her eyes. She let them go. She sat for a few seconds and cried while staring at the phone. Then she got up and threw it across the room with a loud scream.

"You bastard, Joe!! You BASTARD!"

45

MAY 2015

BETH AND I had finished talking to Mrs. Turner, who had lost her husband five years ago. She had cried a lot when we told her what happened to her son, but at the same time, she was happy to finally get closure. All these years, she had wondered where he was and why he didn't come home.

"It gets so bad, you catch yourself just staring out the window, into the street and expect him to walk around the corner any second," she told us.

It was raining when we stepped out of her house. And when it rained in Florida, it poured. We said our goodbyes and promised to keep her updated if there was any news in the case, then ran towards the car and jumped inside. We closed the doors, then looked at each other and laughed. We were both soaked just from that little run. The rain was still pouring heavily on the windshield.

"That was interesting, huh?" Beth said, when I drove into the street, where the cars had slowed down due to the heavy rain. Our wipers couldn't keep up with the amount of water that was being poured on us.

"It definitely was," I said.

"How come she didn't tell the police what she knew?" Beth asked.

"Probably no one wanted to listen," I said. "A black woman from a poor neighborhood back in the nineties? Not a chance."

"So, what do we do now?" she asked.

"I don't know yet. But we need to go talk to the people at the shop tomorrow," I said. "The fact that she had seen the guy in the Ford parked on the street in front of her house every day for at least a week before her son disappeared is certainly something that should have been investigated back then."

"And that she had seen him before? I can't believe it wasn't investigated," Beth said.

"I know. It's mentioned nowhere in the report, even though she did tell the police that she had seen the guy, that she knew where he worked."

"I can't believe that the same roofing company is still there," I said with a chuckle. "This many years later."

"Well, Mrs. Turner said it was a family business, and that the son had taken over now. But there is always work to do in the roofing business, right?"

I looked out the window at the black clouds covering the horizon. "And there sure will be if Anna gets any closer."

I had just parked the car in front of the Sheriff's Office and run inside through the rain when my phone started to ring. It was Shannon. I picked it up.

"Hi, sweetheart."

"Jack, oh, Jack."

She could hardly speak. I could tell she was tearing up. A million thoughts flickered through my mind. Had something happened to the baby? Had she lost it?

"What's wrong, Shannon? Talk to me. Is it something with the baby? Has something happened?"

"I…I…I need you."

"I'm coming home right away," I said, as I grabbed my car keys from my desk. I signaled to Beth that I had to go home and she understood. I ran to the car and got in. The rain wasn't as heavy as it had been earlier. It would soon be quieting down.

"Talk to me, Shannon. What's going on?"

"They've…my lawyer called. They've decided to charge me with first degree murder," she said, her voice trembling.

My heart dropped. I couldn't believe it. I started the car. "Stay where you are. I'm coming home."

46

CUBA, APRIL 1980

"ISABELLA SUAREZ? Have you seen a young girl, sixteen years old? She might be with an elderly couple. Their names are Suarez?"

Everything was chaos. When Raul and Hector finally docked in the harbor of Mariel, boats waited everywhere, hundreds of boats…from tiny skiffs to yachts. On the docks, the crowds of people waited, all looking for a way out. Names were being shouted in the crowds, some screamed in joy when they found each other, others cried. In search of their own family, Raul and Hector talked to many of them and soon realized that the rumors had been true. Castro had allowed everyone with a permit to leave Cuba. They could only hope their family was among those that had been granted a permit.

And they could only pray that they would be able to find each other. Until now, they had met nothing but shaking heads, and people telling them: "Sorry, but no."

Still, they kept going. Yelling their family name into the crowds, tapping people's shoulders and asking them personally if they had seen them, met them, or even heard about the Suarez family, about Isabella.

But, after hours of searching, they still hadn't found them.

As the sun set on the horizon and many boats left with their families onboard, Hector felt the panic spread once again. Would he ever find Isabella? Would he ever look into her beautiful eyes again?

He wasn't ready to give up hope.

Hector glared at the many boats leaving the harbor, at people in warm embraces, holding their family members tight, sailing towards the Promised Land, and he could only dream that it would soon be him, holding his daughter in his arms again.

As darkness lay its thick covers over the harbor, the yelling of names was still heard in the distance, and neither Hector nor Raul was ready to give up for the day. They continued to ask their way through the crowds, and finally found someone who recognized their names.

"Suarez? Yeah. I know them," the young man said. "They were the ones who crashed into the Peruvian Embassy in a bus. They were the ones that started all this."

Hector felt the excitement rise inside of him. He had heard about the crash into the embassy on the radio back in the U.S. He had heard how people had stormed the embassy afterwards. This was good news.

"How many were they?"

"I believe it was a young girl, her grandparents, and her uncle."

Hector lit up. They were together, all of them.

"Do you know if they got a permit to leave?" he asked.

"Yeah, they did. Everyone at the embassy did. I know. I was there and I got my permit this morning."

Hector smiled widely. "So, they are here?" he asked.

The man shrugged. "They should be. I'm pretty sure they were among the first to get permits."

"And when was that?"

"Two days ago," he said.

"Two days ago! But that is such a long time ago." Hector sighed and ran a hand through his hair.

The young man shrugged. "Sorry." He placed a hand on Hector's shoulder. "Maybe they're still here, waiting somewhere. We are all just waiting and hoping to find our families. I hope my brother will come."

Hector thanked the young man and wished him good luck in finding his brother, then walked back to the boat that Raul was guarding so no one would steal it. He sat on his chair on the deck, looking hopefully at Hector.

"Any news?"

Hector nodded and told him what the young man had said. He could tell it gave Raul hope.

"They must be here somewhere, then," he said and got up. He walked up to Hector and patted his shoulder with a wide smile. "You're worn out. Let me take the next round."

47

MAY 2015

I FOUND Shannon sitting on the balcony of my condo overlooking the ocean and the almost black clouds. The rain had ceased, but it still looked like the end of the world closing in on us.

"Shannon. Are you alright?" I asked and hugged her.

She had been crying.

"I don't know, Jack. I am not sure I will ever be. I mean, what am I going to do? I have a baby on the way, but what if I never get to see him or her grow up? We're building this awesome house, but will I ever live in it?"

I pulled her closer to me. My heart was racing in my chest. I was terrified, but I couldn't let her know. I had to be the strong one. But, of course, I was scared. What if I had to raise this child alone? What if I lost Shannon?

I looked into her eyes. "Nothing is decided yet," I said. "You're not convicted yet. You have a very good and very expensive lawyer working your case. You need to keep your head cool and not panic. We'll solve this together."

Shannon sniffled and nodded. I looked into her eyes and moved a lock of hair from her face.

"We can do this," I continued. "You and I can do this together. It's not over yet. But I need you to be strong for me. Can you do that?"

Shannon bit her lip and shook her head. "I don't think I can."

I grabbed her hand and pulled her up from her chair. "Come with me," I said.

I took her to the lot. Our lot. The heavy rain had forced the workers to pause, and their heavy machines stood still on the ground. The rain had turned the soil into mud. We got dirty feet from walking across it in our flip-flops. I pulled Shannon by the hand and escorted her to the middle of the lot. The workers had cleared the ground now and the old remains of the Kingston's house were finally completely gone. There was nothing left to remind us of what had once happened here.

"What are we doing here, Jack?" Shannon asked.

I asked her to stand still, then walked away from her and stopped. "Right here, Shannon," I said, and pointed to the ground beneath me. "Right here is where our bedroom is going to be."

I took ten big steps around to the right, then looked at her again. "And here is where the twins' room is going to be. I know they'll want to keep sharing a room, since they've always loved that."

I took another couple of steps towards her. "And right here is where Angela will be sleeping. I've talked to her about painting her room in a jungle theme with monkeys hanging from the trees."

Shannon chuckled. "She does love monkeys."

"I know she does," I said and walked a lot of steps towards the end of the lot, then stopped. "This is where Emily will be living."

I walked a little back towards her, then pointed again. "All the bedrooms are on the second floor, but on the first, right underneath where I am standing, we have the living room, the dining room, the kitchen, and an office for each of us. Yours will be turned into a studio, so you can make your music at home. I've talked to your producer at your label, and he will be arranging it so it's perfect, with everything you need, since I know nothing about making music, and, as hard as it is for me to admit it, am tone-deaf."

"That's not true!" Shannon said. "I heard you sing in the shower." She chuckled again.

"Anyway," I said, and walked all the way over to her, leaned over, and kissed her. I looked into her eyes. "Right where you're standing, on the second floor, next to our room, will be the best room of all. That's the nursery. I figured we could open the window and let him or her fall asleep to the sound of the crashing waves."

Shannon looked at me, her eyes moist. "Oh, Jack. It's going to be beautiful."

I grabbed her around the waist and pulled her closer. "We're going to be very happy here, Shannon. And you will too. I picture you sitting on the deck in a rocking chair with our baby in your arms, rocking it to sleep while you look at the ocean."

Shannon stared at me, and just as I saw the hint of a smile, a dark cloud seemed to cover her face. She removed my arms and walked away. "But, the thing is, I will never get to experience all that."

"Yes, you will, Shannon. I'm not doing it without you." I took in a deep breath, and then dropped to my knee. Shannon stared at me and clasped her face. I pulled out a small box from my pocket, opened it, and looked up at her.

"Shannon King," I said, my voice breaking. "Will you marry me?"

48

MAY 2015

I HAD been waiting for the right time, and no time seemed more right than this moment. It wasn't spectacular. It wasn't perfect in a traditional way. There were no flowers, no band or violinist. Just me kneeling in the mud at the ground of our future house.

I had bought the ring a long time ago. For weeks, I had been warming up to creating the right situation. I had wanted to invite Shannon out for dinner, then put the ring in the dessert, or maybe in her glass. But, until now, the ring had simply been burning a hole in my pocket for almost two weeks.

Now I was kneeling in front of Shannon in the mud, staring at her surprised face, waiting for her answer, when it started to rain again.

Shannon was still looking at me, her hand clasped to her mouth. We were both getting soaked.

"I…I…" Shannon stuttered.

Please say yes, please say you'll marry me?

The hand holding the ring was shaking and

my knee was getting tired. My heart was racing in my chest. It felt like an eternity had gone by.

Shannon finally removed her hand from her mouth and smiled. "You really think we have a future together? You really think we can get through this?" she asked.

I nodded, tears rolling across my cheeks. "Of course I think so. I know we will find a way."

She chuckled. "You're such a romantic, Jack. A hopeless romantic. How can I not love you? How can I say anything but yes?"

I stopped breathing. Did I hear her right? Had she said yes?

Shannon grabbed my hand and pulled me up. She leaned over and kissed me, then looked into my eyes while holding my face between her hands. "Yes, crazy romantic, Jack Ryder. Yes, I will marry you. Come what may."

I smiled and kissed her, then placed the ring on her finger. "Come what may," I whispered.

We stood in the rain and kissed for a long time, before we finally both burst into laughter. There was nothing like hearing Shannon laugh. It had been awhile since I had seen her happy. She had that light in her eyes again that I loved so much.

"You're crazy, do you know that?" she said and grabbed my hand in hers. "To take a risk on someone like me."

I smiled. We started to walk across the muddy ground towards the car. We were soaked already, so it was no use hurrying back. Instead, we walked hand in hand, with joy in our hearts and wet hair slapping our foreheads. I chuckled in joy and lifted her hand to see the ring again. It fit her so well. It looked beautiful on her. I knew it would.

As we walked in silence, hand in hand, Shannon suddenly stopped. "What's this?" she asked, and bent down to pick something up from the soil. She rubbed off the dirt and showed it to me. It was a ring. It had a deep reddish brown stone in it.

"Wow," I said.

"I know. It's gorgeous," Shannon said.

She turned it in the scarce light.

"I hope you don't like that ring better than the one I just gave you," I said.

"Are you kidding me?" Shannon said and laughed. "I like this a *lot* better." She placed an elbow in my side while putting the ring in her purse with a small laugh. The rain suddenly increased in strength, and we ran for the car.

49

MAY 2015

"SHANNON AND I have some news!"

I stood up during dinner and looked at everyone around the table. They were all there, even Emily, who hadn't touched her food, as usual. We were eating inside the motel's bar because of the heavy rain.

Everyone looked up at us. I grabbed Shannon's hand and showed them her ring. My mom let out a shriek and clapped her hands.

"Oh, my God!" she said and looked at my dad, then back at us. "You're getting married?"

Shannon and I looked at one another, then back at them. "Yes," I said.

Abigail and Austin looked like they didn't understand anything.

I continued, "Shannon accepted my proposal of marriage earlier today."

Austin looked confused. "But I thought you were already married," he said. "I thought you had to be to make a baby."

All the grown-ups around the table laughed.

"What?" Austin said.

"Don't you think we would have been to their wedding if they got married, doofus?" Abigail said.

Austin looked sad. "How am I supposed to know?"

Abigail rolled her eyes at her brother. "Don't you know anything?"

Austin burst into tears. The moment was ruined. "Abigail," I said.

"What?" she asked.

"Say you're sorry to your brother," I said.

She turned and looked at him indifferently. "Sorry," she said in a tone that clearly let him know that she wasn't.

Shannon and I sat down and everyone returned to their food. Emily left the table. Shannon nodded in her direction and I got up to follow her. Emily hadn't said a word when we told the news. I walked after her into the TV room, where she threw herself on the couch. I sat next to her.

"You don't have to follow me, you know," she said.

"I know," I said and placed my feet on the coffee table.

"Sherri is going to kill you for that. You know that, right?" she asked and pointed at my feet. My mom never allowed feet on the table.

"I know," I said. "So, what's going on with you?"

She shrugged. Some show with vampires was on the TV. I knew she loved the stuff. "Just tired, I guess."

"You do like Shannon, right? Or does it bother you that we're getting married?" I asked.

"I love Shannon," she said. "She's awesome. No it's just…well it's all going a little fast, don't you think?"

I nodded. "True. But it is the right thing to do. Shannon is pregnant and I want to do right by her."

Emily laughed. "You're so old."

I chuckled too. "Guess I can't run from that. I know things are changing rapidly around here, and I guess I forgot to think about how it will affect you."

She looked up at me and smiled. "Are you going for *dad of the year award* here? 'Cause you're in the lead as we speak."

I smiled, leaned over, and kissed her forehead. I put my arms around her, and to my terror, realized she had lost even more weight. I was afraid of scaring her away or making her resent me if I kept asking about it, but at the same time, I was afraid of what would happen if I didn't do anything, if I didn't talk to her about it. In this moment, while holding her small fragile body in my arms, I realized I had no idea what was going on with her, and had no clue how to deal with it either.

I felt lost.

50

MAY 2015

NOAH KINLEY had finally fallen asleep. Inside of his small wooden cell, he laid curled up, naked, and hungry beyond starvation. He hadn't heard from his guardian for what he believed had to be days, but he had lost count. He no longer knew if it was day or night, and had no way to figure out if an hour had gone by or just a few minutes. Noah was so weak from starvation that he drifted in and out of this dreamlike state constantly. It was hard for him to tell what was real and what was the dream.

Now he was dreaming of his mother. She was waiting for him in the kitchen of their old house on Merritt Island, standing by the counter preparing him a snack. Peanut butter and jelly sandwich on white toast. That was his favorite, next to Pop-tarts.

She smiled when she saw him. Her warm and loving smile. Noah had missed her smile so much, and he had missed her kisses and warm embrace.

"Are you hungry?" she asked.

Noah nodded. "Yes. I'm starving!"

"Come, sit," she said and pulled out the chair.

Noah threw himself at the sandwich. His mother laughed. At first, her laughter was hearty and warm, but soon it turned vicious. Like the laughter of his guardian. Now she was speaking with his voice too.

"So, you're hungry, huh? Little spoiled brat is hungry!"

Startled, Noah looked into his mother's wonderful eyes, just to realize it wasn't her eyes looking back at him. It was his. His piercing mad brown eyes. Noah gasped, while his mother started to knock on the kitchen table with a wooden spoon in her hand, still laughing maniacally.

Noah covered his ears from the loud banging noise. "Stop it," he yelled. "Stop the banging."

But, she didn't stop. Noah watched her, startled, while her face turned into that of the man, and soon, Noah was violently ripped out of his childhood home and back into the box, where the banging sound was getting louder and louder.

Noah opened his eyes and let out a loud scream.

"Help!"

Still, the banging continued. On the other side of the box, he could hear the guardian's laughter while he banged on the box with a stick.

"You tired, huh? Little momma's boy is tired, huh?" he yelled between slamming the box. "Well, try and sleep now, you little brat!"

The guard laughed maniacally. Noah cried

and tried to cover his ears to block out the sound, but he couldn't make it go away. He was so tired, so incredibly tired. The hunger made him hallucinate, and he kept seeing his mother's face inside of the box, her face with the man's vicious eyes, while slamming the spoon on the table like she had done in the dream.

"Stop it!" Noah screamed in complete and utter desperation. He cried and pleaded.

"Stooooop!"

But the banging didn't stop. It didn't stop for many, many hours. Hours turned into days, and still the banging continued. The man only took a few breaks now and then, just enough for Noah to doze off and get into his dream before it continued again, over and over again.

51

MAY 2015

SHANNON FELT better the next day. Jack had managed to convince her that it would be all right, that they would get through even this, and she was beginning to believe him. After all, it was no use worrying. She got nowhere by worrying.

After Jack and the kids had left the condo the next morning, she decided to treat herself to a day of spoiling herself. She thought she deserved it.

She took the car and drove to the mall on Merritt Island, where she started out getting a manicure, then moved next door to the hairdresser and got a new haircut. It was on her way out of the hairdresser when she was about to pay, that she felt the ring when she stuck her hand inside her purse and pulled it out. She looked at the brown stone and turned it in the light. It was surely beautiful, but very big.

"Thank you so much, Mrs. King," the lady behind the counter at the hairdresser said. She had that smile on her face that Shannon knew so very well. She couldn't wait to tell her friends and family whose hair she cut today. It was always the same.

Shannon gave her a smile, then left the store, thinking she could soon go under the name Shannon Ryder. She wondered if she would take his name. King was, after all, only a stage name.

Shannon turned the ring between her fingers. It was a big ring, and didn't fit any of her fingers. She was on her way to buy herself a new dress, when she found herself stopping in front of the jewelry store. She looked down at the ring, then decided to go in. The woman behind the counter looked at her and smiled.

"Welcome. What can I do for you?" she asked. She looked at Shannon, scrutinizing her. "Say, aren't you…?"

Shannon nodded. "Yes, I am," she said.

The woman behind the counter blushed. "Oh, my. I'm so honored to have you in my store, Mrs. King."

Shannon smiled too. She never knew what to say when people said things like that.

"How may I be of assistance?" the woman asked.

"I…I found this ring. I was just curious as to what kind of stone that it is," she said, putting the ring on the counter.

The lady picked it up and studied it, then froze. She looked up at Shannon with startled eyes. "Where did you get this?"

Shannon felt slightly self-conscious. The way the woman looked at her made her uncomfortable.

"I found it, why?"

"Because it's tortoiseshell. It's illegal here in the U.S. It is banned in most parts of the world as an endangered species."

Shannon looked at the lady. "I'm sorry. I didn't know."

The woman handed back the ring. Shannon took it.

"If I were you, I wouldn't show this to anyone," she said. "It's extremely beautiful, but…"

Shannon put the ring back into her purse, then closed it. "I didn't know. Thank you for your help."

The woman smiled again. "Anytime, Mrs. King. Let me know if there is anything else I can do for you."

Shannon left the store, then drove back to the condo, where she took out the ring once again. She turned it between her fingers, and then decided to put it away. She pulled out a drawer in the hallway and put the ring inside, then closed it.

52

MAY 2015

WE HELD a brief press conference outside of Cocoa Beach City Hall. I was standing next to Ron, who spoke about the search for Noah Kinley and the finds of the two bodies believed to be of Scott Kingston and Jordan Turner.

"Is it the police's theory that this is done by the same guy?" A reporter from *Florida Today* asked.

Ron leaned over the microphone. "That is our theory, yes."

"So, Vernon Johnson is out of the picture?" a female reporter asked.

Ron looked at me. I nodded and took the microphone. "Since Vernon Johnson was in prison at the time both Scott Kingston and Jordan Turner were killed, we don't consider him to be a suspect anymore, no."

"Could he have worked with someone else?" another reporter asked.

"We don't know at this point, but that is not our theory so far," I answered.

"Do you have other suspects?" one of the TV

reporters asked.

"The investigation is still ongoing."

They all knew what that meant. *No, we don't.*

Weasel took over and asked the public for help in finding Noah in time.

"The entire city is holding its breath," she finished.

I drove back to the Sheriff's Office with Ron and sandwiches from Juice N' Java in a bag. We ate at our desks, since I had a ton of paperwork to finish. I kept thinking about Shannon and wondering how this was all going to end. I considered calling my colleagues in Nashville and asking them for details in the case, but was afraid I might end up making matters worse instead of helping her. I had to leave it to her lawyer to fight her case. I just felt so damn helpless.

When I finished my sandwich, I received a call from Roosevelt Elementary. It was Abigail.

"Dad, you've gotta come down to the school. I need new shoes."

I sighed and leaned back in my chair. Abigail's shoes had broken that morning when she was about to go out of the door, and I didn't have another pair for her to wear, so I had let her put on flip-flops.

"I know you need new shoes. I'll buy them after work," I said.

"No, I need them now," she said. "I'm not allowed to wear flip-flops to school. The front office will send me home if I don't get new shoes."

I sighed and ran a hand through my hair. "You're kidding me, right? But I wrote a note and everything? I wrote that we didn't have any other shoes for you to wear."

"I know. But I'm not allowed to be in school wearing flip-flops."

I closed my eyes and rubbed my forehead. I knew the rules, but still, it was kind of an emergency. The schools were so strict about these things, it was ridiculous. Abigail had once been sent home from school for wearing a spaghetti-strap shirt. Apparently, that wasn't allowed either.

"Alright. I'll buy some and bring them to you."

"Thanks, Dad."

I told Beth what was going on and drove to the mall in Melbourne, where I found a shoe store and a nice pair of sneakers for my daughter. I rushed to the school and made it inside just before it started to rain again. The front desk didn't allow me to go down to the classroom, so Abigail came to me. She brought Austin with her and they both hugged me and kissed me. I handed her the shoes, then took the flip-flops and said goodbye to them again. I watched both of them as they disappeared down the hallway. They had grown so much lately.

I walked outside to the car and ran to not get soaked. I jumped in, and then drove into the street, when suddenly I spotted Emily's old truck. It passed me in the middle of the street. I felt confused, since I didn't believe she was off from school till three-thirty. The high school was located right next to the elementary school, so it was very possibly her. It looked a lot like it.

I decided to do what every dad would do. I followed her. She drove down Minuteman Causeway, then north on A1A. I kept my distance and spotted her as she stopped at the fitness center. She parked the car in the parking lot. I caught a short glimpse of her as she ran inside, covering her head with a sports bag to not get soaked.

53

MAY 2015

I DECIDED to let it go. After all, skipping school to go exercise was hardly the worst a teenager could do, right? Except, it felt like she was doing something really bad. I knew she had a membership to the fitness club, but didn't know she really used it. Maybe one of her classes was cancelled, I thought, and decided to not go back to the office for the rest of the day. I could do some work from home, and then maybe hit the waves for a little while before the kids came home from school.

Shannon was sitting in the living room with her computer in her lap when I entered. "You're home early," she said as I kissed her.

"I thought I'd work a little from home," I said.

"You mean surfing," she said with a smile.

"I don't know," I said and sat down. "I feel really bummed out about this case. I can't believe we haven't found Noah yet. Not even a trace. The areas around 4th Street North have been searched over and over again. We've talked to all the neighbors. Still, we have nothing.

"What about that roofing company? You said Jordan Turner's mother told you she had recognized the guy waiting in front of their house as someone working at the roofing company in Rockledge?"

"Yeah, we talked to them, but it is now run by the son in the family, and he told us he had no idea who worked there sixteen years ago. He was just a teenager, and there had been so many men working for his dad over the years. They kept no records."

"That's too bad," Shannon said.

"So, what are you up to?" I asked, and looked curiously at her screen. "You looking at rings? Isn't the one I gave you good enough?"

Shannon laughed. "It's perfect, Jack. I love it. No, I just keep thinking about the ring we found in the ground. I took it to the jewelry store today. The woman there told me it was made from tortoiseshell and that it is illegal here in the States."

"Wow," I said. "I didn't know that."

"Me either," Shannon said and looked back at her screen. "But, I couldn't stop thinking about it. Where did it come from? So, I looked up tortoiseshell and jewelry and guess what I found?"

"What? More rings?" I asked.

"No, it is illegal to sell jewelry made with tortoiseshell in most countries around the world, except one place. And that is where I figure this must come from."

"Where is that?"

"Cuba."

"Cuba, huh?"

"Apparently, they don't care about the rules the rest of the world follows or about the fact that the tortoiseshell is endangered." She shrugged. "Anyway, I just thought it was funny. I mean, how do you think a ring like that would end up in the ground on our land?"

"I don't know. Probably would make a great story," I said.

"It is a very rare piece of jewelry," she said and went to the hallway to take the ring out of the drawer. She came back with it and showed it to me. "It might be something that has been handed down as a family tradition," she said. "It looks old and it has this engraving on the inside, look."

I took the ring in my hand and looked at the engraving. A word. A name.

"Armando?" I asked.

Shannon nodded. "Does sound kind of Cuban, right?"

54

CUBA, APRIL 1980

THEY WAITED nine days at the harbor in Mariel. Hector and Raul became more and more frantic in their search for their family. Every day, more and more Cubans came to the harbor, and more and more left on boats. While they waited, thousands of Cubans had left and new boats come to pick them up.

But still they hadn't found Isabella or anyone else from their family. All they knew was that they were on the bus that crashed the embassy and that they were among the first to receive their permits to leave Cuba.

The more the days passed, the more Hector and Raul started to fear that they had been lied to. They feared their family had been incarcerated for their disobedience by the Cuban government. They heard so many stories of people being imprisoned for standing up against the government.

On the ninth day, Hector and Raul were finally allowed inside the Peruvian Embassy. They were greeted by the diplomat, who told them he vividly remembered all five of them...the Suarez family and the bus driver.

"So, what happened to them?" Raul asked, as they sat down in the cold office at the embassy.

"They were allowed to leave," the diplomat said.

"But, we have been here nine days and haven't found them," Hector argued.

"They have already left," the diplomat said. "They were on the first boat out of here. I personally made sure my guards escorted them to the boat. We couldn't risk the Cuban soldiers changing their minds all of a sudden. The boat took them to Miami."

Hector leaned back in the leather chair with a relieved sigh. He looked at his brother, who smiled and laughed too.

"So, you're telling us they're already in Miami?" Hector asked, when suddenly a new worry appeared. Where had they been staying in Miami for nine days? Did they have any money?

The diplomat laughed and nodded. "Yes, they should be perfectly safe. But I am sorry you have come this long way in vain."

Hector felt tears in his eyes as he got up and shook the diplomat's hand. "It was worth it, as long as they are safe. Thank you so much!"

"You're very welcome," the diplomat said.

Hector and Raul hurried back to the harbor and the old fishing boat. They couldn't wait to get back. They were laughing and running. But as they approached the boat on the dock, they suddenly realized someone was walking around on the deck. And it wasn't just anybody.

They were soldiers. Cuban soldiers.

"What's going on?" Hector asked and looked at Raul. The soldiers were swarming the boat, searching through it.

With shivering steps, the two brothers approached the boat. As they did, one of the soldiers looked up and his eyes locked with Hector's. Hector gasped when he recognized him. He knew the man was a general in Castro's army. He had looked into his eyes once before, right before getting onto the airplane.

The soldier jumped up from the boat and onto the dock, then looked at Hector with a smile.

"Didn't I tell you I would shoot you if you ever came back to Cuba?"

Hector had no idea what to say. He felt his hands get clammy. His legs were trembling, threating to give way underneath him. The general stared at Hector, and then burst into loud laughter. He put his hand on Hector's neck, and then forced him to walk with him.

"Now, how do you suggest we resolve this unfortunate situation, huh?"

PART THREE:

THIS IS MY HEART, IT IS TURNED TO STONE

55

MAY 2015

I WORKED for a few hours more, then hit the waves to clear my mind a little bit when there was a break in the rain. It was warm out and the water was warm too. Waves were good, overhead high, but quite messy because of the wind. I had fun on my short board and enjoyed not thinking about work or Shannon's case for a little while.

An hour later, I went up and showered at my parents' place before picking up the kids at the bus stop. Abigail and Austin ran into my arms, and I hugged them tight. I felt like they were growing so fast now. Angela came off the bus as well and stayed a little behind while I hugged the twins.

Once I had let them go, I looked at Angela, then walked to her and gave her a warm hug as well. "How was your day?" I asked.

"Great," she said smiling. I could tell she was doing well. She had been very happy lately. I believed she enjoyed having a more normal life now, a life where she went on the school bus and went to a normal public school like all other kids.

I walked up to my parents' place, where the kids threw their bags on the floor, then threw on their swimsuits and ran to the beach. I played beach volley with them for an hour or so, before Emily drove up and parked her old truck in the parking lot of the motel.

I looked at Abigail next to me, then threw the ball at her. "I have to talk to Emily," I said. "Be right back."

Abigail made a disappointed sound.

"Let's play hide and go seek in the dunes instead," Austin exclaimed. It was his favorite game of all.

"Okay," Abigail said. "But no hiding in the motel this time. Only outside hiding places."

They all agreed to that and I ran to Emily who was talking to my mother on the deck. I waved and approached them. I kissed my daughter on the forehead. "How was your day?" I asked.

She shrugged. "Okay, I guess. As usual."

"Nothing interesting happen? Any classes cancelled?"

She looked at me, and then shook her head. "No. Not this close to end of the year. Why?"

It was my turn to shrug. "Oh, I don't know. Maybe because I saw you drive away from the school around lunch time?"

Emily snorted. "Are you spying on me?"

"Nope. Was just at Roosevelt with some shoes for your sister. Where were you going?"

Her eyes avoided mine. "Just getting some lunch. The food in the cafeteria is so nasty. I had a sandwich at the Surfnista."

I sighed. "Emily. We both know that is not true. First of all, you hardly eat anything anymore, second I saw you park at the fitness center. Are you cutting classes now to go work out? Look at you. You're skin and bones. What's going on, Emily?"

Emily looked at me. Her nostrils were flaring. "Well, if you already know everything, then why are you asking me?" she yelled, then stormed to her car and got inside. Before I could reach her, she had driven off.

I went back to the deck, where my mother was still standing. "Guess I handled that really well," I said.

My mom put a hand on my shoulder. "She's been through a lot. A girl her age asks a lot of questions. Where am I from, who am I going to be? What will I look like? She can't get many answers when she doesn't have her parents. Plus, everything around her is changing. You're expanding the family, and that means you have less time for her. Give her time."

"But, the thing is, I don't feel like I have much time," I said. "Every day that passes, she seems to be getting thinner and thinner. I can't stand to look at it. I feel like I need to do something. I just don't know what."

"I have noticed she hasn't been eating and the weight loss," my mom said. "I'll try and talk to her, if you think that would help."

"Thank you," I said and hugged her. "What would I ever do without you?"

56

MAY 2015

SHANNON WALKED across the sand, looking at the dark clouds on the horizon. She had just watched the local news, which was all about Tropical Storm Anna. She spotted Angela playing in the dunes with the twins. Angela saw her, then signaled for her to be quiet. Shannon realized they were playing hide and go seek and decided she could hug her daughter later.

She whistled the tune to the new song she had been working on the past couple of days, when she spotted Jack on the deck of the motel with his mother. They seemed to be in a deep conversation. He looked serious, but his face lit up when he saw her. He waved and she approached them.

Shannon kissed her future mother-in-law on the cheek and her future husband on the mouth. "What's going on?" she asked. "Why the serious faces?"

"It's Emily," Jack said. "I'm worried about her."

"Is she still not eating?"

Jack shook his head. "I saw her today skipping

class to go to the gym and work out. I think she is deliberately trying to lose weight."

"That's bad. We need to get her professional help," Shannon said." Before it goes too far."

Jack went quiet. It seemed like he didn't agree.

"I don't know," he said. "I don't trust those kinds of people much. They'll only give her medicine, and that's not what she needs."

"But this is serious, Jack," Shannon said. "She needs help."

Jack and his mother both went quiet. Shannon knew it was hard for relatives to accept the fact that someone in their family was seriously ill and needed help. She wondered if she had gone too far, if she had somehow overstepped their boundaries. The atmosphere was unpleasant. Shannon felt like she had to say something to make things better. She picked the ring out of her pocket and held it in the air.

"Look what we found at our lot," she said and showed it to Sherri.

"It's tortoiseshell," Jack said. "Shannon took it to the jewelry store and they told her it was illegal."

"Isn't it beautiful?" Shannon asked.

Sherri studied it closely. "Armando?" she said, and looked surprised at Shannon.

"Yes. Sounds Spanish right? We thought it might be Cuban, since using tortoiseshell for jewelry is common in Cuba. Interesting, right?"

Sherri frowned. "Armando is Vernon's birth

name," she mumbled.

Shannon stared at Jack, then at Sherri.

"What do you mean?" Jack asked.

"Vernon was originally born Armando, so was his father and his father before him. It's a family name."

Jack looked confused. "So, his name is really Armando?"

"Yes. After his father. Armando Jesus Castro García. It was a family name, but his mother changed it when they came to the States."

"So, Vernon Johnson is from Cuba?" Jack asked.

"Yes. He came here during the Mariel boatlift in 1980. But there was so much hatred against the Cubans back then, so his mother decided to change the name to make it easier on them, to be able to get a job and a new life. Say, do you think this may be his ring?"

57

MAY 2015

VERNON FELT anxious. Sherri had called and asked him to come down to the motel and meet her family. She had something she wanted to show him, she'd said. Something important.

Vernon jumped on the bus and sat by the window as it drove over the bridges taking him to the islands, wondering what it could be that was so important. He wasn't too fond of the idea of meeting her son. He was a detective with the Sheriff's Department and it was his colleagues that constantly came knocking and asking him questions about the disappearance of that boy, Noah Kinley.

Vernon had followed the case on TV closely, and every time they talked about it, his name was mentioned in connection to the case and every time they had talked about the similarities to the old case from '86, the one Vernon had been imprisoned for.

It was like it was happening all over again. When Noah had gone missing, it was just like the first time. The police had been at his doorstep the very next day asking him all these nasty questions. Later that same day, they had taken him in. They had cuffed him again and Vernon had cried and pleaded for them to leave him alone. His mother had seen it and she too had feared it was happening all over again. For hours, they had kept him in custody, asking him questions over and over again.

"Where is Noah? What did you do to him?"

Over and over again. He had felt so tired in the end, he had almost told them he had done it, just to make them leave him alone.

But, luckily, they had suddenly released him. He had gone home to his mother, who had been on the couch, crying since he'd been taken in. She hadn't shown up for her job at Publix, and later they called and told her she was fired. Vernon's mother had been devastated. Her job was her everything.

She had looked at him with big tearful eyes.

"Did you do it?"

Vernon looked surprised at his mother. "What do you mean *did I do it*?"

She threw a cushion at him. "Did you do it, damn it? Did you kill that kid? Did you take that second one? Did you kill him too?"

Vernon had stared at his mother in complete shock. He had been so sure his mother believed in his innocence.

"I can't believe you would even ask that."

The next day, he had moved out. He had bought a condo on the water in Titusville with some of his money. His mother kept saying how sorry she was, but Vernon didn't believe her. Just like the rest of the world, she believed he was guilty. Deep down, she believed it, and that was enough for him.

Vernon went to the door as his stop came closer. He got out and walked towards the motel. He looked forward to seeing Sherri again. He enjoyed her company. So far, she was the only one who had stuck by him and kept believing in him through it all. Even when they started to accuse him the second time around.

"Vernon!" Sherri came down the street to meet him. She opened her arms and gave him a big hug. Vernon closed his eyes and enjoyed the closeness. He hadn't been very close to another human being much during his years in jail. It felt strange for him to hold her in his arms. Strangely wonderful.

"I'm so glad you came," she said. "Come, meet my son."

Vernon smiled, then let her drag him towards the deck of the motel. Vernon recognized them both from the magazines. Shannon King was even more beautiful in real life.

"It's an honor to meet you, Mrs. King," he said.

"Vernon, meet my son, Jack. Jack, this is Vernon," Sherri said.

"Nice to meet you," Vernon said and reached out his hand.

Jack Ryder took it a little reluctantly. In his eyes, Vernon saw the same suspicious look that every one else seemed to have. Except Sherri.

"Sit down, Vernon," Sherri said. "I'll get you a beer."

"Oh, I don't drink, Miss Sherri," Vernon said. "Just water will be fine."

Sherri brought water for all of them and they sat down on the wooden furniture. Vernon loved the motel and fully understood why Sherri loved it here. It had such a quiet charm to it.

"So, what did you want to talk to me about?" Vernon asked nervously. He felt like Jack Ryder was supervising his every move.

"Show him," Sherri said, addressed to Shannon King. The famous country singer put her hand in her pocket and pulled something out. She showed it to Vernon. He stopped breathing. Everything inside of him froze to ice. He took it in his hand, then looked at the engraving. He couldn't believe it.

"Where did you get this?"

"You know it?" Jack asked.

"Are you kidding me?" Vernon said, his voice trembling heavily. "It belonged to my father. I haven't seen it since I was five years old."

58

MAY 2015

Vernon Johnson was crying. He was sitting on my parent's deck and crying. I had no idea how to cope with it. I didn't like the guy, for some reason, maybe because he had spent so much time with my mother and I felt jealous for my dad.

My mom put her arm around him, and that made everything turn inside of me. My dad was in the back working on the pool pump that had broken, and here she was holding someone else. I knew it was wrong, but I couldn't help feeling upset about it.

"I don't remember much of him," Vernon said. "But he used to always wear this ring."

"What happened to him?" My mom asked. "You never spoke of him?"

"He was taken away from us," Vernon said. "They took him one day. "

"Who did?" My mom asked.

"Castro's soldiers. They put him in prison. We never heard from him again. When Castro decided to open the harbor of Mariel to anyone who wanted to leave, my mother decided it was time for us to go. We didn't have any relatives come to pick us up, but we paid someone to take us with them. Cost us everything we had, but it was worth it. We had to get away. My dad had been gone for seven years by then, and we knew we would never see him again."

"Why was he taken to jail?" I asked.

Vernon shrugged. "I never knew. But so many were imprisoned because they spoke up against the regime." Vernon paused and looked at the ring. "Where did you find it?"

"Two blocks down there is an empty lot," Shannon said. "We just bought it and we're building a house on the grounds. We found it in the soil where the former house had been."

"You mean the ground where the Kingston's old house was?" Vernon asked. He sounded surprised.

"Yes. Kind of strange, isn't it?" I asked. "So, how do you figure it ended up there?"

"I...I...I have absolutely no idea," he said, sounding all of a sudden nervous. "Can I keep it, though? It's my only memory of my dad."

"I think we might need to hold on to it for a little while longer," I said. "While the investigation is still going on. I'll make sure you get it once we're done."

Vernon looked anxious. Small pearls of sweat appeared on his upper lip. He wiped them away with the back of his hand.

"Okay. That's okay," he said and handed it back to me.

"Jack!" My mother said. "It's the man's only memory of his father."

"I'm sorry. But I need to keep it for the investigation."

"Now you're just being a bully."

My mother got up and walked to Vernon. "Come. Let me take you home."

Vernon got up. He looked at me defiantly. I didn't know what it was, but I really didn't like the guy. He looked at me angrily. "I can find my own way home, thank you, Miss Sherri," he said. "Good day."

He turned around and walked away. My mom looked at me angrily. "Look at what you did. Don't you think he has been through enough? Can't you show a guy some mercy?"

I stared at Vernon as he disappeared around the corner of the building. I started to feel a little guilty. But I only did what I had to, I told myself. Maybe it wasn't nice of me, but something told me this ring was important.

59

MAY 2015

THE CONSTANT banging on the lid of the box ceased all of a sudden, and then there was nothing but quiet. At first, Noah enjoyed that he could finally sleep, enjoyed the peace and calm in his mind from days of insomnia because of the noise. But soon, another well-known emotion made its entrance. With the quiet came the fear. Where had his guardian gone? Was he all alone now? Would he come back? Had he grown tired of his games and left him to rot inside the box? Would Noah die in the box?

Noah Kinley tried to accept the fact that death was closing in on him. He was lying silently in the box waiting for his body to simply give up. His tiredness had put a damper on the hunger and thirst, and even though he was still only a child, Noah knew perfectly well that his body wasn't going to take much more of this. His back was hurting constantly from the beatings he had to endure, and his head was throbbing with pain from the lack of sleep and water.

He was cold in the box. Constantly freezing.

The lack of nutrition had sucked him dry and he was only skin and bones and couldn't keep his body warm enough.

It had been days since the lid was last lifted and Noah taken out to eat and go to the bathroom. At least he thought it was. He couldn't distinguish between night and day anymore. All there was, was darkness.

"What do you want from me!" he screamed into the darkness when he felt the strength for it. But there would be no answer. Every now and then, he cried. Cried when he thought about his parents, wondering if they were looking for him, if they were worried and sad. Wondering why they hadn't found him yet.

"I want my mommy! I want to go home!"

He had thought his eyes would eventually get used to the darkness, that he would be able to see something like he used to in his bedroom at home, but it never happened. It was like he had gone blind.

He tried to remember his mother's gentle smile, to recall little details that he used to love when looking at her. The mole on her upper lip that moved when she spoke. The vein in her forehead that popped out when she was angry with him. Her ears. Her ears that were uneven on each side of her head.

Noah no longer cared that he peed himself in the box. It had become more and more rare that he had to go anyway, and if he did, he just let it happen. The smell didn't even bother him anymore.

Noah tried to count the seconds and minutes to be able to determine when a day had gone by. But it was in vain. He had lost the will to keep trying to pretend like he was alive.

He had lost hope.

Just as he thought he would never get out of the box again, the lid was opened and light entered. It hurt his eyes and he had to squint. Arms pulled him out of the box and dragged him across the ground. Noah tried to fight, but his guard was too strong.

"Let me go. Let me go home!" he yelled.

He was thrown into another barren room lit up by bright fluorescent lights. He landed on the bare cold floor, his naked body throbbing in pain from being locked in the same position for days. Before he could manage to get up, the door was closed behind him. The light was so bright it felt like an explosion of white suns, and he had to close his eyes and cover them with his hand. It was like the light pierced through his retinas and sent waves of pain into his head. Noah crouched in the corner of the room and pulled his knees up to hide his head in them. His eyes hurt so badly from the bright light.

"Please, turn it off," he whispered feebly.

He felt so tired, all he wanted was to lie down onto the cold floor and fall asleep. But the bright light made it impossible for him to sleep. It pierced painfully through his eyelids and hurt him.

"Please, turn it off," he yelled, even though he

knew it wouldn't help. "Please, turn the lights off!"

60

MAY 2015

"**What's going** on?"

My dad had entered the deck and looked at all of us. My mom hadn't spoken a word to me since the incident with Vernon. She was looking at me angrily. My dad stood with a wrench in his hand, his shirt soaked with sweat.

My mom shook her head. "Nothing," she said, walked past my dad into the motel. I felt awful. In less than an hour, I had managed to severely anger two of the women in my life.

"Jack?" my dad asked.

"It's nothing, Dad."

I didn't want him to know what had happened. He felt threatened by this Vernon enough as it was. He looked confused, then wiped sweat from his forehead. "Well, then, if it's nothing, then I think I'll jump in the ocean. Tell your mom the pool is up and running again when she gets back out here."

I looked at Shannon. I could tell she felt uncomfortable. I sat next to her and put my arm around her. I pulled her closer and kissed her.

"Do you want to go back to the condo and get some take-out instead?" she asked.

"Nah, my mom will be herself in a little while. Don't worry. She can never stay mad at me for very long."

We sat on the bench and looked over the ocean where my dad was soon walking out in the waves.

"She's gaining strength, they say," Shannon said and leaned her back on me.

"Who? Anna?"

"Yes. I watched it on the news before I got here. She's growing."

"I don't think we've ever had a storm stay out there this long," I said. "Usually they pass in a few days…maybe a week, but it has been on its way for at least two weeks now. It has stalled for the past days, moving very slowly while growing bigger and more powerful."

I thought about the storm and then about Noah Kinley, who had disappeared right before the storm had started to build in the Atlantic. I wondered if he was still alive somewhere around here after two weeks. Did the killer keep him alive like he had done to Scott and Jordan? Why? He had the power to kill them whenever he wanted to. Was it because he enjoyed it? Did he get off in some weird satisfaction by keeping them alive? Was it a power trip?

My dad returned with a satisfied look on his face. "That was just what I needed," he said with a deep sigh. Like me, he loved being in the ocean. It didn't matter if I was in the water or on a surfboard or even on a boat. The ocean was my element. It was where I belonged.

"Did you have fun out there this afternoon?" my dad asked and wiped himself with a towel.

"It was okay," I said. "Waves have been building to a good size, but the wind kind of messes it up."

"I figured," my dad said.

My dad used to be a surfer when he was younger. I knew he dreamed about going out there again, but his knees couldn't take it. After two knee surgeries, he was told by his doctor he couldn't surf anymore. I felt bad for him. I dreaded the day I couldn't surf anymore.

My dad sighed with contentment.

"Well, better get dressed before dinnertime."

My dad left us and I smiled and looked at Shannon. I kissed the top of her head and held her body close to mine. It felt good to sit here. To be close to her. I wondered what I would do if she ended up going to jail. I simply couldn't bear the thought.

I reached down and touched her belly and thought about the baby growing in there. I couldn't wait to hold him or her in my arms. It was strange how I, not so long ago, had thought it was over for me, that I wasn't going to have another baby, and didn't feel sad about it at all…how I suddenly longed to hold a baby in my arms again.

Speaking of babies, I spotted Abigail and

Angela walking up from the beach, and I waved at them. "Hi guys. Dinner is almost ready. Where is Austin?"

Abigail looked at me with wide eyes. I hadn't noticed before, but now I did. Her eyes were torn in fear.

"We can't find him, Dad. We've looked everywhere."

61

CUBA, APRIL 1980

THEY WERE packing his boat, cramming people in it. Hector could do nothing but watch as more than two hundred people were being loaded onto the old 70-foot fishing boat by the soldiers. Hector didn't understand where all those people had come from. They hadn't been among the ones waiting at the harbor. They didn't look like ordinary people. Many of them were toothless and their clothing looked like they were beggars.

There was nothing Hector could do, even though he didn't feel comfortable about this. The general had promised him that he and his brother, who was wanted by the police, would be able to leave the island if they promised to never return and if they took a bunch of refugees with them.

It was either that or Cuban prison, where they would probably die. Hector had accepted the terms, and now they were loading the many people onboard. Hector looked terrified at how deep the boat lay in the water with the heavy load and wondered if they would even be able to make it across the ocean to the coast of Florida.

"We can't take anymore," Raul said, as another batch of people were being lined up. He looked at Hector. "The boat is going to sink."

"I know. But we don't have a choice," Hector said. "This is our only chance to get out of here."

Raul knew he was right and stopped arguing. Soon, the General loaded the last passenger onto the fishing boat, then grinning from ear to ear, told them they could leave Cuba.

"Safe travels," he said with a chuckle.

With their hearts in their throats, they started up the old engine and left the harbor of Mariel. The weather seemed to be with them. Clear blue skies and the ocean as calm as possible. It gave them hope. The boat could sail, and soon they saw the harbor disappear in the distance. They went slowly, but steadily ahead. As soon as the coast of Cuba was far behind them, Hector and Raul breathed in a sigh of relief and looked at each other. They hugged once and laughed.

"We did it. We made it out," Raul said. "Again!"

"Not many can say that," Hector replied.

In front of them was nothing but the endless ocean, and soon behind them as well. They were happy to see Cuba go, more than happy, exalted even, but none of them could escape the anxiety that nagged on the inside.

What if we don't make it to land?

The boat was sailing steadily, but they could tell the engine was struggling with the weight. The people were closely crammed, and soon a fight broke out between two of the men.

Hector and Raul looked at one another, not knowing what to do. The fight continued. The two guys fighting were struggling, and suddenly, one of them was thrown over the railing by the other. Hector gasped and looked to Raul. Raul elbowed through the crowd to the railing and looked down. Hector followed him. The man who had been thrown overboard didn't know how to swim, and seconds later, he disappeared and went straight to the bottom.

"We have to do something! The guy is drowning," Hector yelled and looked at Raul.

Raul turned to stare at their passengers, then he shook his head. Hector turned and looked at them as well. That was when he realized. These weren't ordinary refugees. These weren't people waiting to see their family on the coast of Florida. These weren't families with children and grandparents looking for a new and better life.

These were the unwanted people. The undesirables. These were the ones not even Cuba wanted to keep.

62

MAY 2015

"Austiiin!"

I was yelling his name at the top of my lungs as I ran across the dunes, looking everywhere for my son. In the distance, I could hear my family calling his name as well. We had been everywhere. The beach, the area around my condominium, our condo building, the basement underneath, my parents' motel, the pool-area. Everywhere.

And still, he was nowhere to be seen.

"Austiiiin!"

All kinds of scenarios went across my mind. I pictured him going in the ocean and drowning. But, then again, Austin was an excellent swimmer. He was a surfer, even though he didn't enjoy it much, he still knew the ocean.

I pictured him walking into the street behind my parents' motel and being hit by a car. But when I went down there, there was nothing. I walked up and down the road to see if he had been hit and was lying helpless somewhere, but didn't see anything. I even crossed A1A and walked to the houses on the other side. It was mostly condominiums and townhouses. I walked in and out of their areas yelling his name and down to the Intracoastal River to see if he was hiding anywhere down there or maybe had fallen in the water.

But he wasn't there either.

They had been playing hide and go seek when he disappeared, Abigail had told me. Austin had hid in the dunes close to our condominium, she was certain. But when she went to look for him, he wasn't there. She and Angela had then been looking all over the beach for him, but with no luck.

"Maybe we should call for help," Shannon said, as I returned to the motel where everyone was waiting, looking at me for answers. But I didn't have any. I had no idea what to do. I grabbed my phone and called Ron.

"I'll have a search team at your place within the hour," Ron said. "Dogs and everything."

"Thanks, Ron."

I hung up and looked at my family. My heart was racing in my chest and I found it hard to breathe properly. I was so anxious and angry at the same time. I looked at my mother.

"What's Vernon's number?" I asked.

My mother looked at me and shook her head. "No, Jack. No. It's not him. He didn't take Austin."

"I think I need to be sure first," I said. "Come to think of it. I don't need his number. I'll go directly to his place and search it myself."

"Don't, Jack," my mother said. "You're all worked up. Why would Vernon take Austin, huh?"

"I don't know. To get back at me, maybe? Because he is mad that he never got to be with you, I don't know. I guess I don't care why right now. All I care about is getting Austin back home in one piece."

My mother grabbed my arm and pulled it. "It's not him, Jack. He didn't do it. He is innocent."

"I think I'll be the one to determine that," I said, and pulled myself free. I walked to my Jeep, jumped in, and drove off. I called Beth and asked her to find Vernon's address for me.

"Ron called," she said. "I am so sorry, Jack. I was just on my way down to join the search team. I'll call you back as soon as I have the address. Do you want me to go with you?"

"No, I'll do this alone," I said. "Besides, I'm already leaving Cocoa Beach."

"Just don't do anything you'll regret, Jack. You hear me? Jack?"

I heard her. I just couldn't promise anything.

63

MAY 2015

"**Where is** he?"

I looked at Vernon Johnson, who was standing in the door to his apartment. He looked surprised.

"Jack? What's going on?"

"Don't pretend you don't know," I said.

"What do you mean?"

"My son. Where is my son? Where is Austin? I know you have him. Austiin?" I called through the door.

I tried to walk in, but Vernon blocked my way. "You know what? I'm getting pretty tired of you people coming here, constantly accusing me of all these things. I am a free man. I was acquitted, remember? The judge let me go."

"Doesn't mean you're innocent. Just that they don't have enough evidence. I don't know how you did it, but I want my son back."

Vernon shook his head. "I don't have him."

"I want to see for myself. I want to go in and see," I said.

Vernon shook his head. "No can do. I'm done being the nice guy here. If you want in, you go get a warrant."

I felt the blood boil in my veins. I felt like taking my gun out and just shooting him in the leg or shoulder and making up a story later. But that wasn't me. That wasn't who I was.

"How do you believe I would have done it, huh, Detective? I was in jail when Scott Kingston was killed and buried, I was in jail when Jordan Turner was abducted and killed. You know I'm innocent. There's no way I could have done any of these kills. I served my time for something I didn't even do. And now you won't leave me alone? I am still in prison. I am still being a suspect in yours and everyone else's eyes. I can't even go to the store and buy groceries without people whispering behind my back. I am innocent, for crying out loud. You got the wrong guy back then. I have the court's word for it, now please just leave me alone!"

"If you have nothing to hide, then why can't I search your place for my son, huh? Why won't you let me in? I'll tell you why. Because you know I'll find something. Because you're not as clean as you claim to be. You know something. I saw it in your eyes today when I showed you that ring. And now my son is missing? I don't believe in coincidences. If you don't have anything to hide, then let me in."

Vernon Johnson scoffed. "Nice try, Detective. But I'm not letting you inside my apartment. I am sorry your son is missing, but it's really not my problem. Now, if you'll excused me, my dinner is getting cold."

He closed the door on me with a loud bang. I snorted and hammered on it, yelling Austin's name.

"If you're in there, Austin, just remember I'm not giving up. I will come back for you. Don't worry."

I felt like an idiot standing out there hammering on a door and yelling. I *was* an idiot. I knew I was acting like one. But what else could I do? I felt so helpless, so frustrated. I was certain Vernon knew where my son was. If he wasn't here, then he knew where he was.

I decided to go back to my car, and I sat in the parking lot for a little while, slamming my hand into the steering wheel, when my phone rang. It was Shannon. I picked it up. "Any news? Have you found him?"

"No. I'm sorry. But we have found something else."

My heart dropped. What had they found? A piece of his clothes? What?

"What did you find?" I asked and started the engine.

"You better come home and see for yourself."

64

MAY 2015

I WASN'T happy about leaving Vernon Johnson's place. I was still certain Austin was somewhere inside of his apartment, and I feared what this sick bastard might do to him. At the same time, I knew it was going to take a while before I could get a warrant to search his place. If I could find a judge that would grant it to me. I didn't have much solid ground to base my suspicion on.

I drove over the bridges, cursing and yelling my anger out. It had gotten dark when I reached the island and drove up in front of the motel. Cars were everywhere, and I couldn't find a space, so I had to park next to the neighbor's fence. I hoped they didn't mind. Shannon came towards my car. My parents were standing behind her, my dad holding my mom's shoulders. They all had worried faces.

Uh-oh. This doesn't look good.

I opened the door and jumped out. Shannon looked at me. "What's going on?" I asked.

"We found this," Shannon said and handed me

a note.

I took it and looked at it. It was handwritten note where Austin had written his name. Nothing else. I turned the paper to look at the back.

"What does this mean?" I asked.

"We found the note in Austin's shoe. Someone had put it in front of the door to your condo."

Shannon showed me the sneakers. They were Austin's, all right. His favorite sneakers, his Game Kicks, that had buttons on the side and blinked and played music. And he could play some game on them. I never understood what it was for, but I knew he loved them and always wore them. They had been crazy expensive, but I didn't mind buying them for him, since he enjoyed them so much.

I looked at the shoe and then at the note.

"It doesn't tell us anything," Shannon said. "Other than he is alive."

"And that someone has him. Someone who wants to make sure we know they have him," I said.

"What do we do now?" Shannon asked.

I sighed and shrugged. "I…I have no idea. Where are Angela and Abigail?" I asked and started walking up towards the motel.

"They insisted on joining the search team," my mother answered. "They're searching the entire beach area. Emily went with them."

"She came back?" I asked.

"I texted her," Shannon said. "Told her what was going on. She came home right away. She was very upset."

I walked to the deck and looked into the darkness that had swallowed my son. A dozen flashlights flickered in the distance. Austin's name was being called from everywhere. A sudden realization struck me like a blow to the face.

I had to go through the night without my son.

"You haven't told the search team about the note?" I asked.

"I wanted to show it to you first," Shannon said.

"I'm glad you did."

She leaned on my shoulder. "Oh, Jack. This is terrible. I am so sorry."

I kissed her on the top of her head. "I know. We'll find him though. I know we will."

"You think he might have been taken by the same person who took Noah Kinley?" she asked.

I didn't answer. I didn't know what to say. I couldn't tell her that was all I was thinking about. I couldn't tell her I was certain it was the same guy. Except for the note. The note and shoe gave me hope. It wasn't something the kidnapper had done before. Either it was someone else, or the kidnapper was escalating, and that often meant making mistakes.

65

MAY 2015

VERNON WAS upset. He kicked a chair in his apartment and caused it to fall over. Then he picked up a vase and threw it against the wall. It shattered to pieces that landed on the carpet. He had bought the place furnished, since he didn't want to have to go out and buy all this crap that people had in their houses; he just wanted a place to live. Some old lady had lived there, and now she was in a home somewhere, and he was staying in all of her old furniture. He hated this place even more than he hated his mother's place, where he had stayed in the beginning.

Why? Because he wasn't free here either. He felt like he was even more in prison than when he was still on the inside. It bothered him, since all he did when he was on the inside was to dream of getting out.

But that wasn't why he was angry. It wasn't because of the constant harassment from the police or the media that always mentioned his name whenever the case about the missing child came up. No, that wasn't why. He was very angry now because of that stupid ring Jack Ryder had found. It stirred something up inside of him, and he couldn't let it go.

The ring had been his father's. He knew it had. He remembered it vividly. It used to sit on the hand that beat Vernon, and it would always leave a mark somewhere. Vernon could never forget that ring. Not even if he wanted to.

But, he didn't. Right now, he didn't want to forget anything. He wanted to remember. He wanted to know what the heck was going on. And there was only one way to find out. Only one person who knew the truth.

His mother.

Vernon ran down the stairs and found his bike that he had bought at Wal-Mart. He had decided he didn't want a car, since it had been so many years since he had last driven one, and he enjoyed the fresh air so much. So, he had bought himself a bike instead, and now he was riding it through the dark night towards his mother's place.

He parked it outside and stormed up to her condo and knocked on the door. It took a while before she opened the door, probably because she was already asleep. She liked to go to bed early.

"Vernon? What are you doing here?" she asked sleepily.

Vernon pushed her to the side and barged in.

"What's going on?" she asked.

"What happened to my father?" he asked

breathing heavily from the biking and running up the stairs.

Vernon's mother rubbed her eyes and shut the door behind her. "What do you mean, what happened to your dad?"

"What happened to him?"

"I've told you. He was taken by Castro's soldiers. He was put in jail, where they killed him."

"How do you know he's dead?" Vernon asked.

His mother sighed, then sat on the couch. "I...I guess I just thought he was. Since I never heard from him again."

"So, you never saw his dead body?"

"No. No, I didn't."

"You never buried him? You never held his funeral, right?" Vernon asked.

"True, but..."

"Why was he put in prison?" Vernon asked.

"Why? I don't know why. Castro didn't need a reason to put him in jail. Your father was very outspoken. He might have said something against the regime. He wanted to fight for our rights. Castro took everything."

Vernon sat down and covered his face.

"What's going on, son?" his mother asked. "Why all of these questions all of a sudden?"

Vernon looked up. "Because they found his ring, Mama. Do you remember his ring? The brown one with the big stone? The engraving said

Armando. They found it where the kid was taken. The Kingston kid."

Vernon's mother gasped and cupped her mouth. Her eyes grew wide and fearful, then tears streamed across her cheeks.

"But…but how? How did it end up there?" she asked. She looked alarmed. "I don't understand? How?"

"That's what I intend to find out."

Vernon got up from the couch, when his mother grabbed his arm. "There is something you should probably know before you go, son. You better sit down for this."

66

MAY 2015

THE LIGHT was never turned off. Noah waited for it to be, but it never happened. At some point, the door to his room was opened and a loaf of bread and a cup of water were placed on the floor.

"Eat," said the voice.

Noah, who had no idea when he had last eaten or even drunk anything, rushed to it and gulped down the water, keeping his eyes closed from the bright burning light. He ate greedily while his guardian watched him. Noah no longer cared that he was naked or that the guard stared at him. He was too hungry and thirsty. It was all about survival at this point.

When he had finished the cup of water, he licked the last drops on the sides and finally opened his eyes to look up at his guardian.

"Can I have some more, please?"

The guardian slapped him across the face so the cup fell to the ground. "No!"

"Please?" Noah pleaded. Being this thirsty was the worst feeling in the world. It made him feel so desperate. He suddenly understood those stories he remembered hearing about people drinking their own urine in order to survive being trapped in places without water.

He didn't care if his guardian hit him again. He needed water. "I'm so thirsty. Please, Sir?"

His guardian took the cup from the floor, then left, slamming the door shut. Noah stared at the shut door, wondering how long it would be before it was opened again. He prepared himself for a long wait and lay down in the light. The floor was cold and the light hurt his eyes, even when they were closed.

Suddenly, the door opened again, and the cup was placed in the same spot. "Here," the voice said. "Now, never ask for more again, you hear me?"

Noah nodded and jumped for the cup. He placed it on his lips and let the warm water run inside of his mouth. It felt so good when it touched his tongue. Noah enjoyed every second of it. When he was done, he handed the cup back to the man. He looked up at him and their eyes met. In the bright light, he couldn't see his entire face, but his eyes had something in them he hadn't seen in his guardian before.

"You never told me your name?" Noah asked.

The man didn't answer.

"Please? Could I know your name?"

"Why?"

"Because you're the only one I see."

"My name is not important," he said.

"Then, please, tell me why you're keeping me here," Noah asked bravely. The other times when he had asked, it had resulted in a beating. He had learned to fear the man's stick and bad temper. But, today, he seemed different. Like he was approachable. Maybe there was some humanity in him, after all?

"You don't need to know," he said. "Just know that I will be the last person you'll ever see."

Noah's heart dropped. He was scared. It was strange, because he knew that he would probably be killed by this man, but still he refused to give up hope completely. There was something inside of him, a small still voice that kept telling him all hope wasn't lost yet. Not yet.

Your parents are looking for you. The police, everyone must be searching everywhere for you. They'll find you. I know they will.

"So, if you are certain you will kill me, and you will be the last person I ever see, then why not tell me your name? What's the risk? I won't be able to tell anyone else, right?" Noah argued.

The man sighed. He grabbed the cup from Noah's hand and walked to the door. Just before he left, he turned and looked at Noah, who was sitting on the floor, his body trembling in the windowless room.

"The name is Hector. Hector Suarez."

67

MAY 2015

NATURALLY, I couldn't sleep all night. None of us could, except the youngest kids, of course. Abigail and Angela wanted to stay awake, but just before midnight, they caved in and slept on the couch in my living room. Shannon and I sat on the balcony. She held my hand in hers. I couldn't stop the tears from coming.

"You've got to get some rest," she said and wiped a tear from my cheek. "I'm sure we will find him tomorrow."

I stared into the darkness. The beach was empty now. No more flashlights. No more voices yelling my son's name out. Nothing but the sound of the crashing waves. On the horizon, I saw lightning. Anna wasn't far away.

"I just can't bear the thought of him being out there all alone," I said. "He must be so scared. Austin isn't strong like Abigail. He won't survive under much distress for long."

"He might be stronger than you think," Shannon said.

"I sure hope so." I paused and looked at her. My beautiful bride to be. The soon to be mother of my child. I had been so blessed in my life. "The scary part is, if it is the kidnapper that has him," I continued. "He has successfully hidden children from us for many years. He had Scott Kingston for seven years. And no one suspected a thing. They all assumed he was dead. The worst part is not knowing, right? You should have seen Scott's parents, Shannon. They were not alive. They were so dead, so emotionally exhausted. I don't want to end up like them."

"It is a terrible thought, Jack. But you can't do this to yourself. You can't think like that. Yes, Austin is missing right now, but we have no idea what will happen tomorrow."

I stared at her, while a million thoughts flickered through my mind. Something had struck me.

"Wait a minute," I said and got up from the chair.

"What?" Shannon asked.

"The note," I said and pulled it out from my pocket. I unfolded it and looked at it. "Look."

"What am I looking at?" Shannon asked.

"The handwriting. Austin's name. He spelled it wrong. If you look closely, you can see, he wrote AUSTEN. He wrote an e instead of an i."

"So? He was in distress?"

"No. He learned how to spell his name when

he was three years old. He knows how to do it right. I taught him by drawing in the wet sand when he was very little. He must have done it on purpose," I said.

"Why would he do that?"

"Because he's telling me something," I said.

"What is he telling you?"

I looked at Shannon.

"It's a code. We used to make our own code system. That was the only way we could keep secrets from Abigail. A is one, B is two and so on. It's a boy scout thing."

"So, these are numbers?" Shannon asked.

I leaned over and kissed her. "Yes." I got up and went to my desk and started to look at the note. I tried different things, but couldn't get it to be anything but 1-21-19-20-5-14. I stared at it for a while, not knowing what it could refer to, until I realized it. I got up and looked at Shannon.

"It's a phone number. Shannon, it's a phone number. 121-192-0514. You were right, Shannon. Austin is smarter than I give him credit for. He is a survivor. He must be in a place where the number is written somewhere."

Shannon looked at me with her head tilted. "Are you sure about this? It sounds a little far fetched. As far as I know, the area code here is 321. I don't know of any place that has 121?"

"It's all I've got right now, Shannon. It's all I've got."

68

MAY 2015

I DIDN'T wait till morning. It was three a.m. when I called Richard and asked him to try and track the number. He was on it right away, and an hour later, he called me back.

"The area code belongs to Birmingham in England," Richard said.

My heart dropped. England? How was this possible?

"But," Richard added. "I made some calls around. I know a guy with the feds who does this and he helped me track it. We traced it to a neighborhood in Daytona Beach. I can't get closer than that. But it I can tell you it was last used today at six o'clock to make a phone call. You'll never guess to whom."

"I think I might have an idea. Sarah Millman, right?"

"Right."

Richard gave me the address of the neighborhood in Daytona, and I looked it up on the computer. Then I leaned back in my chair with a deep sigh. Shannon came up behind me.

"I'll be damned…" I said.

"What is it?"

"It's the neighborhood where the couple was killed. The couple that held their child in the basement and was killed by the Angel Makers for it. What the heck is going on here?"

Shannon shrugged and sat down next to me. "I don't know. Do you think the Angel Makers kidnapped Austin?"

"I…I don't know. I'm beginning to think so," I said and grabbed my phone. I got up, kissed her on the forehead, and grabbed my car keys.

"Where are you going?" she asked.

"I have to go get him," I said.

"Jack, don't. It could be an ambush."

I shrugged. "So what if it is? I have to go. I can't leave him up there all alone for any longer."

"Think about it, Jack. Austin is smart, but there is no way he could have come up with that code alone. He wouldn't dare to. Plus, how would he know the number of the phone if it is a cellphone? It's not like the number is written on the outside of a cell. They want you to come for him, Jack."

I sighed and kissed her on the lips. "I know. But I have to go anyway."

"Can't it wait?"

"No. I have to go and get him."

"Alone? How about taking Beth with you?"

she asked.

"Beth can't leave her three kids home alone at four in the morning," I said. "It's not like she has a babysitter at hand…or a husband, for that matter."

"What about Ron?" Shannon asked. She sounded desperate. "I'm scared, Jack. Please don't go alone."

"Ron will have to contact the local sheriff, and before they get out of bed, the Angel Makers have left with my son. Shannon. I am a detective. I can defend myself. I will be fine. Don't worry."

She sighed and kissed me twice before I was allowed to leave. I jumped for my Jeep and drove off. I stopped for gas at the local Seven-Eleven on A1A and bought coffee and a Coke to keep me awake.

"Leaving town, huh? Good call. In a few hours, all the roads will be packed," the young guy behind the counter said. "It's going to be complete chaos."

"Excuse me?" I asked.

"Oh, you haven't heard. I just assumed you had and that you had decided to be the first to leave town."

"No, I haven't heard. What's going on?"

"They just announced it on the radio. Breaking news and everything. The National Weather service says Anna is going to make landfall within the next twelve hours."

69

MAY 2015

It was all over the radio as I drove up North towards Daytona. They had all the blaring alarms going and the reports from the National Weather Service, ordering everyone in the coastal areas to evacuate.

I picked up the phone and called Shannon. She sounded tired. "Jack? Is everything alright?"

"Anna is going to make landfall," I said.

"What? When?"

"Within the next twelve hours. I need you to get the children and my parents and prepare to leave first thing in the morning. Make sure to close the hurricane shutters before you leave. My parents know what to do."

"But…but…I have never…"

"It's going to be alright, Shannon," I said. "It's still only a tropical storm. They say it might upgrade to a category one hurricane right before it hits land, but it's not one of the big ones. As long as you go inland, you should be fine. I'm thinking we should find a resort in Orlando and book it for the entire family."

"Sure. That sounds good, Jack. I'll make sure to make the reservations as soon as possible. But, what about you?"

"I'll be back as soon as possible. I have no idea how long it will take me to find Austin or what is waiting for me up there, so that's why I need you and my parents to take care of everything in case I don't make it back in time. Austin and I will just find you in Orlando."

"I have a better idea," Shannon said. "How about we all go to Nashville?"

"Nashville?"

"I still have my house, and it's big enough to house several of our families. Up there, we'll be far away from any storm. And the kids might think it's fun. It's actually more of a ranch. I have horses and everything."

"You don't have to try and convince me, Shannon. You had me at *I have a better idea.* Anything is better than being locked in at a resort while it's pouring outside."

"Good," she said. "I'll reserve the tickets and take everybody with me, hopefully early in the morning."

"And Austin and I will join you later. That sounds like a plan," I said. I liked the idea of my family being far away from the storm. I didn't like it when my loved ones were scared, and a storm raging outside the windows could be very scary.

"Now promise me that," Shannon said. "Promise me you'll be okay and that you'll come with us."

I sighed and turned off towards Daytona Beach. "I promise," I said.

Then we hung up.

The sun would have risen on the horizon by now, if it hadn't been covered in the blackness of the storm threatening us from the ocean. It was pitch dark over the horizon and the winds had picked up. It was shaking the car pretty bad.

I drove over the bridge to the beach shores, towards the neighborhood where the phone had been used last, wondering what I was going to find once I got there. I knew Shannon was right. I knew they wanted me to come. There was a reason for all this, and I was about to walk right into it. But what other choice did I have? The police all along the coast were busy getting people out of their houses and onto the mainland. They had no time to help me out, even if they wanted to. When Anna made landfall, she was so big it would affect the entire coastline of Florida. There would be wind gusts of up to eighty miles an hour and heavy rainfall. It was important to get people out while there was still time. And evacuation took time. It was all that was on their minds right now. A storm was coming, and it could be deadly if you were at the wrong place at the wrong time.

This might turn out to be an ambush, but I had to do it. I feared for Austin if I didn't go and get him. I had to at least try. Even if it cost me my life.

70

MAY 2015

A FEW minutes later, I was driving through the beach-shore neighborhood. Many had already left. Their houses were left with shutters closed and empty driveways. Others were still packing the cars, getting their belongings, children, and pets into the cars. I could tell on their faces they were worried. It was tough leaving everything behind, not knowing what you would come back to. Especially when you lived beach-side...that was usually hit the hardest. You could come back to a house with no roof and water damage inside, windows broken, a house filled with sand or like most did, a house that no longer had a screen around the pool.

I didn't know exactly where I would find Austin, but I had a pretty good hunch.

It was easy to recognize the house. The entrance was still blocked by police tape. I parked my car and got out, holding a firm hand on my gun.

The house was a shabby blue beach cabin from the fifties. It was still marked in the driveway where the bodies had been found. Bullet holes on a tree and a fence behind were marked with red.

A wind gust grabbed me and almost made me fall. I fought through the wind and walked to the front door and looked in the window next to it. It was dark inside.

What if you are wrong? What if he isn't here? Then you've wasted all this time.

It was pretty far fetched. I knew that much. And it would be devastating if I was wrong. That would mean me leaving Austin somewhere unknown while the storm raged. But my gut told me I was on the right track. I had to be. I had to believe I was.

I walked around the house and looked in all the windows, while clasping the gun between my hands in a tight grip. If these insane women wanted to attack me, I wasn't going down easily. I would fight for my life.

I looked inside the kitchen when a gust of wind grabbed the palm tree next to me and a branch was loosened. It fell towards me like a missile from the sky and landed right next to me.

I gasped and stared at the huge palm tree branch. It had sharp pointy edges that would have cut me severely had it hit right.

Luckily, it didn't. I crept along the house wall towards the next window and looked in. Then I let out a small shriek. Inside, I spotted Austin. He was lying on a bed. He was facing the wall, so I couldn't see his face. My heart rate went up quickly.

He is here! I knew he would be! Is he alive? Oh, my God, what have they done to him?

My eyes were glued to the window while I

wondered how to approach this. The Angel Makers were merciless. They had already tried to kill Beth using a bomb. They might do it again. They had also shot Ron from the house across the street. I wondered what their move would be this time?

I decided there was only one way to find out. I had to just go in. I tried to open the window, then used the handle of my gun to break it instead. There was no time to waste. I removed the glass so I wouldn't cut myself, then crawled inside. I landed on the floor with a thud. Austin didn't seem to react. He wasn't moving at all.

Is he asleep? Why isn't he moving? He should have woken up from the sound of me entering? Why isn't he moving?

"Austin?" I said and rushed to him. I grabbed his shoulder and turned him around. When my hand touched his body, he felt warm.

"Austin?"

Austin's eyes met mine. His mouth was covered with duct-tape. His eyes filled with tears. I saw a fear in them I had never seen before. A note was taped to his chest. On the note it said:

WE DON'T HURT CHILDREN. BUT WE WILL IF WE HAVE TO. LEAVE US ALONE!

The note was for me. It was the Angel Makers making a point. They were angry. I had pissed them off by killing one of theirs. I had declared war on them.

"Austin, are you alright?" I asked.

His eyes told me he wasn't. I was about to take off the tape from his mouth, when he groaned and made me look down at his hands. Between them, he was holding a hand-grenade. The pin had been pulled out. The only thing hindering it from exploding was him holding the striker lever down. His hands were shaking with restraint. He was whimpering behind the tape and had tears flooding from his eyes, screaming desperately for my help.

71

MAY 2015

"I'M GOING to take the tape off your mouth, now, alright?" I said, my voice shaking in fear. "It will hurt a little, but it is important that whatever you do, you don't let go of the grenade, alright? Nod to let me know you understand, Austin."

Austin nodded.

"Good," I said, and grabbed the edge of the tape. I pulled it as fast as I could. Austin screamed. I stared at the grenade and his hands, but they didn't move. I was sweating heavily now. My hands were clammy and drops of sweat rolled from my forehead to my nose. The air was very moist and it was hard to breathe properly.

"Dad," Austin said, his voice trembling in fear. "I'm scared."

I forced a smile to try and calm him down. "I know, son. Me too. But we'll find a solution."

I wiped the sweat off my forehead with my arm and looked at my son. I cursed those women for what they had done to him.

"Now, I'll untie your feet," I said and grabbed

the tape used to hold his feet together, making sure he didn't move or try to get out of there. It was so brutal, so cruel to put him in this position. I could hardly restrain my anger.

Why would anyone do this to a child? Why? Just to get back at me? It made them no better than the people they tried to fight, in my opinion. I pulled off the tape carefully, while Austin tried to lie still. He hardly moved.

I looked at my poor son, who was clutching the grenade between his hands. He too was sweating heavily. I kneeled next to him on the bed and stroked his hair.

"You're doing great here, Austin," I said. "You're doing really great." My voice was trembling too. I couldn't hide how scared I was. Austin knew me well enough to be able to tell. "Now, the next thing I am going to ask you to do is to get up on your feet. Do you think you can do that without letting go of the lever?"

Austin looked into my eyes. Never had I seen such an expression on his face before. It was heartbreaking.

"Do you think you can do that?" I asked again.

He swallowed hard, then nodded cautiously.

"Okay," I said. "Let's try, then. Remember, if you let go of the lever, it explodes after four seconds, all right? So, don't let go."

Austin nodded again to show me he understood. My heart was pounding in my chest as I watched him swing his legs to the floor and slowly raise his body from the bed. Tears were rolling across his cheeks, and I could tell the fear had a firm grasp on him.

"Look at me, Austin. Look into my eyes," I said, when he managed to sit up. His eyes met mine. His entire upper body was shaking. "You're doing great," I said. "You're doing really great."

Austin gasped for air. I could tell the fear was overpowering him now. I forced him to keep looking at me.

"Now, try and stand up," I said. "I'll help you."

He lifted the hands with the grenade up in front of him, and I grabbed him around the waist. I lifted him up till he was on his feet. Austin whimpered when I let go. I stared at his hands. They were still firmly attached around the grenade.

"Okay," I said. "So far so good. You're standing up now. You're up. I haven't been this excited about you standing up on your own since you were a one-year-old."

My comment made Austin chuckle. I looked into his eyes to make sure he knew I had this under control. I was trying to ease his fear and I believed I succeeded. At least for a few seconds. Up until the first bullet hissed through the air and hit the wall behind me.

72

MAY 2015

"GET DOWN!"

It was my first reaction as another bullet hit the wall and left a deep hole. It was my instinct to react like this, but Austin didn't throw himself on the ground. Due to the grenade, he didn't dare to. He kept standing on the carpet. He was a sitting duck.

I reacted fast. I grabbed him in my arms and lifted him into the air. Grenade or no grenade, he had to get out of there. But as I grabbed him, the next bullet entered the room and hit me in the shoulder, forcing me to let go of Austin, who fell to the floor. He screamed. I gasped and looked at his hands. They were still in place, holding down the lever.

"You okay?" I asked, while throwing myself next to him with my back against the wall, while bullets were still being fired through the window above my head.

Austin stared at me with wide eyes. "Dad. You're...you're bleeding," he said.

I felt my shoulder. Blood was gushing out of it very fast. My shirt was already soaked. I grabbed the sheet from the bed and ripped it apart. I wrapped my wound with it and tried to stop the bleeding. Austin stared at me, sweat springing from his face. He was clasping the grenade.

"I'll be alright," I said. "It's only a scratch."

I used my gun to fire a few shots out the window, then fell back down next to Austin. He looked tormented.

"I can't hold on to it much longer," Austin whimpered.

I looked at my son and the grenade between his hands. I had an idea, but wasn't so sure it would work. It seemed like the shooting was coming from the house next door. The houses in this neighborhood were pretty close together. Maybe… just maybe. Would he be able to?

"Listen, son," I said. "I need your help."

Austin looked at me. It was risky. What I was going to ask him to do could end up costing him his life. And mine as well. It could also end up saving us both if it worked.

If it worked.

Austin was only six years old…almost seven, he would argue. Would he be able to pull this off? Was it too much responsibility to put on one kid's shoulders? I would have done it myself. But I was hurt now. Austin was my only chance.

"I need you to play a game, alright? Let's say

we're at one of your baseball games. You're very good at baseball, right? You love it, right?"

Austin nodded. "Y-y-yes."

"Alright. Now let's pretend this is one of your games. You're pitching. You can win the game if you do this right. I need you to aim for the house next door. Aim for the window, and then throw the grenade towards it. The best throw you have ever done. The throw of a lifetime. Can you do that?"

Austin stared at me. I could tell he was about to cry. "Don't cry, Austin," I said through the throbbing pain. "You're our only chance now. You can do this. You're a big boy."

Austin bit his lip. He looked at me, determined, then rose to his feet, still with the grenade clasped between his hands. He stood with his back against the wall.

"Good boy. Now, count to three, then walk to the window and throw it. Can you do that?"

Austin went quiet. I feared he had lost his courage. "Daad?" he said.

"Yes, Austin, what is it?"

"I don't want to surf anymore. I don't like to surf."

My heart stopped. I stared at him. Where did this come from all of a sudden? I shook my head with a moan. "You never have to surf again. I promise you. Just help us get out of here alive. Throw that damn thing!"

Austin took in a deep breath, took one step,

and stood in front of the window, then let go of the lever with one hand and lifted the grenade with the other. I stared at him, my heart racing in my chest. Right when he let go of it and it hissed through the air towards the neighboring house, I heard a shot being fired. I got up on my feet, jumped at Austin, and pulled him down. Seconds later, the explosion sent most of the outer wall of the house down on top of us.

73

MAY 2015

I ASKED Austin to stay where he was, once we had gotten out of the debris from the fallen wall. I rushed towards the neighboring house, where the grenade had hit and blown the walls down. I walked with the gun in my hand, pressing through the pain with the adrenalin in my body, across the fallen debris.

I spotted her on the floor of what I believed used to be the hallway. She was lying on her back with the rifle on the floor next to her. Her eyes were staring lifeless in the air, blood running from her head. I pointed my gun at Kelly Monahan, the last of the four sisters, then bent to feel for a pulse. But there wasn't any. She was dead.

Relieved, I ran back to Austin, who was sitting in what was left of the room, shaking, with his knees pulled up against his chest. I kneeled next to him. He looked up. "Is it over?" he asked.

I nodded with a relieved sigh. The adrenalin was still pumping inside of me, but finally, I felt like I could relax. She was gone. The last sister was gone.

"Yes, Austin. It's over."

Austin cried and sniffled. "What about you, Dad?" he asked. He looked at my shoulder.

"That? I told you, it's just a scratch," I said to comfort him. "The bullet barely touched me. Now, come on. Let's go home."

I called 911 on my way out of there and told them where they could find the body, then told them I wasn't going to stay there, since it was too dangerous with the storm coming closer. Then I called Ron and told him everything.

"I'll be..." he said. "We'll issue a warrant for Sarah Millman's arrest again," he said. "As soon as everything is back to normal. This time, she won't make bail."

"Is all the beachside evacuated?" I asked, as we hit the bridges leading to the mainland. I felt a big relief to leave the beach behind me for once. Anna was quickly approaching. I could feel her breathing down my neck.

"Yes. Everyone is out. We have left the area too. I'm in Orlando with my family. Where are you going now?"

I looked at the clock on my dashboard. It was almost eleven. It was too late to make it to the airport and meet with Shannon and the rest of my family. She had left a message telling me they had booked airplane tickets for ten fifty-five. It was the last plane out of Florida for today. Everything was closing down now. She told me she would wait for me at the airport, but leave if I didn't make it. I had tried to call her before I called Ron, but her phone was shut off. So was Emily's and my mother's. I guessed they had already boarded. My shoulder was hurting like crazy, but I pretended to be fine to not scare Austin.

"I don't know," I said. "I think we might drive to Nashville."

"That's one heck of a long drive," Ron said. "Are you sure it's a good idea. What about your shoulder? You said you were hit?"

"It barely touched me; it doesn't even hurt anymore," I lied. I had my phone on hands free and put the speaker on, so I could focus on driving. Austin was listening in. I didn't want him to worry.

"I'll be fine."

"Maybe you should go to the ER once you hit the mainland," Ron said. "Just in case."

"Nah, I'm fine. But thanks for worrying."

I hung up. I could tell Austin was getting concerned. His eyes didn't leave my wound. It looked worse than it was, I thought. I tried to ignore the pain.

"You have more messages, Dad," Austin said, looking at the phone in the holder. "Don't you want to hear them?"

"Sure," I said, thinking it was probably Shannon or my parents calling to ask me if I would make it in time.

Austin pressed the phone and the message came on. But it wasn't from Shannon or my parents.

It wasn't a voice belonging to anyone I loved.
It was Vernon Johnson.

74

MAY 2015

I **KNOW,** *I am probably the last person you wish to hear from now. I have nowhere else to turn. I need to cleanse my name once and for all. But I need you to help me. I know where Noah Kinley is. Meet me at Oceansurf.*

I stared at the phone, then back at the windshield. It was pouring down outside now. It was hard to see the road. I saw lightning in my rearview mirror. It was followed by a loud clap of thunder. The voice of Vernon Johnson wouldn't leave my head.

I know where Noah Kinley is.

I looked at the display. The message wasn't more than fifteen minutes old. What the heck was he up to now? Cleanse his name? I didn't understand. How did he know about the kid? What did he want from me? Was he trying to ambush me? Or was he trying to help? Why did I have to meet him at the surf shop? It made no sense. But there was one sentence that I couldn't stop repeating in my mind.

I know where Noah Kinley is.

I shook my head and tried to think about something else. I reached I95 and turned off towards Jacksonville.

Austin looked at me. "What are you doing, Dad?"

"Getting you to safety," I said.

"Are you just going to leave that boy?" he asked, startled.

"What else do you want me to do?" I asked. "We don't even know if he is telling the truth. It's way too dangerous to go back there."

"But…but you can't do that! You heard what he said. He knows where the boy is. You've got to go there, Dad. He told you he needed your help. You can help rescue the boy."

I sighed. "I can't think about that now, Austin. Getting you to safety is more important for me right now."

"How can you say that?" Austin asked. He looked at me like I had just told him Santa wasn't real. I was his hero, I knew that. And right now, his hero was letting him down.

"It might be a trap, Austin. I just found you. Do you have any idea how afraid I was of losing you? I don't want you to be in danger again. I can't let that happen again. I simply can't. Now, stop it. Let it go. I'm driving to Nashville, and that's the end of the discussion."

But Austin wouldn't let it go. He was suddenly as stubborn as his sister could often get.

"I can't believe you, Dad. The boy needs your help. What if he's killed during the storm? How will you be able to live with yourself, knowing you could have helped him? What if it was me?"

Austin was making all the right arguments. It hurt like crazy. I really didn't want to have to go back. I really didn't. All I wanted was to drive north, get far away from the trouble and the storm, and drive till we reached Shannon's ranch and stay there with my family till the storm was over. Just holding everyone I loved tightly in my arms. That was all I dreamt about right now, after all we had been through. But Austin was so right. It hurt to admit it.

There was no way I could leave the kid in Cocoa Beach.

I looked at Austin with a deep sigh. Austin smiled. "Now, let's go back and get him," he said.

75

MAY 2015

THE FLUORESCENT light above Noah was flickering. Something was going on outside of the room. His eyes were still hurting, and he couldn't keep them open for many seconds at a time without covering them to protect them from the bright light.

But something was definitely going on. For the first time since he had been kidnapped, Noah heard voices. They were coming from behind the door, and when he put his ear to it, he could listen to them.

There were two voices. One belonged to Hector, his guardian; the other, he didn't recognize. Noah hoped it was someone who had come to help him, but he wasn't sure. It sounded like this person knew the guardian. Noah didn't want to risk anything, so instead of banging on the door to let this person know of his existence, he put his ear to the door and listened to them. They seemed to be arguing.

"You sick bastard!" the stranger said. "You kept the kid for years. What did you do to him, huh?"

"I only did what a little boy like him deserved," Hector replied.

"An innocent stranger! A little boy! How could he deserve such a fate?" the stranger yelled.

"You know perfectly well, why," Hector replied.

"Just because of that? Just because of what happened to you more than thirty-five years ago?"

Hector didn't say anything. He hissed at the stranger, and Noah knew the stranger had to be careful now. That was exactly the way he always hissed at Noah when he didn't like his behavior. It was usually the sound he would make right before he did something bad to him.

Be careful, stranger!

Noah wanted to yell it, wanted to scream and bang on the door, but something held him back. Fear of Hector's wrath held him back.

"You're sick," the stranger continued. He clearly didn't know Hector the way Noah did. He would know to stop now if he did.

"A sick, sick bastard is what you are."

Hector still didn't say anything. Noah knew how Hector was staring at the stranger right now. He knew the look in his eyes when he was angry. He always became quiet right before he hit. He would stare at Noah with those piercing brown eyes…stare at him with madness in his eyes. Evil madness.

After spending a long time with Hector, Noah had learned to avoid that anger. He knew to please him to keep that look from appearing in his eyes; he knew what to say to soften him up.

But the stranger didn't know. He kept yelling at Hector. And that was a bad idea. That was a very bad idea. Noah could vividly picture how Hector was now grinding his teeth in anger, waiting for the right moment to lash out.

"What do you want?" Hector asked. "Why have you come?"

"I want the kid," the stranger said. "Where is he?"

Noah gasped. It could only be him they were talking about, couldn't it? Had the stranger come to get him? Would he get out of here?

"I don't know where he is," Hector said.

"You're lying. I know you did it. I know you took him and the two others as well. 'Cause that's just how sick you are. And then you made sure it was all blamed on me."

Two others? Noah swallowed hard. There had been others? It wasn't just him that was being punished, that was being kept like this?

Suddenly, Noah felt the tears well up in his eyes. He felt such anger towards Hector and what he had done. He was no longer afraid of what would happen. He removed his hands from his eyes, turned to face the door, and then slammed both his fists into it, while screaming at the top of his lungs:

"HEEEEEELP! I'M IN HERE!!! HEEEEELP

ME!"

76

MAY 2015

I DROVE up in front of Oceansurf about an hour and fifteen minutes later. The streets had been vacant, so I allowed myself to ignore the speed limits to get there faster. The rain was pouring heavily and the wind gusts pulled and tossed the car.

I assumed Hector Suarez had left town long ago, and didn't understand why Vernon wanted me to meet me here. As suspected, the shop was closed. Shutters covered all the windows.

I looked at the shop through my windshield, shaking my head.

"There's no one here," I said. "Vernon tricked us."

"Why would he do that?" Austin said.

"I don't know. To get back at us."

I was about to put the car into gear, when I spotted something parked up against the façade of the building.

It was a bike.

I knew from my mother that Vernon hadn't

bought a car, since he didn't feel safe driving after all these years, and since he loved being outside feeling the fresh air on his face.

I sighed and put it in park. I looked at Austin. "I better go check to be sure."

Austin smiled. He didn't like the idea of leaving without being certain either. "Okay, Dad."

"You stay here, alright?"

Austin nodded.

"I'll leave the engine running, so you can listen to the radio. I'll be right back, okay? Will you be okay alone out here?"

A thunder clap crackled through the air outside. I could tell Austin was terrified. He never liked thunderstorms, and these were some very severe ones.

I sighed, then opened the door and rushed out. I ran to the door and tried to look inside, but the glass was covered with shutters. I grabbed the handle and realized the door was open. I walked inside and closed the door behind me. The light was on inside the shop, which I found very odd. The lights kept going out, then coming back on. My clothes were soaking and dripping on the floor, leaving a small puddle beneath me. I felt my shoulder. The bleeding seemed to have stopped, but it still hurt like crazy when I moved my arm.

I heard voices coming from the back. I walked to the counter. The door was open behind it. I had never been into the back of Hector's shop. That was where he shaped the boards. He never let anyone in there and always showed us the boards outside in the store.

"Hector?" I asked. "Vernon?"

The voices coming from behind the door were loud and drowned me out. I looked around me, then decided to pass the counter. I pushed the door open and was let into a small hallway with several doors on each side. There was a light coming out from behind one of the doors. I pushed it open.

"Hector?" I asked.

Then, I gasped. Inside the small office stood Vernon. He was holding a gun, pointing it at Hector. It wasn't until I saw them really close to one another that I realized how much the two of them looked alike. Hector had long dreadlocks, making him appear different, but now I saw the similarity.

Behind another door in the room, I could hear the cries of what sounded like a little boy.

"What the hell is going on here?" I said and pulled my own gun.

Hector looked at me, then grinned. He looked at Vernon. "Go ahead," he said. "I know you want to."

He was right. Vernon pulled the trigger before I could stop him. Hector was shot right in the chest, then fell to the ground in a pool of blood.

77

APRIL 1980

HECTOR AND Raul took turns steering the boat and keeping an eye on the passengers. They trusted no one. They had no weapon to defend themselves with if anyone came against them. All they could hope for was that they would leave them alone till they reached Florida, and then they would be someone else's problem.

If only they could keep things calm for that long.

Many eyes were staring at them. The ocean seemed endless. There wasn't a boat in sight. If someone threw them in the water, no one would lift an eyebrow. No one would be able to save them.

Hector started thinking about those swimming lessons he had thought about taking for so long while living in Florida. There was water everywhere, and everyone should be able to swim, his brother had told him. It wasn't that he didn't want to learn, it really wasn't. It was just…well, the timing just was never quite right. Now, he regretted it. Being able to swim would increase his chances of surviving in case he was thrown overboard like that poor guy had been earlier on the trip. At least he would be able to keep himself alive, maybe long enough for another boat to pick him up. At least he wouldn't sink like a rock. Maybe it didn't matter. Maybe he would die anyway.

Nightfall came upon them, and soon darkness surrounded the boat. It didn't make Hector less uncomfortable. A guy was sitting on the deck right outside the wheelhouse, staring at him with this creepy smile on his face. He wasn't very old, early twenties, maybe. But he had been badly beaten. His face was bruised, and so were his arms and legs. Hector could only imagine how he looked underneath his ripped T-shirt. The chill in his eyes said everything. It made Hector shiver in fear.

Raul was steering the boat when the young man later approached them. Hector's heart was racing. Hector could spot light on the horizon and with relief in his heart realized they were getting closer to the shore. Unfortunately, so did the young man. Grinning from ear to ear, he walked inside the wheelhouse.

Hector walked towards him. "No one enters the wheelhouse," he said in Spanish. "Those are the rules. Everyone stays outside. We're almost on shore. You'll be in Florida in less than an hour."

The young man stared at Hector, still smiling from ear to ear. He was missing a few teeth. Hector wondered if they had been knocked out.

"You think I'm afraid of you?" he asked.

"Go back to where you were," Hector said

without answering. He knew very well this man wasn't afraid of him.

And he was right. The man grabbed Hector by the throat and lifted him into the air without as much as a groan. Hector yelled for Raul, who let go of the wheel, then rushed to his rescue. Raul hit his fist into the man's jaw, but the man barely moved. He was skinny, but he was strong. He was obviously used to taking a beating. Raul hit him again, this time in the stomach, but the man barely made a sound. He held Hector in the air, while Hector struggled for air. With the other hand, he punched Raul in the face so hard, Raul stumbled backwards, his eyes rolling back in his face. As he fell backwards, his head hit a sharp edge.

"Raul!" Hector exclaimed, gasping for air. But Raul didn't move. He was lying still on the ground, blood running from his nose and the back of his head. Hector's heart stopped. He felt a deep panic grow inside of him. He looked into the eyes of the man, while desperately holding on to his own life.

"Tell me your name," the man asked.

Hector barely had any air to speak. "Hector," he whispered, in some hope that if he told the man what he wanted to know he might let him go. "Hector Suarez."

Then he felt the man stick his hands inside of his jacket and pull out his passport and papers. The man laughed and showed Hector what he had taken from him.

"Now, I am Hector," he said, while laughing.

He let go of Hector and let him fall to the ground, where he lay coughing and gasping for air for a long time. The man took the steering wheel and soon after, docked the boat. Hector lay still, hoping the man would forget about him, now that he was finally at their destination. The man left, then came back before Hector dared to get up. He smiled from ear to ear, then bent down, grabbed Hector around the throat again, and squeezed so hard everything stopped inside of him. The last thing Hector thought about before he stopped breathing, was Isabella. He was certain he could hear her voice calling for him from the dock of the Miami Harbor.

78

APRIL 1980

SHE WAS calling his name.

"Paaapa?"

Isabella was running from boat to boat in the harbor, asking if they had seen her father, calling his name.

"Hector Suarez?" she yelled.

A man shook his head. So did another one and another one. Isabella kept running. She had been on one of the first boats out. She and her grandparents and her uncle had all made it to safety on the very first day of the boatlift. She had managed to contact her other uncles, who now lived up north in Central Florida, but they had told her that her father and Uncle Raul had travelled to Cuba to find her.

It had crushed her heart.

They had missed each other, and now Hector and Raul were back at the island looking for her. There was no way she could contact them and let them know she was already in Miami. So, all she could do was to approach every boat that docked at the harbor and ask if anyone had seen them or heard about them. This evening, ten more boats had come to the harbor. One was harboring more refugees than the others. She wondered how many were so full they never made it to the other side, and prayed her father and uncle at least would be among those who made it back. She was certain she would be able to find them, as long as they made it.

"Hector Suarez?" she asked a flock of people, who had just jumped off an old fishing boat. There seemed to be several hundred people on this one. How had all of them been able to fit into that old boat? It was a miracle it didn't sink.

"Yes," an old man suddenly said. "Hector Suarez."

Isabella gasped. "You know him?"

The old man nodded.

"You have seen him?"

"Yes." The old man pointed to the old fishing boat in front of her. "Hector Suarez," he said again.

"Hector was on this boat?" Isabella asked.

The old man nodded. "Yes."

She wanted to kiss him. Instead, she shook his small hand. "Thank you. Thank you!"

Isabella ran to the boat, elbowing her way through the crowd, yelling her father's name. She wondered what it would be like to see him again after this many years. Would he recognize her? Would he be proud of who she had become? Would he love her?

"Hector?" she yelled. "Hector Suarez?"

The crowd coming up from the boat were all anxious to get to the shore and paid no attention to her. She was pushed backwards, but managed to fight her way back to the boat, still while yelling her father's name.

"Hector Suarez? I'm looking for Hector Suarez."

A voice suddenly broke through the air and a face appeared in front of her. "I'm Hector Suarez," the voice said.

Isabella gasped, then looked into the eyes of the person standing in front of her. He was smiling widely. Everything inside of Isabella froze when she looked into this man's eyes. The evil that emerged from them was so overwhelming it made her numb.

Isabella shook her head and took a step backwards.

"I'm sorry," she said, the feeling of disappointment eating her from the inside. "I was looking for someone else. For another Hector Suarez."

The man still smiled. Isabella felt very uncomfortable.

"Good luck finding the real one."

79

MAY 2015

HECTOR FELL to the ground with a loud thud, blood gushing out from his chest. I pointed my gun at Vernon, not knowing what else to do. I didn't understand anything of what was going on.

"What the heck is going on here?" I yelled. "Explain!"

Vernon dropped the gun, then lifted both his hands in the air. "I'm sorry. I had to do it," he said.

"Why? Why did you have to shoot Hector?" I asked.

"Can I please explain later?" Vernon asked. "We need to get the boy out of there." He nodded towards the door, where the heavy banging and screaming was coming from. I realized he was right. I didn't trust Vernon one bit, but in this moment, I had to. I should have cuffed him, but wasn't carrying any cuffs.

"Stay there," I said, and pointed the gun at him while walking to the door. Vernon walked backwards both hands in the air. I grabbed the door handle and tried to open it, but it was locked.

Of course it was locked. Meanwhile, the screaming intensified behind the door.

"HEEELP ME!"

"Don't worry," I said. "I'll get you out."

I looked to Vernon for help. "Try to see if he has the key on him," he said.

I bent down and went through Hector's pockets. I found a set of keys in his pants and pulled it out, then sprang for the door. I tried key after key but none worked. I cursed and tried a new one. Finally, one worked. I turned it and opened the door. A light so bright it burned my eyes hit my face and blinded me. I covered my eyes with my hand, as I felt someone throw himself in my arms. I lifted him up, turned around, and carried him away from the burning bright light. Then, I finally looked. In my arms lay Noah Kinley. He was naked and badly bruised on his small body. He was skinny and feeble and so pale. He held on to me so tightly I wasn't sure he would ever let go again.

"There's a blanket over there," I said to Vernon. "Could you grab it and wrap him in it?" I said, fighting my tears. The boy felt so skinny in my arms.

Vernon grabbed the blanket and wrapped the boy. Then, he grabbed a cup and filled it with water from the cooler in the corner. He handed it to the boy. The boy grabbed it and gulped it down.

"Easy there," I said. "I don't want you to choke."

The boy emptied the cup. Vernon fetched more for him, which he drank as greedily as the

299

first, still while clinging to me. I held him up so he could drink again when we heard a loud crash.

Austin!

"The winds are picking up," Vernon said. "This place isn't safe."

"I have my son in the car!" I yelled, then ran out the door with Noah Kinley still tight in my arms. The adrenalin in my body was so strong, still my shoulder hurt like crazy. But I fought my way through it. I was getting all of us to safety, no matter the cost.

Vernon held the front door open for us and as I walked outside I realized what had happened... what had caused that big crashing sound.

A tree had fallen. It had fallen from across the street and blocked the road going south. Luckily, it was still open going north.

"We better hurry," Vernon said. He helped me carry Noah to the car and get him inside the back seat. Vernon jumped in with him and I took the wheel. "Are you alright Austin?" I asked.

He nodded. "Yes. Are you?"

"I will be. As soon as we get the hell out of here."

80

MAY 2015

"**WE NEED** to get him to the hospital!"

Vernon was yelling at me from the back seat. We had made it onto A1A, when Noah Kinley suddenly got worse.

"He's shaking, Daddy," Austin yelled. "His eyes look creepy!"

A wind gust grabbed the car and forced it sideways; the wheels slid on the wet asphalt. I turned hard on the steering wheel and got the car back on the road.

"Just hold on," I said and sped up. The rain was hammering on the windshield. Lightning hit somewhere close by. The thunder clap came right away. It sounded like the entire sky cracked open above us. Austin screamed. I focused on the road and staying on it. Water had overflowed the road and flooding had started.

I grabbed my cellphone to try and call Ron, but there was no service. "I think we can make it to Cape Canaveral Hospital."

The adrenalin was rushing through my

veins as I passed Downtown Cocoa Beach. It was strange to see my town so vacant. All the shops and restaurants were closed up with shutters or plywood. The streets were dark and wet. Not a single car. All parking lots close to the beach that usually were swarmed with cars, even though they charged ten, sometimes fifteen dollars for parking, were empty.

I drove past the Kelly Slater statue and out of the old downtown. A tree had fallen and blocked the street on my side, so I had to drive onto the other side of the road to get past it. The wheels screeched, and I lost contact with the road as we hit the flood of water gushing across the road.

I regained control of the car and managed to continue on A1A. We passed Ron Jon's Surf shop, where the eight-foot surfboard in front of it had fallen and blocked the entrance. I turned left and made it onto 520 towards the mainland. The hospital was located on a small peninsula on the way to the bridges. We weren't far from it.

"Hurry, hurry," Vernon said. "He's cramping."

"Hold on, we're almost there," I said.

I sped up. I could see the hospital now.

"Please, stay with us," Vernon said.

I could feel the desperation in his voice. We were so close now. Just a few more yards.

"No...Vernon said. "No. Don't go. Noah... Noah...stay with us, please, don't..."

"Dad, he's dying." Austin spoke with a

trembling voice.

"Almost there," I said, and turned the car into the hospital's parking lot.

"He's not breathing," Vernon said.

I raced towards the Emergency entrance and pressed the horn down. I knew the doctors and nurses would be there to keep the hospital open and sleep there for days if they had to, as a part of their hurricane preparedness training. I pressed the horn and didn't let go until I saw movement. Two nurses came running to the car as I drove up to the door. I sprang out.

I opened the door to the back and Vernon handed me the lifeless body of Noah Kinley. My heart was pounding so fast in my chest. I put him on the stretcher, and the nurses ran inside with him between them. I watched, panting, my shoulder shooting pain through my body, my stomach turning in anxiety.

Will he make it? Were we too late?

All I had was my hope.

81

MAY 2015

"HE WAS my brother."

Vernon Johnson looked at me from across the room. We had been sitting in the waiting room for half an hour after I had gotten my shoulder checked and my arm put in a sling. Austin was sitting next to me and had fallen asleep in my lap. Vernon had bought coffee from the machine for the both of us. The hospital personnel had told us we were allowed to wait out the storm. They had no idea how long it would last, so they had to ration all their supplies, and that meant food and coffee as well. It was only for the patients. We decided we could live off what we could get from the vending machines.

I sipped my coffee and looked at him. "Hector Suarez was your brother?"

Vernon nodded. "Half brother. We shared the same father. Hector isn't his real name—or wasn't. He was born Alejándro Martínez back in Cuba."

"So, he changed his name when he moved to the States?" I asked. "Just like you and your mother?"

"He must have. I didn't even know he was here. As a matter of fact, I didn't even know he existed. My mother told me about him yesterday. She told me I had seen him when I was just a kid, that he had lived with us when I was younger, but I don't remember. I was too young. My mother told me Alejándro had a troubled upbringing. His mother couldn't care for him properly. Our father didn't want him…thought he was worthless. Nevertheless, he came to live with us for a time when I was two years old. Stayed for a year, but my mother once discovered him inside of my bedroom in the middle of the night with a pillow in his hand, and after that, they decided they couldn't keep him. He was a lot older than me, so I didn't know what was going on. He grew up at his grandmother's house and was beaten regularly by his grandfather. Got himself in a lot of trouble constantly. He came to Florida during the boatlift in 1980, according to my mother. Just like my mother and I did. I don't know how much you know about it, but back then, Castro decided to open the harbor of Mariel to let people leave if they had someone come and pick them up."

"I heard about that," I said, thinking about my time working in Miami. I remembered the stories told by my colleagues about how Miami changed around that time.

"About 125,000 refugees came to South Florida," I said. "It changed everything. The labor market, the housing market, the crime."

"Exactly," Vernon said pensively. "During

this exodus, Castro decided to also open his jails, flooding Miami's streets with criminals, drug addicts, and mentally unhinged people, which contributed to Miami's skyrocketing crime rate and helped it become murder capital of the world just one year later. My brother was one of them."

"He was one of the criminals?" I asked.

Vernon nodded. "He was in prison. So was my father. I was only five years old when they took him. I don't remember him much. My mother told me they were arrested at the same time. She never told me this before yesterday. She kept everything about him a secret from me. My father even remained a mystery throughout my childhood. My brother was only seventeen when he was put in one of Castro's prisons."

"But was released at the boatlift and sent to Florida. What about your father? Wasn't he released?" I asked.

Vernon shook his head. "He never made it. According to my mother, Alejándro came to her one day when I was in school a few years after we had moved to Florida. I went to Cocoa Beach High with your mother and we had a good life. But Alejándro never had any of that. He was angry when he came to see her at her apartment. He beat her badly and told her it was all her fault. It was her fault he had those scars on his body now, it was her fault her husband was gone."

"He died in prison?" I asked.

Vernon sighed. "Yes. He died inside a drawer

cell. You ever heard of those? I looked them up. It's these small boxes they put the prisoners inside of and leave them without water or food for a very long time. They sometimes open the box and throw excrement at the prisoners, or ice-cold water, or they bang on the boxes, making it impossible for the prisoner to sleep. They also put them in small rooms with fluorescent lights for days, so they can't see and can't sleep. My dad died inside one of those boxes. And Alejándro listened to him call for water all night, his voice becoming smaller and smaller, until it was nothing but a hissing sound. Then, Alejándro started to call and yell for help, but no one ever came. When they realized my dad was dead, they took out Alejándro and beat him senseless, then they urinated on him and threw him inside the box instead. He spent seven years in that box. Until Castro decided to get rid of him."

I looked at Vernon and had forgotten all about my coffee. It all made sense all of a sudden. The crouched bodies, the starvation, and the bright light we found in the room where Noah was being kept. "So, Alejándro was doing the same thing to these boys as had happened to himself and to your father?"

Vernon nodded. "Yes. He kept them for years until they died of starvation."

I returned to my coffee and sipped it. It all made sense all of a sudden. Hector had told me he used to be a carpenter. My guess was, he had been working for that roofing company in Rockledge back when Jordan Turner was abducted on his way home from school. Before Hector opened the surf-shop. I wondered where he had kept the kids before he opened the shop? At his home? Maybe we would never know. At the roofing company, he had access to all kinds of wood. Even the very rare birch sort that was very durable and could sustain someone banging on it for hours, weeks and days. My skin shivered at the thought.

Austin mumbled in his sleep. I kept thinking about Noah Kinley. My stomach hurt with anxiety.

Please, let him live, God. He's been through enough. His poor parents have gone through so much. Let them have their boy back.

"But, why young boys? Why not adults?" I asked.

Vernon leaned back in his chair. He rubbed his forehead with a sigh.

"Wait, you were a child back then. Did he do it to get back at you?" I asked. "To punish you for having the life he always wanted with the dad he had longed for all his life?"

"Close," Vernon said. "He did envy me all those things. He did resent me for having all he ever wanted, especially our father's love. But there's more." Vernon emptied his coffee and cracked the cup between his hands. Then he looked at me. "It was all my fault," he said.

"What was your fault?"

Tears sprang from Vernon's eyes now. He wiped them off with a sniffle and tried hard to hide them from me. "That they ended up in prison.

That they had to endure all that. That my dad died. Everything. It was all because of me."

"How so?"

"I spoke up against the regime," he said. "I was just a kid, but that didn't matter. I don't remember doing it myself, but apparently, I had assaulted an officer at my grandmother's house when they came to take her farm. She was an old lady and the farm was her entire life. According to my mother, I tried to tell them they had no right, that Castro was a coward for picking on old ladies. My father was in town spending time with Alejándro for the first time in years when the police came to pick him up at a public park. They told him it was his upbringing of me that had given me those ideas, that he was leading a conspiracy against Castro. He was what they called an *anti-socialist element*. In a way, they were right. My dad was a famous poet and had spoken up against the regime on several occasions. When they came to pick him up, my brother went nuts and started to fight them. So they took him as well. They decided they both were a threat to society and kept them without even a trial. My mother never even got to visit my father. She never knew what happened to him until Alejándro came to her that afternoon when I was in school. He showed her the ring, my dad's ring. That was all he had left of him. When you showed it to me, I couldn't believe my own eyes. But now I know. Alejándro must have dropped it when he took Scott. He still had it when he beat up my mother and left her bleeding on the floor." Vernon shook his head with a sigh. "I found her when I came home. She decided to keep the story a secret from me. She told me it was a robbery. I always believed that was what happened. Up until yesterday when my mom told me everything. Told me how my brother blamed me for everything bad that had ever happened to him. Everything, Detective. She also told me where to find him. She knew he had that surf shop in Cocoa Beach. She had seen his picture in *Florida Today*, the local section in the paper when he opened up the shop ten years ago. But it had been under another name. Hector Suarez. So she knew where to find him when I confronted her. When I came to him, and asked him about the boys, he told me he had done it because he wanted me to be punished. When he was released from the Cuban prison and sent to the States by boat, he was determined to find me. He was so eaten by anger over what had happened to my dad. So when he finally found me here in Florida, he wanted me to suffer in the same way he had. He kidnapped a kid and made sure I was blamed for it. He tipped off the police anonymously, and when they had a witness that identified me in a line-up and said I looked like the guy he had seen with Scott Kingston, then the case was clear to them."

"Except, it wasn't you. It was him. But back then, you looked so much alike," I said.

Vernon snapped his fingers. "Twenty-eight years of my life. Gone. Just like that. All because of one little childish mistake."

"And once your brother started torturing little

kids, he couldn't stop, so once Scott was dead, he kidnapped another one, Jordan Turner, and held him captive in the back of his store for years. Till he died several years later."

"When he heard I was out, he kidnapped Noah Kinley, because he wanted me back inside. I didn't deserve the release, he told me right before I shot him. He wanted me to spend the rest of my life in jail. He knew the police would immediately suspect me."

"And he was right," I said. "We all suspected you right away."

"I shot him because I wanted him off the face of the planet. He told me you would never believe me over him. I had to get rid of him. Even if it meant I would go back to jail."

The door opened to the waiting room and a doctor entered. I stared at him, my heart beating so fast it almost hurt.

"He's stable now. Gave us quite a scare," he said. "His heart had stopped beating, so we had to revive him. Took a while before he was stabilized. I wasn't sure he would make it. He is severely dehydrated and malnourished, but I am positive he will be better soon with the right care. You brought him to us just in time. A few more minutes, and it would have been too late. You saved his life, Detective."

EPILOGUE:

I AIN'T GOT JACK—AND I WANT MY JACK BACK

82

MAY 2015

SHANNON WAS waiting by the front door. She kept gazing out the window to see if she could spot the car down the road. But still, there was nothing. It had been four days since she left Florida with Jack's family and her own daughter, and she had missed him like crazy. He had called her from the hospital to let her know he was all right and that he would ride out the storm at the hospital with Vernon Johnson and Austin. He also told her how he had found Noah Kinley and that the case was closed.

Now he was on his way to her house in Nashville. He had texted her and told her he had landed at the airport an hour ago, and she had send one of her drivers to pick him up. She looked at the clock on the wall, then back at the road outside.

The gate slowly opened, and she spotted the black car as it drove up.

"They're coming!" she yelled into the living room.

There were shrieks and screams, as Angela and Abigail ran out the front door. Jack's parents followed, and Shannon grabbed Emily and walked arm in arm with her outside the house. She looked at the young girl, who had been more worried about her father being alone in the storm than she would care to admit. She had been eating better over the four days she had spent at the house. Jack's mother had spoken with her, and that had seemed to help. Shannon had kept an eye on her, and she seemed to be doing better, even though she was still very skinny.

"Hi, guys!"

Jack looked radiant as he stepped out of the car. Maybe it was just because she had missed him so much. His right arm was still hurting, he had told her, but they had taken off the sling, so you could hardly tell.

She let the children get to him first. Abigail jumped into her father's arms and then continued to her brother.

"Don't you ever do that to me again," she said. "I was so scared."

The twins hugged, while Jack was greeted by his parents in a warm embrace. When they let him go, Angela hugged his legs before she too continued to Austin, whom she had taken a serious liking to. Shannon had suspected them of having a little crush on one another. It was too cute.

"Hi there, sweetheart," Jack said and approached Shannon. She kissed him intensely, even though everyone was looking. He touched her stomach lightly, then turned to look at Emily.

She looked a little shy. Jack smiled and opened his arms.

"How's my girl?"

"Fine, Dad."

He grabbed her and hugged her warmly. Shannon felt all mushy and her eyes got wet. It was silly how this pregnancy messed with her emotions.

"Let's go inside," she yelled and clapped her hands. "Lunch is served at the deck outside."

"Outside?" Jack asked. "But it's so cold here."

She hit him gently on the shoulder. The good one. He grabbed her around the waist and held her tight. "How's my baby doing?"

"I'm good. I stopped throwing up, finally."

"I was talking to the other one," he said with a grin."

"Jack," Shannon said.

They started to walk inside. Jack whistled when he saw the house. It was a little much. Shannon had always thought it was, but Joe couldn't get it big or pompous enough. She couldn't wait to sell it and move on.

"So, how did it go with Noah's parents?" she asked, as the door closed behind them.

"Oh, you wouldn't believe it. It was so great. As soon as the storm stopped, they were flown in from Orlando on a helicopter. The reunion with their son was heartwarming. It felt so good, you know, to be able to save at least one of those boys. It makes it all worth the effort. It is in moments like that that I really love my work."

"And it is a big part of you, Jack. I do realize that," Shannon said.

For a long time, she had tried to convince him to give up his job and just live off her money, but she was beginning to understand more and more how big a part of him his job really was. Even though she hated that he had to risk his life constantly for others. It was also very admirable and very sexy.

"I still can't believe the guy kept Noah Kinley right across the street from us all this time," she said.

Jack looked serious. "It makes me sick to think of. Noah Kinley was right there, in that shop, in the back, without any of us suspecting anything at all. I mean, all the times I have been in his shop and...I keep thinking, why didn't I hear him? Why didn't I hear him scream? But all the rooms were soundproofed. He built his own little torture chambers back there in the rooms we thought he used for shaping boards."

Shannon felt a chill and shivered. "It's creepy."

"And I even thought he was a nice guy. I surfed with him!"

Shannon nodded, thinking it showed how little you really knew about the people around you.

"And, Vernon?" she asked.

"I talked to Jacqueline Jones, and we agreed he was the real hero who saved the boy. There won't be charges pressed, even though he shot Hector

Suarez. The only sad thing is, now I'll never get my new board," he said with a laugh.

"You'll live," Shannon said.

"You said you had a surprise for me?" he asked and kissed her again.

"Yes, follow me."

Shannon walked to the library and asked Jack to sit down in a leather chair, then placed a box on his lap.

"What's this?" he asked.

"Open it."

He opened the lid. Then he looked up at Shannon with a gasp. "Is this what I think it is?"

She nodded. "Yes. He kept it in the safe at the house for all these years. Probably thought he could use it against me if I ever decided to leave him, the bastard."

Jack scoffed. He looked at the gun in the wooden box. "I can't believe it. It has been here all this time. Right under your nose."

"I know. I haven't touched it. I'm turning it in tomorrow, and hopefully they'll drop the charges."

"Let's hope that happens," Jack said, and handed her the box back. "Now, let's get something to eat. I'm starving."

Shannon grabbed his hand and pulled him back. The rest of the family was already engaged in a lively discussion outside; they could hear all their voices talking over each other. It always thrilled Shannon how well their two families did together.

She couldn't wait for them to all live in their dream house in Cocoa Beach. She longed for her new life to begin. Especially now, when the future looked a littler brighter for her.

"I have one more surprise," she said and kissed him gently.

"There's more? I hope it's as good as the first one," Jack said.

"It's better," she said.

His face lit up.

"The scanning yesterday. How did it go?"

Shannon smiled from ear to ear. "Do you want to know?"

"Yes. I do want to know. Don't I?"

"I know."

"Then I definitely want to know."

"It's a boy."

Jack was one big smile. "A boy!! And, you're sure?"

"As sure as I can get."

"Yes!" Jack exclaimed. "No more being the underdogs around here. More manpower to the family."

Shannon laughed and put her arm around his shoulder. " I guess it evens the score a little around here." She opened the door, and they could see the entire family sitting around the table outside on the patio area. "But, we still hold the majority. Remember that."

"Like I could ever forget," he said.

THE END

DEAR READER,

THANK YOU for purchasing *The House that Jack Built*. I hope you enjoyed it. I want to let you know that the inspiration for this story, as in many of my other books, comes from real life. There was a kid that was once abducted from her home in 1979 in Merritt Island, while she was asleep. The killer was allegedly lured in by her nightlight. You can read about it here:

http://www.floridatoday.com/story/news/local/2015/04/24/torres-friends-slain-girl-connect-years-later/26307607/

Furthermore, for those of you that don't know about the Mariel Boatlift, it really happened. Castro opened the harbor briefly in 1980 and let people leave, and he sent a huge flock of criminals, drug addicts, and mentally ill people with them. Even the story about the bus driving through the embassy walls is true. Only the characters are not. I made them up.

http://www.miamibeach411.com/news/fleeing-cuba

The torture inside the prisons is not something I have made up either. The drawer-cells, the fluorescent light, the banging on the boxes, the starvation, and even them throwing excrement on them, but I thought that was too much to put in this book with the children. You can read more here:

http://www.nytimes.com/1986/06/08/books/surviving-castro-s-tortures.html

Don't forget to check out my other books as well. You can buy them by following the links below. And don't forget to leave reviews if possible. It means so much to me to hear what you think.

Take care,
Willow

CONNECT WITH Willow online and you will be the first to know about new releases:
Sign up here: **http://eepurl.com/wcGej**
I promise not to share your email with anyone else, and I won't clutter your inbox. I'll only contact you when a new book is out.

Jack Ryder has his own Facebook page. Follow him here: https://www.facebook.com/pages/Jack-Ryder/1002605086433592

BOOKS BY THE AUTHOR

MYSTERY:

REBEKKA FRANCK series:

- ONE, TWO ... HE IS COMING FOR YOU (REBEKKA FRANCK #1)
- THREE, FOUR ... BETTER LOCK YOUR DOOR (REBEKKA FRANCK #2)
- FIVE, SIX ... GRAB YOUR CRUCIFIX (REBEKKA FRANCK#3)
- SEVEN, EIGHT ... GONNA STAY UP LATE (REBEKKA FRANCK #4)
- NINE, TEN ... NEVER SLEEP AGAIN (REBEKKA FRANCK#5)
- ELEVEN, TWELVE ... DIG AND DELVE (REBEKKA FRANCK #6)
- THIRTEEN, FOURTEEN ... LITTLE BOY UNSEEN (REBEKKA FRANCK#7)

EMMA FROST series:

- ITSY BITSY SPIDER (EMMA FROST #1)
- MISS POLLY HAD A DOLLY (EMMA FROST #2)
- RUN RUN AS FAST AS YOU CAN (EMMA FROST #3)
- CROSS YOUR HEART AND HOPE TO DIE (EMMA FROST #4)
- PEEK-A-BOO I SEE YOU (EMMA FROST#5)
- TWEEDLEDUM AND TWEEDLEDEE (EMMA FROST#6)
- EASY AS ONE TWO THREE (EMMA FROST#7)
- THERE'S NO PLACE LIKE HOME (EMMA FROST #8)
- SLENDERMAN (EMMA FROST#9)

JACK RYDER series:

- HIT THE ROAD JACK (JACK RYDER #1)

- SLIP OUT THE BACK JACK (JACK RYDER #2)

- THE HOUSE THAT JACK BUILT (JACK RYDER #3)

HORROR:

- ROCK-A-BYE BABY

- NIBBLE, NIBBLE, CRUNCH

- EENIE, MEENIE

- HUMPTY DUMPTY

- EDWINA

- CHAIN LETTER

PARANORMAL THRILLERS:

- BEYOND (AFTERLIFE #1)

- SERENITY (AFTERLIFE #2)

- ENDURANCE (AFTERLIFE #3)

- COURAGEOUS (AFTERLIFE#4)

- SAVAGE (DAUGHTERS OF THE JAGUAR #1)

- BROKEN (DAUGHTERS OF THE JAGUAR #2)

- SONG FOR A GYPSY (THE WOLFBOY CHRONICLES)

- I AM WOLF (THE WOLFBOY CHRONICLES)

ABOUT THE AUTHOR

WILLOW ROSE is an international Best-selling author.

She writes Mystery, Thriller, Suspense, Horror, Paranormal Romance and Fantasy. Originally from Denmark, she now lives on Florida's Space Coast with her husband and two daughters. She is a huge fan of Agatha Christie, Stephen King, Anne Rice, and Isabel Allende. When she is not writing or reading, you'll find her surfing and watching the dolphins play in the waves of the Atlantic Ocean. Sold more than 900.000 copies of her books.

Connect with Willow online:

http://willow-rose.net
http://www.facebook.com/willowredrose
https://twitter.com/madamwillowrose

The following is an excerpt from Willow Rose's Bestselling Mystery Novel

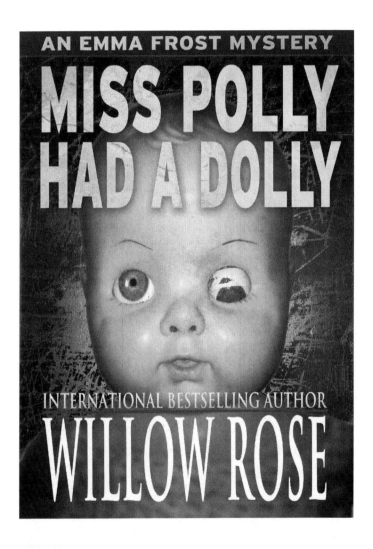

CHAPTER 1

July 1997

MISS POLLY LOVED HER DOLLY. That's what she called her. *My Baby Doll.* Because her beautiful daughter looked just like a doll with her blue sparkling eyes and long blonde hair. And Miss Polly loved to dress her up, just like she was a small doll. She had done it ever since the child was born, but now that she had turned six years of age, she was beginning to resent her mother for doing so.

"I don't want to wear that dress, Mommy," she would say. "I want to wear pants like the other girls."

Pretty dresses weren't currently in style among little girls, and Miss Polly knew she soon faced the end of an era where she was able to decide what her daughter should wear. It wouldn't be long before her rapidly maturing daughter demanded to decide on her own. Miss Polly knew that and therefore she tried to enjoy it while it lasted. This morning she put three different dresses on her little girl and took pictures of her in all of them. Each outfit complete with matching headbands, of course.

"The light blue one is the prettiest," she said and looked at her gorgeous daughter.

Miss Polly had never been beautiful or even remotely pretty as a child, and her own mother hadn't cared about anything other than teaching Miss Polly how to cook so she could be sent away as a maiden at the tender age of thirteen.

So that was her excuse for dressing up her baby girl every day, even if it was only to take her to the playground, like today, and show her off to all of the other mothers.

"You ready?" she asked and put on her hat.

Her daughter appeared behind her. Miss Polly couldn't help but smile when she saw her. She walked to her and set her dress straight and then washed a small smudge off her face by licking her thumb and carefully wiping at it.

"Now there. I think we're ready."

Miss Polly opened the door and let her daughter walk out first. Then they started parading down their street hand in hand, enjoying the many looks from neighbors and by passers whose eyes always smiled when they landed on the little girl. Miss Polly could see in them how beautiful they thought her daughter was and felt a thrilling sensation of pure joy in her stomach.

Her little angel of a doll had given her many hours of that kind of joy ever since she had come into her life. The father they never spoke of. Miss Polly had told her to never ask about him, since he wasn't important to either of them any longer. The fact was that he had run off as soon as Miss Polly had told about the baby. At first he had told her that he wanted her to take care of it, to terminate the pregnancy, but Miss Polly had refused that with a snort. At age thirty-seven she knew this might very well be her last chance to have a child.

"Then I don't want anything to do with it," he had said angrily.

"You don't have to," Miss Polly had answered. "We don't need you or any other man for that matter."

"Good."

Then he got up from the kitchen table in the small apartment that she had rented back then and left. She hadn't heard from him since, and she hoped she never would. They were doing fine on their own, her and her angelic little girl. No need for a third party to ruin the fun.

"Three is a crowd," Miss Polly always said. And it was so true.

When they reached the playground she felt the other women's jealous eyes on her daughter. Miss Polly kneeled in front of her and held her hands in hers.

"Now remember, no getting dirty in there. You're wearing your prettiest dress. Pretty girls don't get dirty. Don't you forget that, my child."

"But the other children..."

"You're not like those other children, sweetheart. You're very special. Some day the entire world is going to admire your beauty and when they do, you'll be prepared for it. Let them look at you, but don't let them get too close."

"But how am I going to play if I can't get dirty or get close to the other kids?" her daughter said with a petulant whine.

"No. No. Pretty girls don't whine, either, my lovely. Or frown for that matter. And don't crinkle your nose like that. It's not becoming. You'll end up getting wrinkles at an early age. Remember, it's all about keeping up appearances, *Baby Doll*. Now go."

Miss Polly drew in a satisfied breath and looked on as her daughter walked towards the playground in her ballerina shoes, taking small feminine steps just like she had taught her to.

Chapter 2

April 2013

"**This book is based on** events that happened to me and my family last year. It is the true story of those events in my own words."

I looked down at the cover of my book, *Itsy Bitsy Spider*, then out on the crowd gathered in front of me. All eyes were on me, expecting me to entertain them, explain to them what really happened and if it *really could be true*? That was the question I got the most at these book signings. People found it hard to believe that all this really had taken place, that all this could have happened to one person, one family.

But it did. None of us had forgotten what happened only six months ago when we were all almost killed by Fanoe Island's first serial killer and now I had written a book about it. Only a month after it had hit the stores, it had become a national bestseller much to my surprise. Everybody loved the story and even if the critics hated it, I was selling a lot of books around the country.

I opened the front cover and started reading out loud. I had been all over the country in the last month doing book signings, but this was a special one for me. This took place at the local bookstore in downtown Nordbo, the town that had become my hometown after my grandmother died and left me her house. I started reading out loud, thinking about my dad who had promised me he would come to hear me today but hadn't arrived just yet, much to my disappointment. Well, he knew the story the book was based on a little too well, so maybe he would peek in later.

I spotted my son Victor and my daughter Maya in the crowd. Victor didn't seem to enjoy being in the crowd too much. He suffered from a form of light autism that the doctors couldn't quite place or put a diagnosis on, but being in a crowd was among the things he didn't cope with too well. My daughter Maya didn't look too pleased, either. On our way down here she had explained to me that she found it so embarrassing that her mom was on a poster outside the bookstore and even worse that I was going to be talking about our family and what had happened. She hated the fact that I had written a book with her in it and even more that everybody in the country seemed to have read it.

"It's so embarrassing, Mom," she had told me when I told her what the book was about. "Everybody is going to know all kinds of stupid things about us. Why exactly do you feel the need to tell them all these things about our family?"

"Because I'm a writer, that's why. It's a great story and I need to tell it."

I had changed the names, but still she had

never forgiven me for writing it. Not even when I told her that with the advance we got I would be able to buy her a new iPad. She had never been easy to bribe, unfortunately for me.

I read out loud from the first chapter of the book that I was so proud of. I glanced up at the audience in between paragraphs. As I did, I spotted Jack, one of my neighbors from across the road and couldn't help but smile seeing him in the crowd. My friend Sophia, who also lived across the road from me, was standing next to him, trying hard to hear me read while two of her kids pulled her arms. She was carrying her newborn in a sling on her front. She looked exhausted, but smiled anyway, which I thought was quite the accomplishment having six kids and being alone with all of them.

I finished the reading then looked out at the many people that had come to hear me. Then I smiled and nodded and received my applause. It was mostly tourists I noticed, but that was no surprise to me, since not many people from the island had liked the idea of me publishing this book. I was constantly receiving remarks, especially from church people that felt they were being put on display in my book, which I admitted they were, but frankly that wasn't my fault. They had done some horrible things in the past and some of them had paid for it with their lives. That was the story and I couldn't change it.

"Now, I'll do book signings over by the table," I said and moved over to the corner where the nice lady named Isabella Petersen who owned the store had put up a table and a chair. She was the first and only bookstore owner on the island who had dared to agree to a book signing by me and I was very thankful to her for that. I had asked my dad to bring her a basket of flowers and wine as a way of showing my gratefulness, so I was getting anxious now that he wasn't going to make it.

A line formed in front of the table and I started signing the books one by one.

"Who is it for?" I asked.

"Me. My name is Alice."

"Okay, Alice," I said and signed the book *To Alice, hope you'll enjoy your reading. Best, Emma Frost.*

After signing about fifty or so, I finally heard my dad's voice behind me. He was out of breath when he spoke.

"Got the basket. I added some chocolate, I heard she likes that," he said and put the basket down next to me. It was nicely wrapped in cellophane. It was perfect.

"Where did you hear that?" I asked, thinking that it didn't matter, all women liked chocolate, right?

Another reader put her book on the table in front of me.

"Sign it to Gerda," she said with a German accent.

"My new girlfriend told me."

"Your what?" I stopped signing and looked up

at my dad who was standing next to me and now I realized he was flanked by a middle-aged woman with very red hair.

"Emma, meet Helle. Helle, this is Emma."

CHAPTER 3

July 1997

NINA HEARD THE ICE CREAM truck from far away. She turned to look in the direction of the sound, but none of the other kids seemed to hear it. She looked in between the houses nearby to see if she could spot it.

Oh how she would like to get an ice cream for once. Nina looked in her mother's direction. She was sitting on a bench smiling while keeping an eye on Nina making sure she didn't get dirty or behave in an unsuitable way for a young girl.

Nina snorted. She was so sick and tired of having to act in a certain way and dress the way her mother directed her to. It took forever every morning for her mother to pick the right dress. When would she get it through her head that Nina didn't care about those things? Nina wanted to be able to play and get dirty like the rest of the kids. She liked wearing pants and a t-shirt and dreamed of the day she'd be able to convince her mother to buy her a pair of jeans. Nina sighed and smiled at her mother. No, that would probably never happen.

"Little girls should have long hair and wear pretty dresses," her mother always said whenever

Nina dared bring up the subject.

Her mother could spend hours just brushing Nina's hair before bedtime. "A hundred strokes a day makes your hair beautiful."

Oh how Nina loathed it when she called her beautiful or pretty. So many times she had wished that she wasn't pretty, that she could just look ordinary like the other kids. She had even once tried to cut her hair off, thinking that if she didn't look pretty then her mother would get off her back.

But her mother had caught her in the bathroom after she had cut off the first piece of the hair.

"What are you doing to yourself!" She could still hear her yelling. And the yelling didn't stop for days. Every time she saw Nina she would start in again. "How dare you. You are blessed with such beautiful hair. Do you know how many small girls would die to have what you have, well do you? You should be grateful that God has given you such a gift. You should cherish it and honor it. Aren't you glad that you're not ugly like those other children?"

"I want to be ugly, Mom. I don't like being pretty!" she had said and run off to her room.

That didn't go down so well with her mother. The next week Nina wasn't allowed to go outside or watch any of her favorite TV shows or even read the magazines that her mother had bought for her, with pretty little girls on the front covers. Not that Nina cared much about them, though. To be honest, she found them to be stupid. Nina had on several occasions asked her mother to bring her magazines with horses or tigers which were the things she was really interested in, but her mother wouldn't hear of it, of course.

Since then Nina hadn't attempted to cut her hair again. She did however dream of the day when she got to decide for herself what to wear and what to look like. When that day came, she was determined that she was never going to wear dresses again. Ever. Her mother would be devastated, but Nina didn't care. She had gotten her way while Nina was young, sooner or later Nina would get her way, as well—whether the mother liked it or not.

A boy approached Nina on the playground with a smile. "Do you want to play?"

Nina shook her head then looked in the direction of her mother. She was shaking her head as well and signaling Nina to *let him admire you, but don't let him come too close.*

"No. I'm sorry. I can't," she said. "I'm not allowed to."

The boy shrugged. "Why did you come to a playground, then?"

"To be seen," Nina said putting her nose in the sky the way her mother always wanted her to. "At least that's what my mom calls it."

The boy shrugged again. Nina looked down at her shiny ballerina shoes. A touch of sand had landed on the top of them. Nina gasped knowing how angry mother would be if she noticed, then she bent down and wiped it off. When she raised her head and looked at her mother, she noticed that she was staring at her. Nina smiled to show everything was fine and her mother's shoulders came down. Nina looked down at her dolly in her hand. *Little Miss Jasmine*, they called her. Nina hated that dolly. It had blue eyes just like she did and wore a pretty dress. Nina suddenly felt like throwing it far away.

The ice cream truck rang its bell again. Nina looked up and spotted it on a neighboring street. She looked over at her mother and wondered if she dared to ask her for ice cream once again.

No, not after what happened the last time.

Nina's mother didn't let her have ice cream—or anything else she considered unhealthy—since she needed to watch her weight and maintain a healthy complexion. Apparently that was very important in life. Her mother had never taken care of herself and *see what she looked like now*?

Nina didn't care. She thought her mother looked fine. She had considered cutting her face, scaring the cheeks once, to get her mother off her back, but she wasn't allowed to play with knives or scissors ever since that incident with her hair.

The bell rang again and Nina was getting hungry. She was sick of having salads for lunch and never having any dessert. She wanted ice cream and candy like normal kids. Nina looked at her mother again and noticed that another woman had approached her and they were now talking.

"Probably talking about me, how *adorable* I look," she mumbled to herself bitterly, thinking that would be the only reason for her mother to want to talk to any stranger that approached her.

Nina looked in the direction of the ice cream truck again, then made her decision. On her way across the lawn she dropped Little Miss Jasmine and never cared enough to go back and look for her.

Nina stormed in between the houses and ended up in a small street. She spotted the ice cream truck a little further down the road and ran towards it. It had stopped and was ringing its bell. Nina was out of breath when she caught up with it. A woman stuck her face out and smiled.

"Hi there you pretty little thing. Would you like some ice cream?"

Nina wasn't supposed to talk to strangers so instead she just nodded.

"Look at the sheet and see if there is anything you'd like," the lady said and blew a bubble with her gum.

Nina pointed at the biggest one with most chocolate on it.

"Ah, that one, huh? Nice choice," the lady said. Then she disappeared for a while and came back and handed Nina the nicely wrapped ice cream. The golden wrapping was sparkling in the sun. It had a picture of the ice cream on the outside of it. Nina couldn't remember ever feeling happier than in that moment.

"That'll be ten kroner," the lady said.

At once Nina froze. Money. She hadn't thought

about money. She felt how the blood left her body when she realized that the dream of ever tasting this small piece of heaven was still as far away as it had always been.

"I...I...I don't have any money."

Nina was ready to give the ice cream back and walk with bowed head back towards her mother who was probably angrier than ever now.

"You don't have any money?" the lady said and tilted her head. She chewed heavily on that bubblegum. "Well you know what?"

Nina looked up with her big blue eyes. Was there still a way? Was there still a possibility that she might get the ice cream after all?

The lady looked to the sides, then whispered. "Come around the back. I have some extra that we usually don't sell but keep for ourselves to eat."

Nina nodded eagerly, gave the glittering ice cream back to the lady who winked at her before she closed the hatch to the magic ice cream truck. Nina looked carefully around to make sure her mother was nowhere to be seen, then walked behind the truck. The lady opened the back door, and peeked out.

"Come on inside, it's in the back."

Nina felt like she had somehow found an escape-way to heaven and was filled with excitement as she took the first step inside the truck. The smell inside was incredible, she thought and she never noticed the door being locked behind her.

It wasn't until the truck started moving that she realized she wasn't going to taste the ice cream any time soon.

CHAPTER 4

April 2013

PATRICK FELT LIKE HE WAS losing control again. It scared him a little, but also filled him with excitement. The frightening part was that he sometimes found it hard to know what was reality and what was his fantasy. Patrick had always had many fantasies, but lately he had begun living and acting them out and that caused him to lose control of reality from time to time. Simply because he slipped into a world of his own and then there was no knowing what he was up to.

He looked at the Asian woman he had just picked up from the street. She was small, and he liked them small. He liked them young too, but he couldn't always get everything, now could he?

He accelerated in the small BMW convertible that the TV-station had rented for him while he was in town.

What town was it again? Viborg, that's right. Gotta keep track of what's going on around you, Patrick. Can't lose complete control.

As usual they were only in for a week, then off to a new town. It was like that all throughout the season of the show. Patrick loved it when a new season started and they toured around in the country. It was the third year the TV show had aired and every year it grew more and more successful. The first three episodes this spring had had the highest ratings any reality show on Danish television had ever had, so it was fair to say it was a success. He was a success. Patrick had been the host for the show since the beginning and his face was synonymous with it to the viewers. When he walked out the door he represented the TV show, they told him. They expected him to act like it.

"Where are we going?" the Asian girl asked with a slight shiver when she noticed they were leaving town.

"I know a place outside of town," he said. "More private like that."

The Asian girl closed her mouth and nodded. Patrick looked at her voluptuous lips. They were painted pink. Patrick didn't like that, he didn't care much for pink, in fact it gave him the creeps. He found a napkin and handed it to her.

"Here wipe that lipstick off. I don't like it."

She did as he told her. Now that was much better. Now her lips looked real. He had offered her two hundred for an hour. Figured she wasn't worth much more. She had accepted and jumped in his car without anyone seeing Patrick's face. He always made sure to use a back entrance when he left the hotel where his fans camped along with the paparazzi and he disguised his face by wearing a hat or a hood from his sweater, since he was, after all, representing the TV show. The girl had recognized him once she was in the car, naturally, but that didn't matter.

She was never going to be able to tell anyone anyway.

Patrick spotted the right place, a rest area far enough from town to be completely left in darkness at night. Not a soul would ever see them. Patrick was beginning to feel worked up, almost high, by the thought of what was about to happen. It wasn't something he was able to control, it just kind of happened, came over him, like a wave inside of him. It was a rush of emotions, of maniac ecstatic feelings that got him so high he could no longer control himself.

"What are we doing here?" the Asian girl asked as he took the exit towards the rest area. Patrick turned off the car's headlights and let it roll into the area. It was empty alright, just as he had expected it to be. He found a spot and parked the car. The Asian girl looked at him and smiled. He could see the contrast of her white teeth on her brown skin in front of him. He fought the urge to knock them out, to smash her face in.

"So you want to do it here?" she asked with an accent.

"Yes, I *want to do it here*," he repeated mocking her accent.

"Okay," she said and took off her small jacket that barely covered anything. She was chewing gum and blowing bubbles while arranging her stockings.

"So what do you want to do first? Do you want me to blow you or do you want to get inside of me right away? Remember, I don't do anal. That's off limits. But tell me your fantasy and I'll try and make it come true. After all, you *are* my first celebrity."

She blew another bubble. It annoyed Patrick immensely. Patrick reached over and grabbed her neck. She shrieked. He put his fingers into her mouth and pulled the gum out, then dropped it in her hair. With a finger he pressed it into her thick black hair.

"Hey!" she yelled and tried to remove it, but it was already stuck. Now it was on her fingers as well. "Do you have any idea how difficult it will be to get that kind of thing out of my hair? That's gonna cost you extra. At least fifty more."

Patrick laughed manically.

"You think it is funny, do you? Well it's not. Why are you being so mean? I always thought you were a nice guy. You seem so sweet on TV," she said, pouting now.

Barely had she finished the sentence before Patrick couldn't hold himself back anymore and he punched her in the mouth hoping it would make her shut up. She screamed and spat out a tooth. Blood was gushing from her mouth. She seemed dizzy from the blow. Her lip was broken and bleeding, too. Her head was spinning and her eyes were rolling up like she was about to fall unconscious. Patrick laughed, mainly because he was happy that he had finally made her shut up. Then he leaned over and kissed her, licked off the blood from her lips and drank from her. She tried to push him away but her small Asian arms were strengthless. Patrick fumbled with his hand in his pants and pulled out his knife. She didn't see it, but protested slightly when he leaned over and held her down. Very close to her ear, he whispered:

"This is my fantasy."

CHAPTER 5

April 2013

I HAD NO IDEA WHAT to say. My dad had taken me and the kids out for lunch after the book signing, along with his new girlfriend that I had heard nothing about up until today.

"So, Emma. It's so exciting with your book, huh?" the woman said.

I was eating my sandwich and had my mouth full when she asked. I stared at her while chewing not knowing what to say to her. That I was in state of complete shock? That I had no idea she even existed? That I had seen my dad at least three times a week since he moved to the island to be closer to us, but he hadn't once mentioned her name? That I thought she looked like an old version of Pippi Longstocking? What? What do you say in a situation like this?

"Well, not everybody finds it so exciting on this island," I answered.

"Helle is not one of them," my dad said.

"Are you a newcomer like us?" I asked.

She shook her head. "I've lived here all my life. But I was never part of the church. My parents stayed away from all that."

"That's good to hear," I said and smiled. She seemed nice. I especially liked her eyes, and I was certain that once I got over the shock, I would be ready to give her a chance. At least my dad suddenly seemed very happy, almost cheerful, and that was a new approach for him, so maybe, just maybe she could do what my mother never accomplished? Could she be the one to make my dad happy finally? I wanted him to move on from my selfish mother who had left him to move to Spain with some guy that I just hated. I wanted him to be happy again, to be at peace and enjoy his life.

I opened my mouth and took another bite of my sandwich, still while staring at her and her very red hair, her fluttering orange dress, and many rings and bracelets. She had that look of an artist or a writer, and I couldn't help but admire her slightly for daring to stand out like that.

"Your children are beautiful," she said.

I looked at Maya and Victor who were both eating in silence. I guessed they were just as surprised as I was. "I know," I said and smiled. "I'm very lucky." I ate more of my sandwich feeling proud of my children. They had both been doing well in school all spring, even Victor had improved, his teacher said. He was interacting with the other children and that was a huge step for him. Maya had gotten good grades and a new best friend named Annika who she spent most of her time with. She was growing up to be such a great girl.

"Do you have any children?" I asked Helle when I was done chewing. I washed it down with a coke that I wasn't supposed to have, since I had once again started a diet and this time I really meant it.

Helle smiled awkwardly. "My daughter is no longer with us."

I almost choked on my ham. "My God. What happened?" I cleared my throat. "If you don't mind talking about it, that is?"

My dad put his arm around Helle's shoulder. "Maybe another day," he said.

Helle put her hand on his arm. "No, it's okay. I don't mind talking about it." She drew in a deep breath. I stopped eating sensing this was too serious a subject. Helle's lips became tight, her eyes moist. "We think she drowned. It's the only explanation they have been able to come up with after all these years. But sometimes kids run out into the ocean by Fanoe Vesterhavsbad and get lost. When it is low tide you can walk to an island there and then they are surprised when high tide comes rushing in. They never found any trace of her though. Not her body or even a piece of clothing and I have no idea what she was doing out there without me knowing it. Last time I saw her we were at a playground, when I looked away for one second to talk with another mother, she was gone. The police think she might have run down to the beach not far from there and then walked into the water thinking she could reach the island, Soren Jessen's Sand. *Maybe she wanted adventure*, they said. But my girl was never adventurous, not like that."

I looked at the woman and suddenly felt the deepest sympathy for her. I put my hand on her arm. "That's terrible, Helle."

She nodded and bit her lip. "I know. Took me many years to accept that she was gone and wasn't going to come back through the front door with some fantastic story about how she'd gotten lost but found her way home. Her father wasn't in our lives. She was all I had. But now I have finally learned to live with it. I still can't help myself though, when I see a girl that looks like her or looks the way I think she would today. I guess I'm always on the lookout for her. I don't know if it'll ever stop."

"How old was she?"

"Six. She had just turned six years old."

CHAPTER 6

July 1997

"**YOUR DAUGHTER IS VERY LOVELY,**" the woman who had approached Miss Polly said. Miss Polly didn't care much about talking to strangers and always told Nina to never do so. But when they complimented her only true love in this world, her beautiful daughter, Miss Polly could never resist answering them.

"Yes, isn't she?" Miss Polly replied happily.

The woman rocked the stroller. Miss Polly could hear a baby fuss inside of it.

"How old is she?" the woman asked.

"Six. She just turned six years old."

"Gonna be some heartbreaker for the boys, huh?" The baby was fussing again and the woman rocked the stroller a bit forcefully while hushing it. Miss Polly stared at the woman feeling her heart accelerate. It was the word she had used. *The boys.* Miss Polly strongly resented the very idea of her precious little girl having anything at all to do with those disgusting…filthy creatures.

Boys. They only want one thing from you. And once you have given it to them, they leave you.

Miss Polly knew the day would come when she would have to face this problem with her Dolly. Up until now she had merely decided that her daughter was never going to be with any boys when she reached her teens. Miss Polly simply wouldn't allow her to be with them. But deep inside she knew that it was going to be a fight that she might end up losing eventually.

Just the thought of one of them ... touching her. Defiling her. I won't let her be besmirched by them. I simply refuse to let that happen.

"So will she start school after the summer?" the woman asked.

Miss Polly was pulled abruptly out of her thoughts. She shook her head. "No, I will be homeschooling her."

"Homeschooling? That's unusual." the woman said.

Miss Polly was getting tired of this conversation and wanted the lady to leave now. All those questions were annoying and tiresome. But she was right. Miss Polly knew it was very unusual in Denmark for people to homeschool their children. It was mostly people who had children with severe autism or other disabilities, and even those had help. Miss Polly was going to do this completely on her own. Even if she had no idea how to. There was no way her precious baby doll was going to go to those noisy, filthy places called schools and be blemished by all those other dirty, filthy children. No she was staying home where it was safe for her to be, where Miss Polly could watch her every moment.

"Yes, well that's what I've decided," she answered a little harshly in the hope that the woman would go away if she sensed Miss Polly wasn't enjoying the conversation. But apparently the woman had no sense of decorum or any sense at all for that matter. She kept right on talking.

"That's really difficult, isn't it? I mean you have to follow a program or something, right? To make sure the child is taught the exact same as the rest of the children. And what about the social skills? How will she learn how to be a team player?"

Miss Polly looked into the woman's eyes while the anger rose in her.

Stupid Danish people. Always talking about everybody being equal, all that socialism is destroying our beautiful country. Don't they see it?

"My daughter will not be a team player," she burst out, knowing very well that her opinion was not like most people on the island, or even in the country. "She is special and I will raise her to know that. She will not go out and be ordinary, she will do many incredible things in life and when she is a grown up everybody will know who she is, since she stood out in the crowd, since she is special and not like all the others. See, I do not believe we are all born to be equal. I believe some are destined for greatness. Now if you'll excuse me, I will take my child home before she catches the bug of mediocrity that has become so common these days."

Miss Polly snorted and stood up in front of the woman.

"I'm sorry," the woman said and held a hand up in the air. "I was just trying to make conversation. Geez."

But Miss Polly was no longer listening. She stormed past the woman and towards the children playing. She tried to spot Nina amidst all the noisy children running around, but she couldn't see her anywhere.

Where are you baby doll? You're not running around getting dirty like all those common children, are you?

Miss Polly was walking faster now while scanning the playground area.. "Nina?" she called out thinking she might be standing somewhere where she could not see her. Miss Polly searched under the slide and on the swings. There was no sign of her precious baby doll anywhere. Now her heart was racing rapidly and she had to put a hand to her chest to calm her breathing down. Where could she have gone? Miss Polly saw the boy that had been talking to Nina earlier and stormed towards him.

"Where is Nina? Where is the girl you talked to earlier?"

The boy looked at her indifferently and shrugged. "I don't know."

Miss Polly grabbed his shoulders and started shaking him, "Where is she? Tell me immediately. What have you done to her, you filthy animal?"

The boy started screaming and a couple of parents ran towards them. They pulled Miss Polly away from the boy. "What's the matter with you?" a woman said to her. Probably his mother; she had the same ugly nose. The ugly mother looked at Miss Polly disapprovingly, but she didn't care. It didn't matter. They didn't matter. All that mattered was finding her precious baby girl before it was too late, before someone... *Don't even think it...* the very thought of someone harming her felt like knives in her body. She could hardly bear it.

"He has done something to my girl. I can't find her," she said. "Where is she?" she yelled at him.

The boy whimpered while his mother put her arm around him and pulled him away. Miss Polly felt the playground start spinning. Could it be the woman that had been talking to her? She'd seemed a little too fond of Nina. Miss Polly started spinning to see if she could spot the woman, but she too seemed to have vanished.

What is happening here? Where is my girl?

Miss Polly was hyperventilating now and could hardly breathe. She bent over and took in a few breaths, while feeling very dizzy. Her poor weak heart couldn't take this. When she lifted her head to start the search again for her precious baby doll, she spotted *it* in the grass. Miss Polly gasped and ran across the lawn. She was panting and pushing kids aside who got in her way. Parents were yelling at her, telling her to *get the hell out of the playground, you crazy bitch*. But Miss Polly didn't hear them. Her eyes were fixated on one small thing in the grass.

Little Miss Jasmine.

Miss Polly was crying hysterical when she picked her up. She held the doll close to her chest while crying.

"Where is she, Little Miss Jasmine? Where did she go?" she mumbled while the tears ran down her cheeks. It felt so good to hold the doll again, just like when Nina had been a baby and Miss Polly would hold her in the exact same way. She held her tight to her body while desperately scanning the area surrounding them. Her lip was quivering and her tears falling to land on the doll's face. Miss Polly wiped the tears away from the doll's face with her hand.

"Can you believe it, Little Miss Jasmine? Can you? Miss Polly can't find her dolly."

CHAPTER 7

April 2013

"WHY DIDN'T YOU TELL ME you were seeing someone?" I asked my dad when we got back to the house. Helle had to go back to her shop where she sold trinkets or something like that according to my dad who apparently didn't really know what it was she was selling.

"I don't know," he said and sat in a chair while I served him a cup of coffee. "I thought it would be better this way."

"You mean a sneak attack on one of my most important days?" I asked with a chuckle.

My dad laughed. "Yeah, something like that."

I found a box of Danish butter cookies and gave him a couple with his coffee. I grabbed a handful myself and started eating them.

"So what did you think of her?" he asked with his mouth full.

I swallowed mine and drank some coffee while choosing my words carefully. "She seemed very nice, actually. I like her."

"Actually? You didn't expect to like her?"

I shrugged. "To be frank, no. It was quite

THE HOUSE THAT JACK BUILT

a shock at first, and then I guess I reacted with resentment. But lunch was a good idea. Talking to her made me like her. But I have to say you didn't give her a fair chance bringing her like that. It wasn't fair towards her. You could have at least told me about her."

He ate another cookie and nodded. "Well, I was afraid you'd be angry, so I thought we should just get it over with."

I chuckled again. "You're impossible. You're lucky she still likes you after that stunt. That proves to me she's a good woman."

My dad smiled in a strange fashion. There was something about him.

Something...like...glowing? Could you say that about a guy? Well, he was glowing. He was happy and I don't think I had ever seen him happy before, not like this. It made me a little jealous. I think a little might be an understatement. Why wasn't I able to make him happy like that?

"She's a great woman," he said with that strange smile on his face. My dad never smiled much. He was grumpy about work, about his medical clinic when I was a child, he was angry at my mom for leaving him and moving to Spain the last few years, there had always been something for him to be moping about. But not now. Now he wasn't even grumbling. That was very new to me and a little odd when you've become accustomed to such different behavior. Thinking about it while sitting in front of him, he had been a lot happier lately. I had just thought it was because of him finally being able to retire from his clinic and moving closer to his daughter and grandchildren.

I smiled with a sigh. "Well as long as she makes you happy, Dad, then I am too. We should invite her over for dinner and get to know her a little better. If she is going to be in your life, then we should make her welcome."

My dad grabbed the paper and nodded. "Sounds great, sweetheart."

His face disappeared behind the local Fanoe paper where pictures from the TV show *Shooting Star* were plastered all over. *Shooting Star* was a TV reality show that featured children singing. A little like *X-factor* and those kinds of shows, only for children. It was the biggest talk of the island these days. The TV show was coming to Fanoe for the first time and everybody wanted their kids to audition. The show's host was a young guy in his twenties who simply went by the name of *Patrick*. He was the most talked about host in Danish history, a horrible drama queen and primadonna, but always fun to watch. Especially when he whined excessively into the microphone in enthusiasm.

He *was* the show and most people liked to see the children sing, but they watched it because of him. He was funny, witty, and very very handsome. And he wasn't afraid of acting crazy. People never knew what he would do or say next and I had a feeling neither did the producers. He always did or said something that created headlines everywhere and made people talk. That made it the most popular show in Danish television history. Me, unlike most people my age, I wasn't afraid to admit it. I liked to watch *Shooting Stars* and I was definitely going to go down there for the auditions. Just to see the set-up, I didn't have any children that wanted to do it, but Sophia did. She had six kids in total and she had managed to persuade two of them to audition for the show. I was naturally going to be there to support her and of course, hopefully catch a glimpse of the spectacular host.

Chapter 8

April 2013

Josephine Gyldenstjerne knew she was born for greatness. She also knew children weren't born equal and that she was among the few born to rule others. At the age of six, Josephine knew all about class distinctions and she knew her place in this world. As the daughter of a Count and Countess of Denmark, she knew she was destined to live a life of luxury.

As always in the spring, the family moved to the small island of Fanoe and lived at their residence close to the beach. And as always, Josephine was followed closely by her governess, Ms. Camilla, even when they took a rare break from her schooling and walked to the beach. Josephine adored the beach. She loved the mighty dunes and wide stretch of sand, and she particularly loved the huge ocean with nothing but water as far as you could see. Every afternoon this week she had begged Ms. Camilla to take her down there and watch the waves coming in from afar. And every day Ms. Camilla had said no, they had work to do. Until this Wednesday afternoon, when the sun was shining from a clear blue sky and even Ms. Camilla felt the calling of the birds and the alluring spring outside of the windows of the mansion they called their vacation residence.

"England is on the other side of the ocean," Ms. Camilla said when they stopped at the top of the dunes. She pointed to make sure Josephine watched.

But Josephine didn't care. She knew all that and even more. She closed her eyes and breathed in the salty air blowing in from exotic places far, far away. She imagined a small boy at the shore in England standing just like she did and breathing in the same air, just hours earlier before it blew across the North Sea. She chuckled at the thought and opened her eyes. Ms. Camilla was still talking about England and trying to teach her stuff that she already knew. Josephine had spent most of her life reading and learning about other countries, but she was never taken anywhere, not even when her parents travelled to all kinds of places all over the world. No, she had to stay and get her education she was told when she pleaded with them to take her along for an adventure. She had obligations. There was going to be a day when she would be able to travel and see the world as well, just not now. Education was more important.

So Josephine had to just dream about all of those exotic foreign places for now, but one day she was going to see them all. No one was ever going to stop her from doing that. Not even her absent parents who only spent time with her when they quizzed her on her knowledge and what she had learned in school so far. They never even ate together, since Josephine was supposed to eat with her governess and was only supposed to see her parents when she entered their chambers every evening at seven forty-five to say goodnight. If she was lucky her mother would come and listen in during her lessons every now and then, and she would get to hug her afterwards, even if it was only a short hug.

Once they took her with them to a gallery opening where they were invited as guests of honor. Josephine had enjoyed that immensely. Especially when all the photographers were yelling and taking pictures and asking her to smile for them. That was a lot of fun. But it had only happened that one time. She was hoping for more.

"So tell me Josephine," Ms. Camilla said. "How many people live in London, the capital of England?"

Josephine sighed. "Do I have to? I want to just enjoy the sound of the waves and the fresh air."

"Yes, I know. But learning is important, too. You know that."

Josephine sighed again and looked up at her governess. How she loathed the woman. She was the person closest to her, but sometimes Josephine wondered if she was even human at all. Sometimes she would imagine her being a robot that her parents had bought to mind her. Josephine would picture her in her chambers putting in new batteries or charging herself up by plugging into the wall outlet. That always made Josephine laugh.

"So? I know you know this one, Josephine. I'm taking it easy on you now."

"Twelve million people," she answered. "Making it the largest city in Europe. The country of England is one of the world's most famous and wealthiest. The country is seventy-four times smaller than the United States. The people of England consume more tea per capita than in any other country in the world. Most police officers in England do not carry guns with them unless it is an extreme emergency. The oldest zoo in the world opened in England, in the city of London, in 1828. In Medieval England, beer was a common breakfast beverage. Shoelaces were invented in England in 1790. England is home to the famous rock and roll band *The Beatles*, as well as *The Rolling Stones, Pink Floyd,* and many other rock bands."

Josephine breathed and looked up at Ms. Camilla waiting for her reaction. Ms. Camilla nodded with tight lips. "Very well then. If you insist on making fun of me, then maybe I should talk to your parents."

Josephine stopped smiling. She shook her head. "Sorry," she said.

"Maybe it was a mistake to come out here. Let's get back and finish our work," Ms. Camilla said.

Josephine felt the tears pressing. She really wanted to go down to the beach first. She wanted to put her feet in the ocean and feel how cold it was. She wanted to breathe the salty air for at least a few minutes more, she wanted to run across the sand even if her dress might get sandy or wet. She just wanted to have a little fun for once.

Is that so hard to understand?

Ms. Camilla grabbed her arm. Josephine pulled it out of her grip. "I don't want to," she said with tears in her voice. She knew she sounded like a small child with her shrill voice, but enough was enough.

"What are you saying? Miss Josephine Gyldenstjerne. You are to obey whatever I tell you to do. If I say we go back, we go back immediately. It's not up for discussion. Would you rather have your father send you away to boarding school?"

Josephine snorted. Her heart was racing and she didn't know what to do. She only knew that she was determined not to go with the governess back to that boring old house and all the boring books. She stomped her feet like a four-year-old.

"I want to go down to the beach!"

"But we have just been to the beach," Ms. Camilla said.

"I want to go all the way down there. I want to have my feet in the sand. I want to feel the ocean. I want to make a sandcastle!"

"Miss Josephine!" Ms. Camilla was yelling now, dismayed. "Are you raising your voice to me? Because I will not have that. You come here this instant and follow me back to the house. I will have to call up your parents and have them come up with a proper punishment for this behavior. Never have I…" Ms. Camilla put her hand in her pocket and pulled out a cellphone. "I'm calling them now. They should know what is going on. Your father will be very angry. He is at a very important meeting today and has no time to deal with this. And your mother is getting ready to go to Skagen for a couple of days. She has to meet with the jeweler about the earrings she ordered and try on the dress for the Royal wedding next month." She looked at Josephine who had started to back up. "Come back here, young lady."

Josephine shook her head. "No," she said. "You're gonna call them anyway. I might as well have my fun first." Then she turned around and started descending towards the beach.

"Miss Josephine!" she heard her governess call behind her, but she didn't care one bit. She ran and felt the wind lift her hair and it was almost as if she was flying. She couldn't help laughing and smiling while she ran down the dunes and into the sand where she felt it tickle her toes in the sandals. Finally, *finally* she was going to feel the ocean. Finally she was on her own. Ms. Camilla was probably still yelling but the wind drowned out her voice much to Josephine's pleasure. She pulled up her dress to better run faster, something she hadn't been allowed to do for a very long time, except during her tennis lessons with Mr. Henrik. It felt so good that she had to laugh as loudly as she could and scream out her joy.

CHAPTER 9

April 2013

THE WATER FELT AMAZING TOUCHING Josephine's feet and covering her expensive sandals. She chuckled and looked down as a wave came in and it reached her knees. Even if she had lifted up her dress it still got wet on the bottom, but she didn't care. Not about the dress, not about her parents, or even about Ms. Camilla who was probably still yelling at her from the dunes. She didn't even care enough to look back and see if she had followed her or was coming for her. It didn't matter. All that mattered was that Josephine had a few minutes to herself doing exactly what she felt like.

She laughed out loud again and stomped her feet making the water splash up high. She closed her eyes and danced while soaking her dress and thighs in the ice cold water. When she opened them again, she spotted someone at the beach, someone walking a dog. Josephine looked at where she had come down to the beach and spotted Ms. Camilla still standing up there, probably just waiting for her to come back, since she couldn't walk in the sand with her high heeled shoes and she was too prim and proper to take them off. Josephine waved at her, then ran towards the dog that was playing in the water just like she was.

"Be careful, he's a little playful," the owner said as Josephine approached the dog and it started jumping around her in joy. Josephine laughed and looked at the owner. An old lady wearing a green rain jacket with the hood covering her head.

"Can I pet him?"

Josephine was filled with joy once again as the old lady nodded with a gentle smile. She wasn't allowed to have pets and the only dogs she ever saw were the ones her dad used on his hunts with his friends. They weren't playful and friendly like this one. Josephine laughed when it jumped her. She touched its ears and face and felt how incredibly soft it was.

"Django," the owner said and walked closer. She grabbed the collar and pulled him down from Josephine. "We don't jump on people. Especially not small girls in very pretty dresses."

"Is that his name?" Josephine asked. "Django?"

The old lady smiled. "That it is. Do you like it?"

"I love it. It's so cute."

The old lady chuckled. "I thought so, too."

"Is it gonna rain soon?" Josephine asked.

The old lady looked confused. "I don't think so. The weatherman on TV this morning said sunshine all day."

"Why are you wearing a rain jacket, then?"

The old lady chuckled. "Oh that." She leaned over and looked into Josephine's eyes. Josephine liked her eyes, they were nice and friendly. "That is just for fun."

Josephine laughed. "That is funny."

Django started licking her hand and Josephine chuckled. Oh how she had always wanted a dog like this one, a friend to keep her company during the long days, a friend she could walk with outside in the yard or at the beach like the old lady. She looked at the woman in the thick raincoat and suddenly spotted something sticking out from inside of the coat.

"What's that?" she said.

"This thing?" the lady asked and pulled out the most beautiful old doll that Josephine had ever seen. She showed it to Josephine.

"Yes, that. Is it yours?"

The old lady nodded. "That's my dolly. Do you like her?"

Josephine nodded eagerly. Like any other six-year-old girl, she could never get enough of dolls. "I love it. Does it have a name?"

The old lady nodded with a big smile. "It does. Her name is Little Miss Jasmine. Do you want to try and hold her?"

Django was running around playfully in the water still as Josephine was handed the doll. She looked at it with stars in her eyes. "She is so beautiful."

"It's an old doll. My daughter used to play with it. The one eye is broken, but she is still pretty, I think."

"Your daughter is very lucky."

The old lady tilted her head and looked at Josephine. "I have more at my house. Would you like to see them?"

END OF EXCERPT

Get *MISS POLLY HAD A DOLLY* here: http://www.amazon.com/gp/product/

Printed in Great Britain
by Amazon

30856813R00207